**THERE'S A NEW SHERIFF IN TOWN,
AND HE'S ARMED TO THE FANGS.**

After fending off an attack by the werewolf pack, the saloon is in shambles and half of the dead outlaws have been sent to hell. Nigel, the lone vampire, takes up the job of sheriff in order to protect the only living boy in Damnation.

A second vampire, with whom Nigel has some history and still bears a grudge, comes to town. To make matters worse, an army of angry Indian warriors arrive, and they're not too keen on sharing their spirit world with the soldiers who killed them.

A sudden scarcity of food and booze spurs the election of a hawkish mayor, who controls the vampires with an unlikely source of warm blood. Buddy and some ragtag gunslingers are left to defend their territory against an entire nation of dead Indians led by an invincible brave.

Books by Clark Casey

Dawn in Damnation
Dead Indian Wars

Published by Kensington Publishing Corporation

Dead Indian Wars

Clark Casey

LYRICAL PRESS
Kensington Publishing Corp.
www.kensingtonbooks.com

Lyrical Press books are published by
Kensington Publishing Corp. 119 West 40th Street New York, NY 10018

All Kensington titles, imprints, and distributed lines are available at special quantity discounts for bulk purchases for sales promotion, premiums, fund-raising, and educational or institutional use.

To the extent that the image or images on the cover of this book depict a person or persons, such person or persons are merely models, and are not intended to portray any character or characters featured in the book.

Special book excerpts or customized printings can also be created to fit specific needs. For details, write or phone the office of the Kensington Special Sales Manager:
Kensington Publishing Corp.
119 West 40th Street
New York, NY 10018
Attn. Special Sales Department. Phone: 1-800-221-2647.

Kensington and the K logo Reg. U.S. Pat. & TM Off.
LYRICAL PRESS Reg. U.S. Pat. & TM Off.
Lyrical Press and the L logo are trademarks of Kensington Publishing Corp.

First Electronic Edition: May 2018
eISBN-13: 978-1-5161-0497-0
eISBN-10: 1-5161-0497-8

First Print Edition: May 2018
ISBN-13: 978-1-5161-0499-4
ISBN-10: 1-5161-0499-4

Printed in the United States of America

Thanks for the input of my first readers Jennifer Brinsdon, Susan Forste, and Daniel DeCicco, and to my agent Doug Grad for bringing me to the table.

Dedicated to Uncle Bob.
Though he wouldn't have approved of any of the violence in this book, he was a cowboy in his own way. He always gave everyone a fair shake and faced tough odds with humor and courage, never afraid to demonstrate love in word or deed.
He showed me what it's like to be a human being, when it's done right.

"Out of the crooked timber of humanity, no straight thing was ever made."
—Immanuel Kant

Chapter 1

Luther

"Hey, blondie!" one of the soldier boys called out. His sleeve was decorated with the silver eagle insignia of a colonel and, judging by the pain-in-the-ass tone of his voice, he reckoned it still meant something. He'd been teasing the other newbies all afternoon. Now, he figured the big fella in the duster was due for some good-natured ribbing. Even a large newbie was easy pickings. Usually. The colonel strolled up with his shit-eating grin and said, "What's with the—"

Before he could finish his question, the sandy-haired giant reached out and grabbed his face. His long fingers stretched from ear to ear and nose to scalp. In a single motion, he drew the colonel in and cradled his neck. Yellow fangs, much longer than Nigel's, dropped below his lip. His gumline was high, like a mare that'd seen more winters than nature intended. He pierced the soldier's flabby sunburnt neck and sucked hard. His blue eyes immediately widened in horror. He spit out the cold blood, then collapsed to one knee in a coughing fit. Some of it must have slipped down his throat and was cutting up his insides like shards of glass.

"*Scheisse!*" he yelled, then tore open his shirt, revealing a stack of muscles like a gorilla. He began beating desperately on his chest. Men dove under tables, fearing he might explode and send vampire guts all over the room.

"I see you have endeavored to sample the local fare, old chap," a voice teased from the doorway.

"Nigel!" he said, still gasping for air. "So that would mean I'm... Is the dark one here?" he asked nervously.

"No, I believe we are just short of his domain—though you may still reach it."

Nigel suddenly dashed forward, closing twenty paces as if they were one, then hammered a clenched fist into Luther's chest. It sent the big fella to the floor with a thud. He wasn't down for long. His eyes glowed yellow with anger, and he popped straight to his feet. The whole building shook as Luther charged Nigel, lifting him onto his shoulder like a bull between the horns. The two of them struck the bullet-ridden wall, then broke clear through to the other side. They tumbled across the road, knocking over a passing sodbuster. As soon as they stood, they began trading blows.

Luther had the advantage with his reach, but Nigel wasn't weakened from drinking cold blood. He crouched low and worked away at Luther's midsection. Finally, the big lug got fed up and smashed his knee against Nigel's face, then gripped him by the slack in his shirt and heaved him through the air. His body landed ten feet away on the boardwalk. Luther quickly grabbed Nigel's legs and dragged him back to the center of the road to finish him off. The crafty Brit managed to take a piece of wooden plank with him, and when Luther flipped him over, he met with a two-by-eight to the face. A twisted nail at the end of the board pierced his forehead, and blood poured over his face.

They both lunged for each other's throats at once. Nigel's short powerful forearms were locked inside of Luther's, both squeezing with all their might as they hissed breathlessly. Neither would let go to try to save his own windpipe from being crushed. It was clear that whoever could hold on the longest would be the winner.

"Not even sure who I should be rooting for," Sal said. "Can't tell if the new vampire'll be better or worse than the old one."

There'd been bastards like Jeremiah Watson running things, then worse bastards like Jack Finney. Buddy was about the nicest top gunslinger we'd ever had. Nigel was cranky, but he usually let folks be. This new vampire might be more of the meddling sort. On the other hand, it looked possible that they might just suffocate one another at once.

Just then, the clouds shifted, and the blanket of gray slipped back to reveal a sliver of the brightest light I had ever seen. We all shielded our eyes. The years of dusk had made us too sensitive for anything brighter than candlelight. I squinted up, but it hurt too much to look at it directly. A single beam shone down on the two vampires in the center of the road, and their clenched hands immediately began to smolder. A flicker of blue flames shot across the length of their interlocked arms. They had to release their grips to pat it out, but it kept spreading over their bodies. The skin on Luther's cheek melted like lard in a frying pan. He threw his duster over his head for shade. Nigel had already put his arms over his face with his back to the sky. Their closest escape from the light was the saloon. They both bolted for the hole in the wall and dove through it at the same time, breaking off bits of wood to make it even larger. A moment later, the clouds shifted again and the sky darkened.

The blisters on Nigel's face looked like they'd heal, but Luther hadn't been as lucky. Smoke was still rising from his blackened skin. It made his blond hair look even lighter. Where the skin had melted away, much of his jawbone and teeth could be seen.

"That was for killing me," Nigel said after dusting himself off, then extended a hand. Luther stared at him silently for a moment.

"I suppose I had it coming," he admitted, and took Nigel's hand.

"Two gins," Nigel called out. Sal hustled out and put a bottle and two glasses on the bar.

"Odd, isn't it?" Nigel remarked. "To feel such pain. Those blows would have been like mosquito bites when I was alive and well fed."

"*Ja.*" Luther rubbed his battered ribs. "Also, you put up a better fight than last time. *Prost!*" He lifted his drink, and they knocked glasses.

The two vampires sat chatting in the room they had just destroyed. Everyone gave them a wide berth, but I situated myself just within earshot and scribbled some notes with my head down so as not to attract their attention. Luther had a funny way of talking, but not in the same way as Nigel. His speech wasn't as proper-like.

"Hear that?" Luther asked.

"What?"

"Absolutely nothing."

Nigel smiled knowingly.

"These humans have no thoughts for me to hear," Luther said in surprise.

"Yes, I find it a welcome silence."

"It is rather nice," Luther agreed, "especially for an old vampire like me."

"If not for the hunger and boredom," Nigel said, "it might make this place bearable."

"So *none* of them have warm blood?" Luther grew worried.

"Tell me." Nigel changed the subject. "Who finally defeated the Scourge of Saxony?"

"The council turned against me," he replied bitterly, pushing his yellow hair out of his charred face. "We disagreed on ideology. They wanted to permit mixing with the humans."

"Still a hardliner, old boy?" Nigel grinned.

"Speaking of that, is your woman here? The one you killed your brother for."

"No, I suppose she went someplace else."

"So you're not going to hold it against me, what I did to you?" Luther asked.

"Ah, you were just doing your job," Nigel replied a little too breezily. Luther studied his face. He probably didn't have much practice in reading a bluff since he was accustomed to hearing thoughts. "Besides," Nigel added, "it can get rather boring here when there aren't any gunfights to watch. The Americans are no great conversationalists. They lack our European sensibilities."

"*Ja,*" Luther agreed.

"So why did the council finally decide to allow relations with humans?" Nigel prodded delicately, like he was hunting for something.

"They believe it is inevitable, the next stage in evolution."

"And you don't agree?" Nigel was surprised. "I suppose you wish to keep our bloodline pure, not muddied by those human traits you abhor."

"I don't hate humans. In fact, I'm looking out for their best interest. I want to spare them from our offspring."

"You fear the mixed-breeds' appetites would cause our kind to be discovered."

"*Nein,*" Luther scoffed. "I fear the hunger of the mixed-breeds could bring about our starvation. They consume too much! If one of them can dispose of an entire town in a matter of hours, what would a dozen do, or a hundred? Let alone thousands! The only way to keep up with their demand would be to farm the humans, keep them caged and continually reproducing. They'd be nothing more than sacks of blood. I wish only for them to remain free as nature intended, and happily ignorant of us!"

"But only one in a thousand mixed-breeds become vampires."

"It is still too risky. Ah, but now we are both beyond the world where such things matter. So you say the dark one is not here?"

"Not openly, but I've sensed his presence," Nigel said hesitantly. "I was never a believer when I was alive, and the last hundred years have given me little reason to think otherwise, but there have been signs recently." Nigel became very serious. "Like that blast of light that separated us."

"The dark one using light!" Luther scoffed.

"I never would've thought it possible either, but things are different here. Even the human priests kill in Damnation."

"Is that the name of this place?" Luther bowed his head solemnly.

"Oh, don't get so high and unholy!" Nigel teased. "The name was given by me in jest. Just after I arrived, some cowboy asked me where he was and I told him Damnation. He got shot not long after, but the name stuck. They have no idea it is the name of our Eden."

Just then, Whiny Pete barged into the saloon. He nervously eyed the hole in the wall, wondering if he should scatter. Nigel looked at him expectantly, and Pete nodded eagerly, perhaps a little less subtly than Nigel would have liked. Luther took it all in wordlessly.

"What's that all about?" Sal whispered to Pete.

"The vampire asked me to move Ms. Parker and Martin to the general store."

"You think that other vampire can smell the warm blood in Martin?" Sal asked.

"If Nigel can smell it, he probably can, too," I said.

"Think he'll wanna drink Martin's blood?" Pete asked.

"Why else would Nigel have you move 'em?" Sal barked. "Better get the word out that nobody should mention the kid in blondie's presence."

"Ain't gonna be easy with all the loudmouths around here," I said.

"Then we gotta put the fear of hell in 'em."

After it was scrubbed down real good, Luther moved into Ms. Parker's old room, and Buddy was left in the room between the two vampires. Everyone reckoned the new vampire was going to cause a big hoopla, but nothing much happened right away. Since he wasn't accustomed to going without warm blood, he was real tired. For the first few weeks, he slept pretty much around the clock. But there were other things to worry about aside from the new vampire.

Chapter 2

The Unknown Soldier and the Apache Woman

"Am I dead?" a new soldier asked as he sat down at the bar. Wedged between his shoulder blades was a tomahawk with greased goose feathers dangling from the grip. It had a pipe bowl opposite the blade and a hollow handle. Presumably, the owner didn't find occasion to bury the hatchet in the earth and smoke in peace. The edge of the blade was peeking out from the front of the soldier's sternum, where chunks of heart muscle had been pushed out. They clung to his shirt like dinner scraps, and his arms were red from trying his damnedest to push the blade back out the way it came. He literally wore his heart on his sleeve.

"Yup," I told him. "You're as dead as a doornail, but twice as useless."

"Figured I was done for when they ambushed us." Judging by the silver strands in his beard and the medals on his tits, he'd been soldiering awhile. "This hell?" he asked matter-of-factly.

"Nah."

"Then why's there so many dang Injuns outside?"

On account of the wars going on back in the states, more and more of them were coming to Damnation every day. Swarms marched out of the dust with their headdress feathers swaying in the wind. Some came hooting and hollering atop dead-eyed ponies, still rallying the bucks with war cries. Others were shot in the back, likely on the run from much larger forces.

They built teepees on the outskirts with scrap wood from old covered wagons. The barren flatlands between the buildings and the dust cloud quickly filled with their camps, and eventually the town was surrounded.

The tribes might not have gotten along so well when they were alive, but in Damnation the Apache, Navajo, and Sioux all banded together. Their ideas about the spirit world were somewhat vague, so when they wound up in a place with tumbleweeds, horses, and a few white men, they reckoned it was close enough.

"I suppose them Injuns weren't good enough for heaven," I told the soldier. "Nor bad enough for hell—like yourself—so they were sent here. Some miner called it *hell's sifter*. He reckoned the Lord was giving us all another look-see to check if any of us might be worth saving from the fire. Another man thought that if you could manage to keep from shooting anyone for a whole year, the gates of heaven'd open up for you. Nobody's managed it so far. Truth is, I can't say for sure where we are. Alls we really know is that you can stay here and play poker as long as you like. But if you get shot, you don't get to see your cards."

An Indian brave on horseback came riding by, shrieking and howling angrily at the window. Then he threw a rock that shattered the pane of glass. It wasn't meant to be an attack or anything. He just wanted to let us know he was out there and didn't care much for our kind. The soldier took it as an omen, though.

"Shoulda known what we done would come back to haunt us," he said uneasily. "Government gave 'em land, but it weren't near enough and the soil no good for growing nothing. Meat rations were slim and often spoilt. We lost ten men in my battalion when they finally revolted. Guess I was the eleventh."

A strong breeze blew the doors open, bringing with it a mess of dust and rattling the rusty fixtures. Nigel burst in like a twister and stopped in front of a toothless man who was huddled in the corner. A shiny tin star was fastened to his lapel. As sheriff, Nigel found he could make good on his promise to look after Mabel while remaining impartial. Otherwise, she might be inclined to let Buddy know it wasn't him who shot John Wesley Hardin. Nigel still reckoned Buddy needed all the confidence he could get to protect Martin, especially with another vampire in town.

Nigel's wounds from the fight with Luther had healed up good as new, though every passing day without warm blood made him weaker. He was still a far shot stronger and faster than any man or wolf in town—just not stronger than the other vampire. Luther had healed up as well, except for his blackened skin and the cheek that had melted away. Nigel might have missed his only chance to take out the big blond in a weakened state.

"This is a child's toy, sir. Not a derelict's!" Nigel yanked a wood-carved rattle out of the toothless fella's hands, then tore out of the saloon as quick as he'd come.

"Who was that?" the soldier asked.

"The sheriff," I told him.

"How's he move so quick?"

"He's a vampire."

"There's vampires here?"

"Just two, and some werewolves," I added. "But most of them got wiped out when they came after Ms. Parker's baby."

"So there's babies?"

"Just Martin. Only living thing in Damnation."

"*Shh*, keep it down," Sal scolded. "Luther might come in and hear ya."

"The other vampire don't know about the child," I explained to the soldier. "We're afraid he might eat the little bugger. So if you see a tall blond fella missing half his face, pipe down about the kid."

Ever since Martin was born, the wolves were afraid to attack because they believed Nigel had a steady supply of warm blood to keep him strong. Nigel never had a drop of the kid's blood, though. Some folks reckoned he was just waiting till Martin got bigger, fattening him up like you would a hog.

There were also worries about a vampire being sheriff, so Buddy was made deputy. At first, he took some pride in the position, but when Ms. Parker began spending more time with Nigel, his mood quickly soured. Eventually, Buddy stopped interfering in any quarrels unless one of the rules was broken, and he was a little loose on their interpretation. One hungry man pointed out that rule number one said *everybody eats*. Buddy lifted his face from his glass, squinted angrily, and told him, "It don't say what, though." Then he shoved a gun barrel in the man's mouth.

"Got any whores 'round here?" the soldier asked.

"Whores go to heaven," I told him.

"So there is a heaven then?"

"Wherever they end up must be heaven," Red added. "'Least you can get a reg'lar poke there."

"It wouldn't be heaven for the lady suffocatin' beneath you!" Mabel laughed.

"I can't stand that damn racket!" Sal complained as he peered out the window to the half-finished building across the road. "The hammering is driving me crazy."

Mabel had hired a bunch of dead carpenters to build her saloon just opposite the Foggy Dew. She used Lucky's poker winnings to pay them. On account of their thirst, they worked fast. They had framed up the walls with a balcony and a pitched roof in just a couple of weeks. The top floor was already finished, too. It was going to be larger and grander than Sal's dingy saloon. They were using some brand new wood for the exterior that had come in from the dust on a lumber wagon. There weren't any new nails, though, so they had to yank old ones out of the rotted-out buildings. The rusty round heads stood out from the shiny new cedar, giving it an odd look, like the new was being held together by the old. Mabel was going to call the place the Rusty Nail on account of it.

"Why we need another saloon anyway?" Sal complained.

"Town's growing." Mabel smiled with no apologies. "'Sides, a girl's gotta keep herself busy somehow."

"Don't think about underpricing me," he warned. "If folks start crossing the road for cheaper whiskey, I ain't gonna bother feeding 'em for free."

"Who says I won't serve food?" Mabel said. "Just 'cause you got a frying pan don't mean you have claim to every dead pig that wanders out of the dust."

"The whole system's going to pot!" Sal huffed, then he counted out ten chips for the new soldier. "We'll all be in hell before the year's through. Mark my words!"

The tomahawk sticking out of the soldier's back parted the crowd as he stood. He took his money straight to the poker table, where he lost a few hands. The gray in his hair had long overtaken the brown. He was likely the grandpa of a little tot he'd rather be holding than a straight flush somewhere shy of hell. When he got down to his last chip, he bought a bullet and borrowed a gun. He stuck the barrel in his mouth and squeezed the trigger. As the bullet broke apart the back of his skull, the piano player paused till the body hit the floor. Then he took up the song again right where he left off.

"Imagine that," Old Moe remarked. "He didn't even make it to lunchtime!"

"Just another soft army boy who didn't care much for whiskey or poker," Sal said. "Third one this month. Get the Chinaman to haul that sad sack away."

As the day wore on, more dead soldiers arrived with stunned looks in their eyes and loads of fear-shit in their drawers. There'd been another battle in Florida, and for every soldier that came out of the dust, four Seminole followed. Their hooting and hollering made the army boys as nervous as a cat in a room full of rocking chairs. Some of the same Indians they'd killed were right outside the door with their war paints on, making bows and arrows out of scrap wood.

"I seen that prairie coon before!" a soldier barked angrily. "He followed me here, damn it! How many times I gotta kill that sumbitch?"

Sal tried to calm them. "Simmer down now, boys. You may've been winning the battle, but you're losing the war here. We're outnumbered! Best you can do is keep your head down and hope they don't dig up the tomahawk to start a war."

"What them red bellies want anyway?" an old sodbuster asked.

"So far, they just wanna dance around the fire, hootin' and hollerin' same as always, but if you stir up trouble, they might wanna kick us out of their spirit world."

"They gonna chase us outta here like we done to them in Oklahoma?" a soldier asked.

"I expect they'd like to," I said.

At night, the rooming house was packed as tight as a barn during a twister. There was hardly a foot of floor not covered by some wretched body. Smelt worse than a slaughterhouse, with all the open wounds festering. I stayed at the saloon as late as I could to avoid it.

As the evening crowd was dwindling down, a squaw in a buckskin dress staggered through the door. She was skinnier than a desert steer, but feisty. Her shawl had been torn and muddied in some sort of scuffle. Her hair was tied up in braids, revealing a round pretty face. Rough as she was, her skin was as smooth as any powdered society lady I'd ever seen. She didn't have a single blemish, except the bullet hole in her temple. The flesh around it was singed, probably from a hot barrel pressed against her head while someone had their way with her. It would've explained the crazed look in her eyes. Her own kind probably chased her away for causing a ruckus. In the Indian camp, they didn't stand for their women getting out of line. She sidled up to the bar, and a few of the fellas offered to buy her a drink.

"This is gonna be trouble," Sal warned.

"Think the teepee creepers will come looking for her?" Whiny Pete asked worriedly.

Sal shrugged. "Who knows, but if she's trading her wares for drinks, there's bound to be a fight over her."

The soldiers didn't much care for her kind, and most hadn't been dead long enough to change their minds. To the rest of the fellas, a woman was a woman no matter what her color or how many bullet holes she had. The squaw accepted a drink from Red. Then one of the loggers put his hand on her thigh.

"Get your own damn woman, you tree humper!" Red hollered. "I done called her first."

Normally, a fella wouldn't take insult to slurs about his former line of work, but a woman was watching, even if she couldn't understand what it meant. Some dead pride surged within the chubby logger, and he lunged at Red. Their bellies knocked together as they swatted each other like a couple of walruses. Red got the upper hand and shoved the logger to the ground. As he went down, his foot kicked the poker table, sending stacks of chips to the floor. The card players jumped up and started shouting in an uproar.

"Ain't you gonna do something about this?" Sal asked Buddy. "You're the dang deputy."

Buddy sipped his beer. "They ain't broke no rules."

"Rule number five says *no killing over dumb shit.*"

"There's only one dang woman in the saloon and thirty men," Buddy told him. "I'd say that's a darn good reason for fighting."

"All right, you fellas take it outside." Sal grabbed his scattergun from the umbrella stand. "I ain't having you break apart what's left of my bar over some dirt-worshiping woman."

Red and the logger headed out to the road, while the squaw stayed at the bar drinking. Nobody was interested enough in the outcome of the fight to vacate a stool.

"Ain't you gonna watch?" I asked her.

"No matter who win," she snarled. "Somebody get shot. Somebody buy me whiskey. All white man same. All filthy dog." She spat on the floor.

A gunshot sounded outside, and a moment later Red trotted back into the saloon, rubbing his hands in satisfaction. "Now that that's all settled," he said, "what do you say to a poke, little lady?"

"How the hell'd you shoot that logger so fast?" Sal asked. "You're so drunk, you couldn't shoot a barn if you was standing inside it. Wasn't even out there long enough to count off ten paces. Musta shot him in the back," he decided.

"You calling me a back-shooter?" Red was feeling bold after shooting the logger, and Sal's scattergun was on the other side of the bar.

All the bickering was starting to annoy Buddy. "Simmer down!" he called out. "Rule number five says *no killing over dumb shit.* Now Sal, if you cared so damn much about whether or not it was a fair fight, you shoulda went out and watched it for yourself. It's over now, and both of you better quit your jawing, 'cause it's giving me a headache."

The squaw's eyes wobbled in her half-closed sockets, looking off in different directions at once, like a blind man who couldn't focus on anything in particular. When she noticed all the pale faces around her, she sneered with real hatred. Red was no friend of mine, but it was only fair to warn him. I pulled him aside and told him to watch himself.

"Ah, you'll get a poke if you wait your turn, pencil pusher."

"You ain't listening. She ain't right in the head," I told him. "She got it in for the white man."

He just brushed me off. "They all got it in for the white man. Makes 'em feisty in the hay." Red laughed and pinched the lady's backside. She squirmed away, saying she wanted another drink, so he ordered more whiskey. She kept gulping it down like there was a bottomless pit inside her. Probably already put away more than a man twice her size. Might've been trying to blot out whatever horrors had been done to her.

The piano player was playing a quick little ditty, and it spurred the lady to dance. She started hopping from foot to foot, like a caged rabbit rearing to be free. Red took her for a whirl around the floor. She shook her hips savagely and kicked her dark legs in the air. Soon enough, they caught Buddy's eye. He wandered over like a cow to hay and cut in on Red. She didn't seem to care much who her partner was.

"Better get the sheriff," I told Whiny Pete.

"Hold it there," Sal interrupted. "When Red and his boys came after Buddy, he shoulda shot him then. I say he'd be in the right to do so now."

"You really changed your tune," I said. "Wasn't so long ago you were trying to have Buddy kilt."

"I did no such thing, Tom. I've always backed the deputy. 'Sides, Red ain't paid his tab in weeks."

"We can't go back to killing each other over grudges," I argued. "Especially with all these dead soldiers in town. Ain't like managing a bunch of cowpunchers and churn-twisters. They actually know how to shoot—some of 'em anyways. If they start settling old scores, there's bound to be a war with the Injuns."

Red stood stupidly for a few minutes, eating drag dust as Buddy sallied about the room with the squaw on his arm. Finally, Red blurted out, "What's the big idea, Buddy?" Buddy just ignored him, which made Red angrier. There was nothing else for him to do but draw. He lifted his gun just as Buddy turned his back. Even stinking drunk, the portly gunslinger had a sense for these things. He must've seen the glint of the metal out of the corner of his eye, because he spun the woman around an extra turn and pulled as well.

"Buddy!" Nigel yelled from the doorway. Both men froze with their fingers on the triggers. "As deputy, you are supposed to maintain order here, not steal other men's women and provoke them into fighting you."

"But he drew first! 'Sides, who's to say I stole her. He don't have no claim on the lady just 'cause he bought her a few drinks. You woulda seen so for yourself if you wasn't playing house with Ms. Parker." It was clear that Buddy reckoned all the time Nigel was spending with Ms. Parker was akin to him stealing *his* girl. Nigel weighed his words before responding. It wouldn't have been prudent to go against his own deputy. Besides, Nigel wasn't heeled, and if anybody was fast enough to shoot a vampire it was Buddy. Each day without warm blood made Nigel slower, and Buddy had gotten quicker. He'd taken to shooting bottles on the outskirts of town like Hardin used to do.

"We've got more pressing problems," Nigel said. "There are a few hundred Indians outside and only thirty soldiers in here. If a gunfight breaks out, *somebody* could get caught in the crossfire." He winked slowly. Buddy just looked at him blankly, so Nigel whispered, "*Little Martin.*"

"Fine." Buddy shrugged and let the squaw go.

After Nigel was gone, Red didn't waste any time in leading the lady upstairs. She swayed drunkenly, nearly falling over the banister, so he threw her over his shoulder and carried her the rest of the way to the storage room. A few minutes later, her screeches could be heard above the barroom.

"Red's really givin' it to her!" Whiny Pete snickered.

A moment later, Red started screaming even louder than the woman.

"Or maybe *she's* givin' it to *him!*" Jarvis said, and everybody laughed.

Then a gunshot sounded.

Chapter 3

The Warrior

The following day, just before lunch, a tall bare-chested Indian brave showed up at the Foggy Dew. He was nearly as tall as Luther, though not quite as thick. The front of him was covered with so many bullet holes that everyone gaped silently, not knowing what to make of him.

Finally Old Moe asked, "How the heck did they shoot 'im so many times?" When Moe was still alive, it took nearly a minute to reload a musket, and the repeating rifles they made nowadays still mystified him.

Even the newer boys who knew something about the latest guns were puzzled by his wounds. A soldier who'd been scalped took off his hat in admiration. "Says a lot about a man that he didn't turn and run from that kind of firepower. Most fellas would've taken those bullets in the back."

The brave's face was striped with black war paint, which meant he had proven himself in battle, presumably before the one that had sent him to Damnation. His bottom lip hung low, like he wasn't much impressed with the lot of us. With the little English he knew, he managed to get across that he was looking for his sister. He had followed her to the spirit world after their tribe was attacked. He probably reckoned one of us had had our way with her and was aiming to scalp the fella, soon as she pointed him out.

"Ain't seen her," Sal said flatly.

The brave stood still as a post with his arms crossed, patiently scanning the room. Looked to be counting heads, maybe trying to figure out how many of us he could take on. For several minutes, he watched each person that came and left the saloon.

"What's the hatchet-packer doing in here?" Red asked as he sat down.

"Looking for his sister," Sal answered.

"What'd ya tell 'im?"

"What ya think I told 'im? I didn't say a damn thing!"

"Well ya better not!" Red chewed his fingernails worriedly.

"See them bullet holes in his chest." The scalped soldier pointed. "They was done by one of them rapid-fire Gatling guns. Shoots near four hundred rounds a minute! Took a lot to bring him down. Boy, I tell ya. I wouldn't wanna face him with no measly Colt—that's for sure!"

Ms. Parker and Nigel came into the saloon for some lunch, but Martin wasn't with them. Mabel often kept an eye on the child. She relished the time with the tot, since she knew there wasn't any chance of her ever having one of her own. Her motherly impulses had followed her to the grave. Ms. Parker had already lost most of the baby weight, so the wedding dress she'd taken out for the pregnancy now hung slack. The bullet-ridden brave took notice of her immediately. Sensing something amiss, Nigel put himself between Ms. Parker and the man.

"I come back," the brave announced. "If Running Horse no return"—he turned his head from side to side as if to address the whole room—"big problem." Then he headed to the door, pausing on the way to lock eyes with Ms. Parker.

"Did someone steal that man's horse?" she asked.

"I think he was referring to his sister, ma'am," Sal explained.

"The squaw from last night?" Nigel asked. Sal nodded silently.

"What you suppose he aims to do?" Whiny Pete fretted.

"He will likely let the matter drop once he locates his sister," Nigel assured Pete.

"How the hell's he gonna find her?" Sal said. "We're eatin' her."

"Huh?" Everyone stopped chewing. Red looked ready to air his paunch.

"Well, not directly," Sal explained. "The pigs ate her up last night." The men at the bar shrugged and continued eating.

"How did she die?" Nigel asked.

The saloon grew quiet. Whiny Pete finally piped up, "Red kilt her."

"Oh my Lord!" Ms. Parker was horrified. "Did you rape her?"

"It weren't rape, ma'am. She was plenty willing," Red defended. "Y'all seen her come upstairs with me. I didn't carry her, least not the whole way. She took off her dress on her own, too. Well, maybe I helped her a little. But she certainly spread her legs on her own. Then when I was on top of her, she tried to stick me in the neck with a knife."

"Where were you while this was going on?" Nigel asked Buddy.

"Sitting right here. You tol' me to let him have her so I did."

"And you didn't arrest Red after he killed the lady?" Nigel asked.

"He didn't break none of the rules. It just says *no rapin' or killin' Ms. Parker.* Doesn't say nothing about no squaw. 'Sides, sounds like self-defense to me."

"Her brother isn't likely to see it that way," Nigel said. "He's liable to start a war over it. And it won't take much to get the rest of those natives riled up."

"I ain't fightin' a hundred Injuns with just thirty of us," the scalped soldier griped. "We barely won when the odds were the opposite, and it cost me my damn hair. They can have their spirit world. I can't believe I died for my country just to end up in a place with watered-down whiskey and no women. I coulda just stayed in St. Louis."

"These drinks ain't watered down," Sal argued. "I wouldn't waste good water on this rotgut."

"What if we just give Red up to the Injuns," Pete suggested. "Wouldn't be no reason for them to attack the rest of us then."

"You ain't givin' me up!" Red yelled. "I ain't done nothin' wrong!"

"We'll just have to detain you until we decide what to do," Nigel said.

Red tried to protest, but Buddy knocked him over the back of the head with the handle of his pistol. The chubby carrot top dropped to the floor like a sack of dirty grain. There wasn't a jail in Damnation, so they hauled him down to the cellar and put a couple of barrels on top of the trap door.

"I didn't know there was a cellar below us," Buddy said.

"It's where I store my whiskey and beer," Sal said.

"That woulda come in handy when them werewolves were raiding the place," I said.

"I didn't want everyone knowing about my stash," Sal said. "And I probably shouldn't be telling you about it now that that woman is opening a saloon across the way."

After lunch, most of the men headed back to the rooming house to nap. Only a handful of restless souls pushed through the dull afternoon hours at the bar. Mabel dropped in for a cocktail after Ms. Parker relieved her from babysitting. Old Moe and Whiny Pete sipped their beer so slowly they seemed to be in a competition over who could finish theirs last. The barroom was even quieter than it normally was between lunch and dinner. Wasn't any bickering or bullying to listen to.

It took a moment to realize that there was peace and quiet only because Red had fallen asleep. When he finally woke up, his hollering could be heard through the floorboards. After a half hour or so, he resigned himself to the situation and simmered down. It turned out that there wasn't much difference between having Red *at* the bar and having him *under* it. The most annoying part was that he couldn't hear as well, so he kept asking folks to speak up or repeat themselves. Also, since he couldn't see anything, he had to know what was going on at all times. A fella couldn't pass wind without Red questioning what the sound was.

"Mind your business," I told him.

"Ya farted again, huh? Better check your draws, Tom. That one sounded kinda wet."

Chapter 4

The Fact-Checker

Jarvis sat in the corner of the bar reading old issues of *The Crapper* to pass the time, just like Ms. Parker used to when she first arrived. He didn't use the information to his advantage in cards, though. The boy had no interest in gambling or drinking, and since food was free, he had no need for money at all. He was entirely free of the system. Jarvis read those old issues for what you might call *academic purposes*.

Though only eighteen years old, Jarvis had an old soul, probably from listening to so many of his pa's sermons. The constant threat of eternal damnation could make a young fella mighty serious. He reckoned the preaching was all hogwash, but going to mass five times a week gave him a lot of time to think about the ways of the world. Now he wanted to know about all the folks who had passed through Damnation and what their lives had amounted to. He believed every single one of them must've had some sort of meaning—at least to them. Before I finished my coffee, he started quizzing me about the particulars of the folks I had written about, and he wanted to know every little detail I'd left out.

"Are you after my job?" I asked him directly.

"No, sir. I don't need a job," he replied. "I don't need anything at all. Just wanna know is all."

"Speak up, boy!" Red called out from below the floorboards. "There's a quarter inch of timber between us. What'd he say, Pete?"

"Says he ain't after Tom's job," Pete yelled to the floor. "Just wants to know is all."

"Well, what are you waiting for, Tom? You're the dang reporter." Red laughed. "Now, report!"

"Fair enough," I said. "But don't go telling me my business, kid. I write it as I see it. When folks pick up a paper, they wanna know three things: where a person comes from, what they done for a living, and how they died. If I put a bunch of other nonsense in there, they'll get bored and think twice before buying the next issue."

If Jarvis had his way, each issue would be a thousand pages thick. "There's so much more to their lives!" he argued. "Take this one. Alls it says is: *he was originally from Virginia, died during a battle in Pensacola, Florida, against the Seminole, and played four hands of poker in Damnation before he shot himself.* That's all you have to say about him? His whole life only amounted to one sentence?"

"Ah, there's too many damn soldiers coming to town these days for me to write much more."

"But some of these aren't even accurate," he said. "Ain't it important to at least record the truth?"

"Like what?" I was beginning to get irritated.

"Well, in this other one here, you say a man was mowed down by the Comanche in northern Tennessee. But that's Cherokee territory! Comanche are plains Indians. Never went east of Kansas. Even the ones that were relocated never stepped foot that far north."

"Ah, Cherokee, Comanche... what's the difference?" I said. "A man got shot by an Injun. That's all anyone wants to know. I ain't gonna listen to some boy with buckshot in his brain tell me how to do my job."

Jarvis glared at me like he wanted to plug my cheeks with as much lead as his had. Lots of men had worse-looking wounds than him, but they were hardened from drinking all day and teasing one another to pass the time. Jarvis was young and cold sober, so he was sensitive about his looks, even if there weren't any young gals to impress. Fortunately for me, he wasn't heeled.

"What's going on now?" Red hollered. "Is the boy still moping 'cause he got half his face shot off and he ain't never gonna find a sweetheart?"

Jarvis kept pouting, but he didn't want to give Red the satisfaction. Even though the kid didn't care for the drinking or teasing, he still enjoyed the atmosphere of the saloon. Said it was like going to a mass where everyone got a chance to do some preaching. But as much as he wanted to feel like one of the boys, the truth was still more important to him than fitting in. As he read on, something kept bugging him, and he couldn't let a thing be when he felt like he was in the right.

"How about this one?" he finally spoke up. "I thought you said that little baby Martin was named after his father?"

"Shush!" Sal said. "Luther might come in and hear you talking."

"That's what Ms. Parker told us." I leered at Jarvis, letting him know he was testing the limits of my patience.

"But this issue from last year says that Ms. Parker died on her wedding night after being caught in a compromising position with another man."

"And what of it?" I scowled, ready to smack the boy.

"You wrote: *Her fiancé, a luckless and no doubt regretful man named Henry, mistook the situation and ran off before she could explain.* Then it goes on to say she drowned herself."

"Lemme see that." I grabbed the paper before anyone else could get a hold of it. Sure enough, it was printed right there. "Guess I musta wrote it up wrong," I said, then tore the page up and tossed the pieces into a spittoon. "You're right, son. I may have made a few mistakes from time to time. Let's not make a big thing of it."

"Hold on there a second, Tom. That ain't wrong," Sal interrupted. "I remember the night she first arrived. She came in wet as a fish and kept crying, 'Oh, Henry! Please forgive me, Henry!'"

"It's true," Old Moe confirmed. "I heard it myself. I remember thinking that Henry fella had been a lucky man. She was the prettiest lady I'd seen in more'n fifty years."

"Well, I wasn't there when she arrived," Mabel added. "But I was right beside her after Martin was born, and she clearly said that she was naming the child after his father."

"I don't get it!" Red yelled from below. "How can the tot be named after the father if her fiancé's got a different name?"

"They might not be the same person." The scalped soldier put two and two together for him.

"So if her fiancé ain't the father, then who is?" Jarvis asked.

"Could be the fella who forced himself on her the night of her wedding," Sal suggested.

"Nah," Red bellowed from below. "I was there when she tol' the story. She stuck a knitting needle in the man's arm before anything happened, 'member?"

Sal wasn't the persnickety sort. "Ah, it's just some other fella named Martin. She probably had relations with him before she died is all. Ain't like none of y'all are saints."

"What's the pencil pusher think?" Red asked. "He ain't sayin' nothin'."

"I might have an idea about who the father is," I confessed, "but I gotta have words with Buddy first."

"Who is it?" Sal asked.

"Not sure yet, but it might account for why baby Martin didn't die when his mommy drowned."

"What's that?" Red hollered from below. "How come Martin ain't dead?" Luther came in just then, so we all hushed up. The blond giant was even scarier-looking now that his face was charred-up and there was no skin covering half his jaw. He took a seat at the end of the bar. Sal placed a bottle of gin and a glass in front of him.

"Who's Martin?" he asked with an evil smile that showed right through to his molars. He might not have been able to read minds anymore, but his hearing was still spot on.

The Crapper

Comings: *As you are all surely aware, a tall yellow-haired vampire has come to town. His name is Luther, and he hails from Germany, by way of England, and most recently America. He worked for a council of vampires, acting as a sort of sheriff, and he died as a result of a falling out he had with them. About a hundred years ago, he killed our current sheriff, Nigel. Luther has not granted an official interview yet, so we can't say as to what good he might've done to earn himself a spot here instead of hell. Then again, we can't really say if that lying bastard Sal is right and that it's necessary to do any good at all to wind up here.*

A mess of soldier boys have come to town recently, but I ain't had a chance to interview any of them yet. Quite a few of you have noted that the more Indians arrive in Damnation, the less soldiers we see, and vice versa. Stands to reason, it's a result of who wins the battles back home. Seeing as how the Indians who wind up here ain't too happy with us, we can only hope that the ones left behind have more success. Otherwise, we might all be sent to hell soon, like we probably deserve.

Goings: *Luther tore the neck out of a foolish soldier named Carl, who had called him "blondie." Seems like he was a colonel and an asshole. The man was only here a month and I didn't have time to speak with him, but I'm told he was from Michigan* *and joined the army when the fur-trapping trade dried up. If any pissant says my facts are wrong or there's more to it than that, well then he can just go write it up himself.*

Also, another soldier shot himself after finding out he wasn't very good at poker. Nobody got his name. I guess he was a chickenshit and not much of a runner, because he caught a tomahawk in the back.

Red shot a crazy-eyed Apache woman, so Nigel had him locked up in the cellar. Keep it under your hat, though, since her brother is looking for her, and he's likely to start a war if he finds out she's smelling sulfur.

I've also been informed that Mabel shot a lecherous logger who squeezed her behind, though I was not there to witness it. I didn't get a chance to speak with that man either, and nobody could recall much about him other than that he had large hands.

Chapter 5

Low and Slow

The smell of charred pork drifted into the window of the rooming house while I was still sleeping. I was dreaming that I was in my old newspaper office, and George Hearst had just told me the way he wanted me to write up the slaughter out in the Black Hills. This time, I clenched his neck and began choking the life out of him. A moment later, I was scarfing down the cooked flesh that I had cut from his gut. When I awoke, my pillow was torn up, and there were feathers in my mouth. There wasn't much use in trying to get any more shuteye after that. Once you smelled smoked meat, you couldn't dream of anything else.

"Smoked ribs day, huh?" I said as I walked into the Foggy Dew.

"Seems so," Jarvis replied. "All morning Sal's been mixing up a dry rub of cayenne pepper, paprika, and salt."

"Gonna be a rough one," I said.

"Oh? Why's that?"

"Always is on smoked ribs day. You'll see."

Sal might've been sloppy with his pouring of drinks, but he was a stickler when it came to smoking ribs. It took all of his attention to maintain the right heat for a low slow cook that'd get the meat falling off the bone after eight or ten hours. The process didn't leave any time to fix a proper breakfast or lunch, so he set out a large pot of day-old beans, which gave rise to endless pissing and moaning. Wasn't much to look forward to in Damnation, so the prospect of two lousy meals in a row put all the newbies in bad spirits. The fellows who'd been in town a spell knew it was worth the wait, though. They just hoped to make it to suppertime without getting shot. Smoked ribs day only came once a year, and those who survived it spoke of little else for some days afterward.

"Why's smoked ribs day so rough?" Jarvis asked.

"Just is," I shrugged.

"But there's gotta be some reason why."

"Wait'll ya taste 'em," Red called out from beneath the floorboards.

"Some fellas mark their time by smokings," I added. "Like how old folks wonder how many more Christmases they got to look forward to. Keeps 'em going."

"It's true," Old Moe agreed. "I went twenty years just tryin' to hold out for one more smoked ribs day. Stakes get higher when there's only a few hours to go till supper. The thing is, by the time you eat 'em, the meat tastes bitter with all the gun smoke in the air—and you gotta count the empty seats at the table from friends who didn't make it. Nowadays, I'd just as soon have beans."

"It don't help none having two shit meals in a row beforehand neither," Red hollered. "Pass some of them Mexican strawberries down the hatch before they're all ate up."

A newbie came in the door and swaggered by everyone else in the chow line. He marched to the front, where Old Moe had been waiting patiently with a bowl and spoon in his hands while everyone else was still in bed. As soon as Sal lifted the lid on the pot, the newbie cut the line in front of Moe. The room silenced. Most fellas would lift metal over less, but Moe wasn't the sort to cause a fuss unless he had to. You didn't get to be the oldest man in Damnation without practicing some restraint.

"See that?" Whiny Pete gasped.

"Course I seen it," I said angrily. "Happened right in front of me, didn't it?"

"Ain't nobody gonna do something?" Pete asked

The newbie couldn't have been more than twice a sheep's age and he was lanky as a beanstalk, with hardly the muscle to lift a plow. His name was Francis, and I'd been told that his appendix had burst some weeks earlier on the Oregon Trail. A few of the fellas had seen the long gash that stretched across the left side of his gut. Apparently, a trail cook had tried to remove the inflamed tissue with a hunting knife in a covered wagon. The cook claimed to have studied doctoring some, but he must've missed anatomy class since the appendix is on the right side. He made a mess looking around for the swollen tube as the boy bled out in agony. He never wanted to end up at the mercy of another cross-eyed trail cook, so he was keen on showing folks in Damnation that he was in charge of his own fate.

"If it weren't smoked ribs day, I'd put a bullet in the lad," an Irishman declared. "But it ain't half noon yet, and the lad's not been tested. Can't be sure he ain't some kind of maverick wid a knife, or just lucky wid a pistol." "True enough," a sodbuster agreed. "I don't mind getting stabbed on a reg'lar day, but there ain't no use going to hell when the ribs are already in the smoker."

"Move aside, old-timer!" Francis ordered loudly, with a venom in his voice that barely hid how scared he was. Clearly, he had singled out Moe because he didn't look like much of a threat. Killers have a shifty look in their eyes, always scanning people coldly like objects. Over the years, the killer in Moe had faded. You'd hardly know he had shot hundreds of men in order to last so long. But putting lead in corpses eventually bores a man, same as everything else. The shifty look was entirely gone. Now he had the cloudy gaze of sick folk waiting to pass on.

Moe just shrugged at the boy and stepped aside. After Francis finished filling his plate, Moe helped himself to two scoops of beans just the same. The beanstalk had gained some ground, so he decided to ride the old-timer even harder, reckoning the crueler he was, the less inclined others might be to hassle him. He stood blocking Moe's way and said, "Beans could use a little seasoning, old man." Then he scooped up a pinch of sawdust from the floor and sprinkled Moe's plate.

Moe winced with real sadness, for he surely liked his beans. The bitter gun smoke that came along with the ribs reminded him of all the friends he'd lost through the years, but beans didn't bring back any such bad memories. Nobody got shot over beans, ordinarily.

The chow line now stretched out the door and onto the boardwalk, some thirty men long. If Moe got on the end of it, the pot would be empty by the time he reached the front. A layer of dust had collected on his pistols, but he didn't seem inclined to give them a shine today. Instead, he just blew the splinters of wood off his plate.

"You ain't gonna eat that, are ya?" the kid scowled.

"Ain't like it's gonna kill me," Moe said with a humble shrug. A few of the fellas laughed. The boy reddened, thinking the old man had gotten the better of him.

"Well, if you ain't the yellowest wood-chewer I ever seen! We're gonna have to call you Termite from now on. How you like that, pop? You got yourself a new nickname."

"He's already got a name, whippersnapper. It's Old Moe!"

Everyone in the room turned around to see who was speaking so loudly, and most of them looked surprised to find out it was me. Buddy wouldn't stir from his bed for hours, and the sheriff wasn't obligated to interfere until somebody got shot. Nobody else seemed inclined to step in, but I couldn't let it pass. There weren't many folks in Damnation I considered a pal, but Moe certainly was one through thick and thin. Before I could measure my words properly, I let the young fella have it.

"Don't you know who you're pickin' on, sonny? That there's the oldest man in town. Show some dang respect, for Chrissakes! He was firing at red coats with a flintlock musket while your grandpappy was still browning his britches in a crib. If there's any wisdom at all in this godforsaken town, he's got it!"

The kid glared at me stupidly for a moment. "He don't look much older'n you," he finally blurted out, which brought some snickers from the crowd. Francis might've suspected then that things weren't as they seemed. Half the town was watching, though, so he couldn't back down now. How would it look if he tried to squash a bug and then backed down to a pencil pusher? His eyes fell on the cane at my side, and he perked up, reckoning I was an easy target, just like Moe.

"Mind your business, cripple, 'less you want a bullet for breakfast."

I wasn't heeled on account of I had my sights set on heaven once again. The clock had been reset when I shot a wolf during the last attack, but I had a couple of months under my belt now. If I didn't carry a gun, I reckoned it wouldn't be too hard to make it a full year without shooting anyone—that is, if someone didn't shoot me first. Because of my hobbled leg I couldn't move too fast, but the boy had only been in town a few weeks, so he didn't know how dead men fight: with little grace and no honor.

"If I wanted lead for breakfast," I barked back, "I wouldn't fuss with a two-bit cowpoke like you."

"I have a mind to... to tan your hide," Francis stuttered.

He had clearly lost his nerve, so I stepped forward to press my advantage. "Shit, slim," I laughed. "You ain't never felt a hide as hard and lumpy as mine. Them frail wrists of yours would prolly shatter if you tried to tan it."

The boy began waving his dukes in the air. Then he bobbed his head like we were in a boxing ring instead of a saloon. He looked ridiculous. The living fight with a measure of respect that seems comical once you've been dead awhile. They throw punches till one man knocks the other down. Then the winner helps the loser to his feet and buys him a drink. Dead men don't bother with such shenanigans. Ain't no use in shaking the loser's hand because he's going to send you to hell the first chance he gets.

Sure enough, the cowpoke wound up and threw a broad haymaker like he was reaching for the fancy whiskey on the top shelf of the bar. On account of my bad leg, I couldn't move back in time to dodge the blow, so I stepped inside his arm's length and was on him like a weasel on goat tits. His arm knocked weakly against my back while I found my target and made him regret he ever said a word to Old Moe.

"Git 'im, Tom!" someone hollered. The crowd circled around us like roosters in a cockfight. The Foggy Dew hadn't seen so much action that early in the morning since Jack Finney was a newbie and Jeremiah Watson made him draw for his breakfast.

Any dead man worth his salt would tell you that if you wanted to finish a fella off with your bare hands, the most fragile place on the body was the eyeball. The living never thought of such things, since they weren't really aiming to kill, but a fingernail could tear the lens like paper.

I plunged my thumb knuckle-deep into the fool's socket and he squealed like a slaughtered pig. Then I twisted my wrist till I sliced a vein. A mess of cold blood came pouring out, sopping his young face. My whole sleeve was dark red and dripping wet. If I had stepped away just then, that would've been the end of it. If a man couldn't see, he couldn't fight. He'd just hear the laughter of the crowd as you readied to smash a chair over his head.

The cowpoke was scrappier than he looked, though. He took hold of me with one hand and with the other he boxed my ear so hard that I could hear church bells ringing. The pain shot through my skull, but you can shake off just about anything when you know it ain't gonna be the end of you. I jabbed my thumb into his other eye for good measure and twisted away. Francis screamed even louder than the first time. His eyeball broke apart like a soft-boiled egg and dropped to the floor. A piece of the pupil clung to my finger as blood leaked from the socket onto my shoe. Then his body buckled and collapsed to the ground.

"Look at the damn mess you made!" Sal hollered at me as he came out of the kitchen. "Couldn't ya have just shot the runt instead of tearing up his peepers?"

"I ain't heeled," I answered. "Been trying not to shoot anyone, remember?"

"Oh yeah, trying to get into heaven again," Sal teased. "How long you got now?"

"Almost two months," I told him. "Since I shot that wolf. I suppose now I gotta start all over again, though."

"Maybe not," Sal said. "Could wrap that fool's eyes up and maybe he won't bleed out."

"He prolly ain't got more'n a few drops of blood left in him," a farmhand remarked. "Doubt he'll last the hour."

"I'll take some of that action!" A cowboy threw a coin on the bar.

"I got a dollar that says he won't make it to supper," said a soldier.

The boys all crowded around to place their bets. It got boring just wagering on cards and dice. They wanted the thrill of something less predictable. Then a gunshot sounded and all bets were off. One of the old Christian ladies playing cards in the corner had a gun in her lap, and the barrel was still smoking.

"Guess that settles it," Sal remarked with no small disappointment. "At least you're still in the running to pass the pearly gates, Tom."

"What happened?" Red asked from the cellar. "Who shot who?" He wouldn't be ignored, so one of the sodbusters went over to the hatch in the floor and gave him the lowdown.

"Gut-Shot Granny done it," he explained. They called her that on account of her delicate wrists slowed her down while raising the barrel of her pistol, but she didn't wait to pull the trigger. She usually ended up hitting fellas lower down than intended. Granny had been in town the second longest, after Old Moe. Even the most hardened outlaws gave pause when they saw a face that could've been their mother's mother. Meanwhile, she'd blast a hole in their tummy because she thought they were being disrespectful to their elders.

Old Moe nodded his thanks to Gut-Shot Granny, then picked up the eyeless kid's plate of beans. The only real loss of the day so far was the bloodstain on my sleeve, since I didn't have another shirt to wear. At least the next whippersnapper might think twice about messing with a man with a red right arm.

"You should tell folks you reached into a man's chest and yanked out his heart," Sal joked. "That's the only way you're likely to make it a year without shooting no one!"

Chapter 6

Skinny Willy and the Coins

"Thanks for sticking up for me," Moe said. "Guess I don't have the grit to draw no more. Even with that boy ridin' me, I couldn't summon the anger. Glad you didn't lose your chance of gettin' to heaven on my account, though—thanks to Gut-Shot Granny. I'd a felt real bad about that."

"Ah, it's prolly silly for me to believe that nonsense anyways," I said. "Like some beam of light's gonna lift me to heaven just 'cause I didn't shoot no one for a spell."

"Gotta believe something," Moe said.

"You know who it was that first started sayin' it?" I asked. "About going to heaven'n all."

"That'd be Skinny Willy. He was the one who started us using money, too."

"Oh? Guess I reckoned money'd always been in use in Damnation."

"Uh-uh." He shook his head doggedly. "Back in the day, there wasn't anything to bet with. Poker is boring enough. 'Magine playing all day with no stakes! You could hardly get through a hand without some fella complaining about being dead, then someone else shootin' him for it."

"So how did it start?" I asked.

"One day, a Wells Fargo stage coach came down the road with a shot-up driver. Must've been a thousand dollars on board, which would've been great if there was anywhere to spend it. One fella wanted to throw it in the fireplace to get the chill out of the room. Willy had the idea of divvying it up to play poker with—just for bragging rights. Willy wasn't much of a card player. He lost his bankroll first, but he was happy enough pouring drinks for the rest of us. The whole afternoon passed without a single fight. After that, we kept playing with the money every day like it was real, just to pass the time. Even with nothing to spend your winnings on, it still meant something when you had a bigger stack than your friend and could lord it over him how shitty he was at cards."

"Skinny Willy didn't charge y'all for drinks then?"

"Nope. He filled glasses and cooked just 'cause he liked doing so—though he wasn't much of a cook. And he was happy enough till one day a loud-mouthed cowpuncher came in and started bossing him around. He made Willy miserable going on about how the grub wasn't fit for a dog. We chided one another to pass the time, but this fella had it in for Willy, wanted to humiliate him. Now, Willy never claimed to be any great chef, but he took some pride in his work, and the taunting soon broke his spirit. Looked like he might jump in front of a bullet just to be done with it.

"After a few weeks, a couple of real gunslingers came to town. Willy poured them whiskey and gave them each ten bucks to play cards. After they lost, they wanted more whiskey, but Willy laid down the law. Told 'em they needed to pay for drinks in Damnation. It was the first anybody had heard of it, but we didn't say nothing. Willy made a deal with 'em that if they shot a certain blowhard, they'd each get ten more dollars and free whiskey for the rest of the day. Musta seemed like a pretty good deal to them, considering there was no sheriff to arrest 'em for it. They put a mess of lead in that cowpuncher as soon as he came through the door."

"Didn't the gunslingers realize no one else was paying for drinks?" I asked.

"They prolly reckoned everyone had a tab. But the next day, after they sobered up, they heard a card player who just got cleaned out say the coins didn't mean nothing anyway. They weren't pleased to know they'd been tricked. One of them put a knife to Willy's gut. That's when Willy told 'em if they lasted a year without killing no one, their sins would be forgiven and they'd go to heaven. They weren't about to be made fools of twice, though."

"So who kept repeating that hogwash like it was true?" I asked.

"Hmm. Not sure. Maybe Gut-Shot Granny can recall." She was sitting at the next table, so I turned and asked her if she remembered who started repeating Willy's tale about going to heaven as truth.

"That'd be Sal," she replied without having to think about it. "He came to town a little after me and was Willy's barback."

"Oh, yeah. That's right!" Old Moe remembered. "He must've been right there beside Willy when the gunslinger stabbed him."

"He was," Granny confirmed. "I was sitting at the bar not five feet away when it happened. I could even hear Willy's last words to Sal as he bled out on the floor."

"What were they?" I asked.

"*Never give nothing away for free.*"

"That's prolly why Sal's so damn cheap," I said.

"I reckon so," Moe agreed. "Sal turned out to be a fair hand with a skillet, and nobody else wanted to cook, so he took Willy's place. He began charging folks, but nobody minded dropping a nickel for a drink and a pork chop since at least the cooking was better, and it made your winnings worth something. When new folks came to town, they just figured that's how things were. They were pleased as punch just to wet their whistle anyhow."

"And rightly so," I said. "It never crossed my mind to question it when the first one was on the house. So Sal kept on repeating the story about going to heaven if you don't shoot no one?"

"Darling, he told it to *all* the new arrivals," Gut-Shot Granny said. "I can't say for sure whether he believed it or not, but it made some tough customers think twice about shooting him. Then, about a year after those two gunslingers came to town, one of them vanished. It could've been the wolves that got him for all I know, but Sal claimed he saw a beam of light lift the man into the sky. The thing was, nobody could recall the last time they'd seen that gunslinger shoot anybody. His friend was always the trigger-happy one. Somebody reckoned he hadn't kilt anyone since he stabbed Skinny Willy a year earlier. And that was enough for folks to believe that whatever Sal said was gospel."

"Anybody else see that gunslinger get lifted into the sky?" I asked.

"Just Sal," Granny said.

The saloon started to clear out as the air became taken over with the stink of flatulence from the beans everyone had eaten. As soon as the first fart sounded, it was wise to stretch your legs and head for the door.

"So what do you make of Mabel opening a new saloon?" I asked Moe as we returned our plates and cutlery.

"Be nice to have a change of scenery," he smiled.

"Think Sal's gonna let it happen?"

"Don't expect he'd like to. He ain't got much power if folks can go across the street. I expect he's most afraid he'll end up like Willy."

"I suppose so."

"I 'preciate ya stickin' up for me, Tom."

"No thanks necessary, pal," I told him. "Termite ain't got no ring to it anyways. If we ain't gonna stand up against bad nicknames, what good are we? We wouldn't be no better than the wolves!"

Chapter 7

Suppertime

Sal's meat smoker was made out of two steel drums that had been welded together. It sat in the courtyard behind the kitchen, leaking plumes of smoke from the seams. He fueled it with scraps from broken-up wagons and boardwalk planks that'd been soaking in buckets of spilt whiskey and beer runoff. The cayenne pepper-scented clouds drifted into the barroom, making everyone even hungrier.

A soldier who woke up after the beans ran out remarked, "I'm so hungry, I could eat my dang boots!"

As the day wore on, the pressure built up. Dead folks carried such an awful hollowness in them that all they could do was try to fill it with as much whiskey and meat as they could stuff down their gullets. Being hungry while the smell of roasting meat was in the air made everyone twice as irritable. If you wanted to make it to chow time without getting caught up in a scuffle, your best bet was to keep your head down and not look anyone in the eye. Couldn't tell who might take advantage of someone's reluctance to pull just to settle an old score.

"Thought you was gonna find out who Martin's *real* daddy was," Jarvis said to me in a tone that fell just short of an accusation. It was hard to tell if the boy was sassing me. He had earnest eyes, but spoke with a forked tongue.

"Yeah," Red joined in from below. "You said it'd account for why Martin ain't dead like the rest of us!"

"Hobble your lip, ginger boy," Mabel scolded. "You already got Luther suspicious with your yapping about the child."

"I still have to confirm something with Buddy," I explained.

"Ain't he up yet? The ribs are nearly done!" Whiny Pete said. "I don't know how anyone could sleep with that blasted smell in the air."

"He musta tied one on last night," I said. "But his hunger'll wake him soon enough."

We wet our whistles with some pre-chow beers. The barroom started to fill in. To pass the time, I interviewed a newbie who'd come to town the previous week. He'd worked as a fur trapper in the Great Lakes region. One of his hands had got mangled in a trap and the wound became corrupted. The boys called him Lefty on account of his right hand was little more than shreds. When he tried to lift his beer, he ended up swatting the glass with the crumpled flesh and withered veins. He was the shy sort, not used to being around people after so many years alone in the woods. When they teased him, he reddened and stormed out of the saloon. As he left, Buddy came barreling through the door like a man on a mission.

"Hey, I need to ask you something," I told him, but just then the dinner bell rang.

Sal yelled, "Come and git it!" as he placed a heap of steaming ribs on the bar.

Buddy's eyes widened and drool fell from his lip. "Not now, pencil pusher," he said. "Ain't gonna be nothin' left but bones if you get gabbin'."

A mob of hungry men swarmed the bar, pushing and shoving to get to the front. As Sal went back to the kitchen to fetch another rack of ribs, there was nobody to make sure a line formed. You might have taken them for a pack of swine crowding a trough if that hadn't been what was being served for dinner. One of the soldiers stepped on a cowpuncher's foot, and he took offense.

"I just shined them boots, you buffoon!" the cowpuncher bawled. "You're gonna clean 'em or you're gonna draw!"

The other army boys were backing the soldier up, so he just snickered carelessly. The cowpuncher wasn't pleased to be ignored, so he got in the soldier's face. While they were bickering, a cockeyed outlaw crept up and stole the cowboy's gun. I'd had my eye on the fella ever since he arrived a few days earlier. Folks called him Stupid Simon on account of he was a little touched in the head.

Simon started firing the gun into the crowd without much concern over who he hit. At first, it seemed like he just wanted to drop a few bodies so that he could get to the ribs faster. But the sight of the corpses made him laugh, and he couldn't stop. Folks in front of the bar couldn't tell where the shots were coming from, so they drew their guns and started firing at the back of the room. A cloud of gunsmoke soon filled the air, and nobody could see who was shooting who. Men were moaning and squirming on the floor. Eventually, Simon ran out of bullets and the gunfire stopped. Then he grabbed a gun from the holster of a wounded man and started shooting in both directions. It began all over again, with the people in the front firing at the people in the back, and there didn't seem like there would be any end to it.

In the middle of all the chaos, a new fella came through the door. He had dark skin and a colorful bandana tied around his neck. He was wearing leather chaps, and if I had to guess I would've said he had tried to ride a steer that didn't want to be ridden. The new fella didn't stop to ask what was going on. He just walked up behind Simon, grabbed an ear in each hand, then gave his head a twist. A loud crack sounded, and the cockeyed outlaw fell to the ground with a busted neck.

The stranger didn't wait for anyone's thanks. "Ooh, ribs!" he said, looking at the bar, then stepped up and served himself a plateful. Buddy was the first one to follow. Then everyone else quickly lined up, a little more orderly this time.

"Hell of an entrance that bronc buster made," Sal remarked. "Ain't ya gonna go find out what his story is, Tom?"

"I'll speak with him later," I replied. "First, I gotta ask the deputy something."

Buddy scarfed down a half dozen ribs without taking a breath. Finally, I managed to pull him aside so that I wouldn't stir up suspicions in case I was wrong.

"Do you recall the night we first sat down with Nigel?" I asked.

"I guess so. What's this about?"

"Remember how Nigel told us he had killed his older brother to protect his wife?"

"I do, indeed. It was after them wolves attacked Ms. Parker in front of their saloon. We sat over in that corner and drank a bunch of gin."

"Nigel told us he had a younger brother, too," I said. "He ran off after Nigel killed his older brother. Later on, the vampire council read his mind, so they sent Luther after Nigel when they learnt what he'd done."

"Sounds about right," Buddy said.

"Do you happen to remember the name of Nigel's younger brother?"

"Hmm. I don't recall," Buddy said. "Now, what's this all about?"

"Not sure yet." I sipped my beer. "Just speculatin'. Mind keeping this to yourself awhile?"

"Sure, Tom."

"If you'll excuse me, I gotta greet this new fella."

The Crapper

Comings: Eight more soldiers came to town. They were hunting Choctaws in a Louisiana swamp when they got ambushed, so they all smell like waterlogged corpses. Also, Lefty, a fur trapper, arrived after succumbing to blood poisoning from an accidental self-inflicted wound. I didn't get his full name since he stormed off in embarrassment when folks teased him about his klutziness.

A cockeyed newbie, who folks called Stupid Simon, arrived from Delaware a few days ago and spoiled some folks' supper last night. Thankfully, another new man arrived in time to send him to hell before the ribs got cold.

Bill Pickett goes by Rodeo Bo. His parents were freed slaves, and he believes he is a quarter Cherokee as well. He was born in Liberty Hill, Texas, where he rode broncs to some acclaim. He claims to have invented a technique for wrestling steer to the ground while biting their lip. Calls it "bulldogging." The technique backfired on him yesterday when he received a kick to the head.

Goings: While the ribs were being served, fifteen men got shot, but only five went to hell, including Stupid Simon. The ruckus all started, as it often does, because someone stepped on the foot of a man who had spent entirely too much time shining his boots.

Also sent to hell were Slippery Silas (a crooked shopkeeper from Idaho), Big Billy (a prospector from Arkansas by way of California), and Little Billy (a dairy farmer from Pennsylvania). They had died of cholera, consumption, and pneumonia, but no one could recall who had which.

In addition, Gut-Shot Granny shot a newbie named Francis after I whooped him in a fight. From asking around, I found out that the boy had a hard time of it while growing up in Cincinnati. He was as poor as a church mouse, and his pop ran out on the family. Francis did what he had to do, including stealing, and he once killed a man for a ham hock—none of which excuses disrespecting his elders or trying to saddle Old Moe with a piss-poor nickname like Termite.

I can't really say much about Stupid Simon, except that he really enjoyed shooting folks, and he didn't get to eat any ribs.

Chapter 8

The Red Gem

Most of the cowpunchers didn't care much about the color of Rodeo Bo's skin. Out on the frontier, there were lots of freed slaves looking for opportunity. Since ranches were often understaffed, many of the men ended up herding cattle, and whites and blacks worked side by side, eating from the same chuckwagon. The ranch bosses I'd met said black cowboys proved to be reliable workers who never shirked their duty during a stampede or an Indian raid. The older Confederate soldiers, on the other hand, had no such occasion to change their opinions. They made spiteful remarks behind Bo's back. But when his talents came in handy to save their hides, they forgot all about the flag they had died fighting for.

It was just a few days after Bo's arrival when a whole sounder of wild boars came out of the dust. Usually they came just one or two at a time, so nobody was ready for so many at once. Sal had hired an army boy named Kenny to help him round up pigs, but these swine were too numerous and ornery to tackle, especially for a lazy redneck soldier with bad knees.

"They're headed for the teepees!" Kenny shouted.

"Well get after 'em," Sal hollered.

"Them Injuns'll stick those hogs—after they get a *surprise*."

"We can't have those bow-benders gettin' in the habit of eatin' pork," Sal said worriedly. "It blurs the lines. Could make it harder for us to get our share in the future. You better shoot them suckers, Kenny, 'fore the red men get the taste of ham on their lips."

"Are you kiddin' me?" Kenny balked. "I ain't wastin' no bullets on boars—not with half the Navajo nation out there looking to give me a haircut!"

"Either you waste five bullets now or you're gonna need five hundred later on to keep dinner on the table."

With all their bickering, the opportunity was lost as the herd sped across the plains, kicking up a heap of dust. They must've caught the scent of chickens roasting in the Indian camp, because they were heading straight for it at full speed.

"Them hogs is outta my range," Kenny said and put down his rifle. He had been at the Battle of the Alamo, and didn't have any problem accepting defeat. He claimed that surrendering to Santa Anna would have been far better than starving and sweating under the Texas sun for three days before dying. "Guess we're just gonna have to eat something else," he told Sal.

A horseback rider suddenly bolted from the other side of town. He was swatting his mustang's rear with his hat like it was on fire. Turned out to be Rodeo Bo chasing those boars. First thing he did when he caught up with the herd was corral them away from the Indian camp. They began running back toward town, which bought him some time.

"I can pick 'em off now," Kenny said, raising his rifle.

"Hold 'er there a sec," Sal told him. "Let's see what this fella has in mind."

Bo had several lengths of rope on his saddle, and he started swinging a wide loop in the air while bearing down on the smallest suckling. When he was just beside the hog, he released the rope and lassoed its neck. As the rope slid down to the animal's ankles, Bo gave it a quick tug. Sure enough, the fuzzy piglet tripped and tumbled onto its back. Bo quickly let go of the other end and was on to the next slowest of the pack.

"What ya waiting for?" Sal scolded Kenny. "Go stick that sucker in the eyes before he breaks the rope!"

Bo lassoed three more medium-sized boars just as quickly and efficiently. Kenny had a hard time keeping up. He could barely run the pigs down before they broke free of Bo's ropes. The largest and meanest of all was the mother. She had a red mane running down her back that looked like a flame for how fast she ran. She was headed straight into town with her head down and her powerful neck ready to ram someone. The old-timers in front of the general store heard her squeals and jumped up on barrels just in time to avoid getting trampled. One sodbuster wasn't quick enough, though, and he got gored by the curved tusks pointing from her bottom lip.

The sow must not have taken kindly to the treatment of her kin, because she was charging with a vengeance toward a gaggle of soldiers in gray uniforms that had long faded to a butternut brown. They had served under General Lee, and they were lazing on their backs, complaining about how they could have won the war. Two of them even had their shoes off, never reckoning two hundred pounds of angry swine would come thundering down the road.

They finally looked up when they heard hooves crashing down a few feet from their heads. Bo threw a double length of rope over the sow's shoulders just in the nick of time. She was too strong to take down with bare hands. Bo would've been yanked clear off his horse. Instead, he tied the other end of the rope to the horn on his saddle, then turned and sallied his horse in the other direction. As the rope pulled tight, she rolled over in midair before flopping down on her back right in front of the defenseless soldiers. Bo didn't waste any time in hog-tying her, since Kenny was still way out in the plains.

"Pretty good roping, pal," one of the soldiers complimented Bo, trying to sound casual, though all three had probably browned their britches. There were no mutterings about an inferior race then. The Confederates looked downright worshipful of the dark-skinned rodeo rider.

The Chinaman soon came along with a wagon. It took five men to lift the great red hog onto the back, and afterward they all complained of aching backs.

"Big sucka!" the Chinaman remarked, petting the sow's head as she snorted and squirmed restlessly beneath the ropes. "I name her Mei. It mean red gem."

"Well, that red gem'll get you through a famine," Bo remarked.

"Let's hope we don't have to find out about that," one of the Confederates said with a chuckle.

Bo eyed the soldier's broad belly. "You might wanna keep a close eye on this hog, partner." He laughed. "It don't look like you're accustomed to missing meals."

Chapter 9

A Damsel Causing Distress

"Ain't gonna be no more hen fruit," Sal announced as he came into the saloon holding a basket under his arm.

"Say again?" Old Moe cupped his ear.

"Chief wants all the eggs now. Since they come from the chickens, he reckons they're entitled to 'em."

"Well, in a manner of speaking he ain't entirely wrong," said the scalped soldier.

"Just whose side you on?" one of the Confederate soldiers asked.

"Not yours, gray coat!"

"Ah, shit!" Red grumbled from below. "What the hell we supposed to have for breakfast now?"

"I don't know why y'all are complainin' anyway," Kenny interrupted. "With all them boars that dark fella roped, we don't need no eggs. Hell, I could eat pork three meals a day."

Red pounded at the floorboards below to show his disapproval. "Ain't no Squanto gonna tell me I can't have an omelet when I want one!"

"Indians outnumber us now," I pointed out. "We should be happy they ain't asking for the pigs as well."

"I reckon that's next," Sal said. "Prolly just testing the waters with the eggs. Injuns keep coming at this rate, they're gonna need the cows, too."

"I'd like to see 'em try," Whiny Pete put in. "Wolves won't lie down to a bunch of red bellies with bows and arrows, even if there's a thousand of 'em."

"Anyway, these are the last eggs we're gonna get," Sal said. "I grabbed 'em from beneath a chicken roosting in a wagon that just came out of the dust. Injuns twisted the chicken's neck, but they didn't notice me taking these eggs. Hey, this one's still warm."

"Crack it open!" the scalped soldier suggested. "Might be a chick inside."

"Let me take a gander at that," said a farmer named Jake. He wasn't your run-of-the-mill dirt-tiller. Jake was more of the studious sort. He held the egg up to a candle and squinted like he was examining a diamond. "You can see some veining in there. It ain't a chick yet, but if you keep 'er warm, who knows? Maybe it'll hatch."

"Are you saying something's growin' in there?" Whiny Pete asked. "How could it still be alive?"

"If Ms. Parker could carry a baby here in her tummy, why couldn't a chicken bring a fertilized egg?" Jarvis said.

"Give 'er here," Buddy ordered, growing oddly possessive of the hen fruit. He gathered up a handful of dry hay to line his pocket, then nestled the egg in there. After it was nice and cozy, he turned and fled like he was late for something. On the way out, he nearly ran into Ms. Parker while she was coming in. First thing he did was check to make sure the egg didn't break. As an afterthought, he dipped his hat and begged her pardon.

It was an awkward moment because the two of them hadn't spoken more than a few words since Martin was born. She'd been spending most of her time with Nigel on account of the protective role he'd taken. Buddy quickly scurried out the door.

It wasn't often that I had the opportunity to chat with Ms. Parker alone, so I sat down beside her at the bar. "Not sure if it's a good time, but there was something I've been meaning to ask you about, ma'am."

"What is it, Thomas?"

"I just can't figure out why you ended up here," I said flatly.

"I beg your pardon."

"It couldn't have been just for killing yourself or having premarital relations—excuse me for being indelicate."

"We all have our sins," she reminded me.

"I know it better than most, ma'am," I admitted.

"It sounds like you have a theory you're about to tell me, Thomas."

"Your fiancé wasn't Martin's father, was he?"

"Why would you say that?" She was taken aback, but not entirely surprised.

"On the night you arrived, you told us the man's name was Henry. You screamed out, 'Please forgive me, Henry!' But after Martin was born, you said you named him after his father."

"Very keen of you to notice," she said.

"Much as I'd like to take the credit, it wasn't me who figured it out. It was that boy Jarvis with the shot-up face. He was reading old issues of *The Crapper*, like you used to. He's keen on pointing out my errors and such. Not much slips by him, I'm afraid."

"Does Nigel know?" she asked worriedly.

"I can't rightly say, ma'am."

"You might as well hear the whole story then. Just promise to keep it out of your paper."

"Fair enough," I agreed.

"My fiancé Henry and I had a tiff a few weeks before our wedding. The next day a handsome foreigner came into our dry goods shop. Normally, I wouldn't pay any mind to strangers, but when he spoke I found I couldn't take my eyes off him. It was like he cast a spell on me."

"And you think he was Nigel's brother?"

She gasped. "How do you know?"

"I wasn't for certain, ma'am. Jarvis got me to thinking, and I seemed to recall Martin was the name Nigel called his younger brother by. At the time of the telling, I was more struck by how unsettled you were. Guess now I know why."

"You won't tell anyone, will you? You heard those awful things Nigel said about half-breed vampires, how they slaughter entire towns just for fun. And who knows how Luther would react? Wasn't it his job to keep vampires from mixing with humans? I wouldn't want anyone to harm Martin for fear of what he might become."

"I don't think there's much cause for alarm, ma'am. Nigel said half-breed vampires gotta drink warm blood to become full vampires, and there's none in Damnation."

"I know that, but when folks get to talking, who knows what they'll speculate, and with the rain and lightning and all the odd things that have been going on..."

Sal served up the other eggs that showed no signs of being fertilized. There was a lull between breakfast and lunch when most folks took a nap, so there were enough scrambled eggs to go around.

"Oughta make this a regular thing," Farmer Jake said, "like a combination of breakfast and lunch."

"That's the dumbest thing I ever heard," Sal said. "But I wouldn't mind doing it once a week just to break things up. Folks might get shitfaced and pass out, so I wouldn't have to cook no supper."

Just then, a girl in a fancy blue gown walked into the saloon. She was a few years younger than Ms. Parker, but the paint on her face and the cut of her mop gave her a womanly appearance beyond her years. She turned around and her whole back was scorched black like she'd been lying facedown during a fire. The men still found the front of her worth ogling, though.

"What's your name, honey?" Sal asked.

"Annabelle, sir," she sniffled. "Where am I?"

"I'll let you handle this one, Thomas."

"Well, young lady, what's the last thing you remember?" I asked.

"I was getting ready for the cotillion ball, where I was being presented," she said with a southern accent. "I had my hair just right, and my gown looked perfect." She looked down at the smudges of ash on her dress. It dawned on her then what had happened. "Charlotte came in with a can of kerosene..." A look of horror came over Annabelle's face as she recalled it. "She splashed the drapes, and when she lit a match the whole room brightened. Then she locked the door behind her." Annabelle held up her hands, and her fingertips were covered with splinters from clawing at the door.

"Why would someone do such a thing?" Mabel gasped.

"She was jealous," Annabelle replied flatly.

"Was Charlotte your sister, honey?"

"Oh, we were much closer than that," she said with a naughty look.

Mabel gave the girl a handkerchief and led her away from the prying eyes. She might have been little more than a child, but she'd stirred the men's longings. Once awoken, there was little else they could think about.

There weren't any empty rooms in the hotel, so Mabel put Annabelle up in hers.

"It's nice to see Mabel take a motherly interest in the young lady," I said after they were gone.

"That tomcat don't do nothing that ain't in her own interest," Sal snarled.

"What you mean?" I asked. "That girl ain't got nothing but a charred-up back. What can she give Mabel?"

"Oh, she's got something she can pay with," he nodded insinuatingly.

"Does that mean there's gonna be sporting ladies in the new saloon?" Whiny Pete asked.

"Could be," a soldier speculated.

Sal's face grew red with anger at the thought of it. "Damn that woman!" "Reckon I'll be drinking at the Rusty Nail," Red hollered from below. "Whenever it's finished."

"I don't think that'll be possible," one of the carpenters teased. "The floor plan don't include no cellar."

Chapter 10

Sightless Sal and the Buzzard

Early one morning, a dead mule came out of the dust pulling a wagon. Perched on top was a redheaded turkey vulture pecking away at something we couldn't quite see. As the wagon rolled closer to town, I nearly aired my paunch at the sight of it. The driver's shattered eyeball was dangling from the bird's beak. The man soon awoke with a horrified screech and shook the buzzard off his chest. Both eyes had already been gobbled up. As the bird flew off, spots of the violet sky showed through the bullet holes in its wings.

"Drag that unlucky bastard into the saloon," Sal told Kenny.

"I weren't hired for that," Kenny argued. "The agreement was for hogs, not men with no eyes." His argument fell on deaf ears.

"And wrap up his empty sockets real tight first," Sal barked. "I don't need him bleeding all over my floor. The mop's already stained red. It's darn near useless!"

After the newbie had some whiskey to dull the pain, it was left to me to tell him that he was both blind and dead, which is about the most hopeless news a person can hear. Some reckoned there wasn't any use in even telling him that he was dead, since he couldn't see everyone's wounds or that the sun never rose.

"He'll prolly get sent to hell by the end of the day anyway," Kenny said.

"I'll take some of that action!" said the scalped soldier.

As the betting went on, I gave it to the newbie straight. He took it well. It turned out he had known it was coming for a while. He'd even been looking forward to it.

"I ran out of water in the middle of the Mojave," he explained. "That damn buzzard was circling me for weeks. I used my last bullets trying to keep from becoming his lunch. I guess my eyes didn't make it."

"What's your name, friend?" I asked.

"Salvatore," he said. "But folks call me Sal."

"Oh, no! Not here they don't," the other Sal said sternly from behind the bar. "We can't have two Sals in the same saloon. It just ain't done. Somebody shoot that sightless sack of shit."

"Now hold on a minute," Rodeo Bo interrupted. "There's gonna be a new saloon across the street soon, right? You can have one Sal for each saloon, can't ya? Maybe this here Blind Sal will wanna drink at the other saloon instead of this one."

"Yeah," Whiny Pete added. "After all, they're gonna have whores over there!"

"Easy, Pete. Don't go spreading no rumors," I warned him. "You get these fellas expectin' a cathouse, and they're gonna tear the place down if it turns out to be a reg'lar thirst parlor."

Red was just rousing from his nap below, and he only heard bits and pieces of the conversation. "Just what in tarnation is going on up there?" he asked. "I nod off for an hour and now y'all got a whorehouse for buzzards and blind men!"

Even though lots of the fellas had bet the blind newbie wouldn't last the day, nobody was inclined to shoot the man. They liked that he got under Sal's skin. The money they had lost was worth the entertainment of seeing the cranky old bartender in a tizzy. If anything, Sal's fits assured that his sightless namesake would hang around for a spell.

The vulture seemed like it might last awhile in Damnation, too. On account of the constant swirl of the wind, it could stay up in the sky, coasting for hours just by tilting its wings. When it finally set down, the cowboys took aim, but nobody could hit the ghost-bird. After a few days, they all gave up, not wanting to waste valuable bullets on an unhittable target.

I was friendly with an Iroquois fella named Little Bear, whom I traded with from time to time. From him, I gathered that the Indians didn't like the buzzard much either. They reckoned it was a bad omen. Whenever one of their own got stabbed or shot in a squabble, they didn't feed the body to pigs like we did. Instead, they put it up on a scaffold, as was the custom of some tribes. The stilted platforms stood between the Indian camp and the dust wall.

The Great Plains tribes had originally used the scaffoldings to keep animals from digging up the bodies of their loved ones. There was no need to worry about that in Damnation since we ate all the animals soon after they arrived. Regardless, the dry silt made grave-digging a tiresome task. The Indians reckoned it was easier to build the scaffoldings from the wood of old wagons, and more respectful than leaving one of their kin on the ground. The horizon was lined with dozens of raised platforms piled with rotting bodies. Right away, the buzzard began feeding on those hell-sent Indians. No matter how many arrows they shot at the pesky bird, they couldn't hit it.

I reckoned this problem might have arisen back on Earth, so I questioned Little Bear about it. Though we were friendly, his mysterious manner of speaking didn't lend me to believe we were true pals.

"They say when bird peck at body, it carry soul off to spirit world," he explained.

"But since we're already in the spirit world, where's that buzzard gonna carry off the souls that it eats here?"

"Some say because bird is here, this not true spirit world."

"Where are we then?" I asked.

"White man spirit world," he said. "They believe we must conquer it and get rid of all white men because we failed to last time." Then he gave me a creepy smile.

"Do you believe that, Little Bear?" I asked.

"Don't matter," he answered. "I am Iroquois. There are very few of my people here. My belief only matter if many more Iroquois come."

Chapter 11

Just Sal

"What's for breakfast?" Rodeo Bo asked.

"Sal says pork and beans," Whiny Pete answered.

"Which one?" Bo asked.

"What do you mean which one? Both pork *and* beans."

"No, which Sal?" Bo grinned playfully. "There's two now."

"What the hell you askin' that for?" Sal the bartender hollered angrily. "There's only one dang Sal who makes breakfast, ain't there? You don't see that blind fool using a spatula and a frying pan, do you?"

"Dunno," Bo shrugged. "He could be a swell cook for all I know. They say when you lose one ability, the Lord gives you another. He might even be a better cook than you. Could be the best cook there ever was!"

"The Lord ain't doling out any special skills after you're born," Sal grumbled. "If he was, how come Tom didn't get any when he was hobbled as a boy?"

"Ain't he good at scribblin' that paper y'all read?" Bo asked.

"He was a dang reporter his whole life! That's how he got good at scribblin'."

"Well, he might not have been if he weren't hobbled," Bo pressed.

They looked to me, and I just shrugged. "I can't rightly say how things might've turned out if I wasn't injured as a boy."

"Oh, I ain't listenin' to this nonsense. If you want some blind fool making breakfast, it's fine by me. And if you want some hussy pouring drinks in a new saloon across the street, be my guest. This whole town's goin' to pot anyhow. The damn Injuns are prolly gonna send us all to hell soon!" At that, Sal stormed off to the kitchen.

"What the hell'd you do that for?" I asked Bo. "You know he's sensitive about there being two Sals. You ain't gotta needle him about it."

"It's a fair question," Bo insisted. "How am I supposed to know which Sal is being spoken about?"

Old Moe had the final say on the matter. "The new Sal is Blind Sal," he declared. "And that's how you should refer to him. Old Sal is just Sal, and you don't have to call him nothing else."

"Okay," Bo conceded, and he was quiet for a full minute before he spoke up again. "Hey, I need a refill. Where the hell is Just Sal?"

Although most folks enjoyed having Blind Sal around, a few of the newbies had their eye on him. He was an easy target to show some grit without much risk of being shot. He was also easy pickings for stealing sips. Sneaky Jim didn't even wait for him to visit the commode. He reached over from the end of the bar and began lifting the blind man's beer stein.

"Hey there!" Blind Sal shouted and slapped Sneaky Jim's hand. Jim slipped off the stool he was balancing on and fell to the floor.

"I tol' ya," Rodeo Bo said. "The Lord gave 'im special abilities to hear sip stealers since he can't see." A few of the other fellas nodded, suspecting Bo might be right.

Mabel suddenly burst through the door, asking if anyone had seen Ms. Parker.

"Who's watching the baby?" Nigel said worriedly, then bolted out of the saloon. He returned a few moments later with the child safely in his arms.

"Ms. Parker wouldn't have left Martin all alone," I said.

"I'm afraid there's a rather unsettling explanation for that." Nigel held up a bone choker necklace with turquoise beads. "I found this on the floor."

"That's an Apache necklace," one of the soldiers pointed out. "Our scout was Apache and he had one just like it."

"The big buck with the shot-up chest was wearing that when he came into the saloon looking for his sister," Jake pointed out.

"Ms. Parker musta tore it off 'im during the struggle when he took her," Sal said.

"See!" Red called out from under the floorboards. "Y'all shoulda sent his ass to hell when you had the chance!"

"Quiet!" Sal scolded. "This is clearly revenge for what you done to his sister."

"Yeah," a soldier interrupted. "We should just turn you over to him and be done with it."

"Now wait a minute!" Red argued. "I was only defending myself. You can't turn a white man over to a bunch of hatchet-packers. It's against the code."

"There ain't no code in Damnation," the soldier said.

"Simmer down, boys!" I said. "The brave still thinks we're hiding his sister. If he finds out what really happened to her, he won't have much reason to keep Ms. Parker around."

"Y'all can flap your gums as much as ya want." Buddy rose. "I'm gonna get her back."

"They'll cut you down before you get within a hundred yards," Kenny said.

"Nigel can dodge their arrows," Whiny Pete said.

"I am not quick enough to evade a hundred arrows. Besides, if I am shot, who would protect Martin?"

Buddy looked at Nigel with a scowl. "You don't even care about Ms. Parker as long as your nephew is safe."

The room silenced.

"You knew?" I asked.

"Course I knew. Nigel told us his brother was named Martin. How many people are there running around the frontier with a namby-pamby name like Martin?" Nigel must have known all along, too, because he didn't show any surprise.

While Buddy was speaking, a pickpocket named Amos used the distraction to take Blind Sal's money off the bar. Blind Sal grabbed his arm. Amos pulled his pistol, but before he could shoot, a blast exploded into his gut. Blind Sal was holding a smoking gun in his hand.

"Nice shot, partner," Rodeo Bo complimented, tipping his hat at the blind man.

"Where you suppose he got that pistol?" I asked.

Sneaky Jim looked down at his empty holster, then called out, "Hey, that's my gun, you thieving bastard!"

Blind Sal pointed the barrel in the direction he reckoned Sneaky Jim's voice had come from, and it was a pretty good estimation. Some sighted men had worse aim than him.

"All right, you can borrow it for a spell." Jim raised his hands skyward.

"I've had enough of this nonsense," Buddy declared and pulled Sal's scattergun from the umbrella stand. "I'm gonna go get Ms. Parker back before them Injuns harm her."

"Hold on a moment," Nigel said. "It won't do much good for you to go off on your own and get shot down. I may not be able to dodge the Indians' arrows in my weakened state, but Luther is still strong. I'll inquire if he might assist us in a proper plan."

"Why would he want to do that?" I asked.

"We have a shared interest," Nigel answered.

The Crapper

Comings: *As you've probably already noticed, there's a dead buzzard circling in the sky that not even the sharpshooters can hit. It came to town while making a meal of Salvatore Taranto's eyeballs. Blind Sal, as he has come to be called, was born in Brooklyn, and his parents were from Naples. He left the city to make his fortune in the West, but he ran out of water in the desert. While dying of thirst, the buzzard pecked out his peepers. To his credit, he managed to shoot a few holes in its wings—a feat no one else can claim—so he must've been a fair shot. Seems the bird bled out about the same time as Blind Sal died.*

You are also sure to have noticed a southern belle in a blue gown that's all burnt up in the back. Annabelle Constantine hails from Georgia. A jealous lover set her on fire before her big coming-out party. Mabel has taken the girl under her wing, so don't go getting any ideas about mistreating her. If you do, you may not be welcome at Mabel's new saloon.

Goings: *Just after he arrived, Blind Sal shot Amos the pickpocket, who had been in town for about a year after dying from dysentery in Denver. He proved useful with a rifle when we were fighting off the wolves. He might've come in handy in the event of a similar situation with the growing Indian population.*

Lastly, Ms. Parker has gone missing. On account of an Apache necklace found in her room, it is believed that the big brave who came into the Foggy Dew is ransoming her for his sister, which won't be possible since Red already sent her to hell.

Chapter 12

Fanatics of Scripture

Lots of the army boys had trench foot. The soggy flesh on their toes would flake off when they removed their boots at night. It made the bunks smell worse than an undertaker's house, so I stayed at the Foggy Dew as late as possible to avoid it. After writing the latest issue of *The Crapper*, I fell asleep at the bar. Just before closing, I was awoken by the sound of laughter.

"Why would I bother?" Luther asked Nigel. I kept my eyes clenched so they wouldn't know I was listening. "Their blood is cold," he continued. "Who cares if the humans destroy one another?"

"As I recall, old chap, you said that you upheld vampire law in order to keep the humans from becoming 'mere sacks of blood that we feed on.' Have you no sympathies for their lot now?"

"But what does it matter to you if the red men take some woman?"

"She reminds me of someone."

"Your human wife?" Luther asked. "The one you killed your older brother for?"

Nigel didn't say nothing, but he must have nodded.

"Interesting," Luther chuckled. "When you can read minds, you never notice these things."

"What's that?"

"You scratched your ear, just like those poker players do when their cards are no good."

"Are you insinuating that I am lying?"

"You deny it then?"

"What would I have to hide from you? We are the only two vampires here."

"Who is Martin?" Luther asked.

Nigel didn't say anything, but I could hear him fidgeting uncomfortably.

"I may not be able to hear thoughts anymore, but I'm not deaf." Luther laughed loudly. "They talk about the child constantly."

"I wasn't sure you'd cooperate if you knew."

"Knew what?"

"You asked me if *He* is present here."

"The dark one?" Luther shuddered.

"I sense a presence within the child."

"He is a vampire?" Luther was taken aback.

"A half-breed born of my younger brother and a human."

"So what?" Luther chuckled in disbelief. "You think he is *the son?*"

"The child was born beyond the grave. He is part living and part dead."

"There is a *living* creature here?" Luther's eyes lit up with a yellow glow.

"Don't you see?" Nigel's voice rose. "His blood is unholy. Not only would it be sacrilegious to consume, but also poisonous. You've read the scriptures."

"I didn't know you were so devout," Luther teased. "But those are just stories that the old ones told to scare the young ones."

"But what if they're true?"

"As I recall, the scriptures refer to him as 'the destroyer of all things.' Why would you even want to summon such a thing?"

"The scriptures also say he is supposed to turn the afterlife into actual life. He could give birth to a new world here, where warm blood flows through the veins of living creatures. We could feed again!"

"But first he would annihilate everyone?"

"Except for the forgetful remainders," Nigel said. "Remember, he will spare those select few who will bear witness to the event and make a record of it before all memory of it is erased."

"So you think you'll be one of the forgetful remainders?" Luther scoffed.

"We are vampires, like him," Nigel said proudly. "Why should he slaughter us? Besides, if there is a chance we might feed again, what choice do we have? Would you rather spend a thousand years withering away in this dusty town, listening to cowboys bicker over games of chance?"

"So why is the woman so important?"

"The destroyer must be reared on his mother's milk until he can be weaned onto warm blood."

"And what warm blood will you feed him if he lives long enough?"

"We'll figure that out when the time comes. You never know what will come out of the dust. A living creature already came inside of a dead one. Maybe another pregnant woman will arrive, or perhaps just a pregnant animal. Besides, what else do you have to do tomorrow? I should think you would find the slaughtering of a few dozen red men amusing."

Luther smiled. "Why not?"

"Cheers!" Nigel lifted his glass.

"*Prost!*" Luther replied and they finished their drinks. After they left, Sal came by to collect their glasses.

"Why are you looking so haggard, Tom?"

"I overheard Nigel and Luther talking while they thought I was asleep."

"Oh, and what were they gabbing about? Some kinda vampire gossip?" he snickered.

"Nigel thinks Martin might be some kind of half-breed vampire who'll destroy the whole town."

"But he's only a child. When's that supposed to happen?"

"When he grows up some, I suppose."

"Ah, I can't be worryin' over that now. I got my own problems," Sal griped. "That hussy's building a saloon across the way. And there's another Sal in town now. Folks are saying he might be a better cook than me, even though he can't even see. 'Sides, we'll probably all get sent to hell long before Martin grows up. You see how many dang Injuns are out there?"

"That's a good point. Also, Martin's gotta drink warm blood first."

"Well, there you have it! No use in worryin' about another live baby comin' to town," Sal decided. "I was here nearly a hundred years before the first gal came in wearing the bustle backward. What's the odds of it happening again 'fore someone shoots me?"

"Ever seen any pregnant animals?" I asked. "They might have warm blood."

"Butchered a few stillborn piglets," he said. "Blood was cold as ours."

"How about that egg Buddy's holding? Think it'll hatch a living chick?"

"Ah, Buddy's more likely to squash that egg before anything could hatch from it."

"All the same, vampires seem keen on Martin getting warm blood and wiping everyone out, 'cept a few witnesses."

"Sounds like a buncha wingnut nonsense to me," Sal said. "Reminds me of that gibberish the preacher used to spout. Guess vampires ain't no smarter than men. Did Luther say if he was gonna help get Ms. Parker back?"

"He did. They need her to nurse Martin till they get him some warm blood."

"Good." Sal collected the glasses and wiped down the bar. "Kinda nice having a respectable lady around. Not like that Jezebel Mabel and that new southern floozy."

"I suppose it is a long time before we have to worry about Martin growing up and sending us all to hell."

"Just the same," Sal added. "I wouldn't go sharing it with the others. 'Less you want 'em to tear the child to pieces. You know how folks get worked up about things."

Sal had a point.

Chapter 13

The Unkillable Indian

The plan was for Buddy to cause a distraction while Nigel slipped into the back of the Indian camp and found Ms. Parker. If anything went wrong, Luther would attack from the other side to divide the forces.

"What are you doing?" Nigel asked Buddy as he staggered to the door.

"Ya said I should get drunk and cause a fight with an Injun," Buddy slurred.

"No," Nigel reminded him. "I said you should *appear* inebriated and start an argument with one of the Native Americans."

"Who's that?"

"The people who inhabited your land before you arrived?"

"You mean the Injuns? Yeah, I'm gonna fight one!"

On the way to the door, Buddy reached into his pocket and pulled out a ball of hay, whispering to me, "Hold onto 'er for me, Tom." He stuck it into my hand before I could refuse. The egg was still nestled safely inside. It didn't have a single crack on it. "If I don't come back, keep 'er warm till she hatches!"

Sal gave me a nod, as if to say it wouldn't be so bad if I happened to drop the egg. My fingertip tingled as I touched it. Felt different from all the other dead objects in Damnation. It wasn't that I could feel anything moving inside of it. It seemed more like the whole thing was made up of tiny moving stuff, shell and all. I slid it in my pocket before Luther or Nigel could see it, fearing they might be able to tell if there was a living creature inside. There was no use in letting them know about the possibility of warm blood if their plan included us being destroyed by baby Martin someday.

Buddy marched out the door and headed into the flatlands. A few hundred yards of barren dirt and withered cacti separated the town from the Indians' camp, and Buddy looked winded after just fifty feet. Meanwhile, Luther and Nigel slipped out the back door and raced toward the least crowded section of the camp. Teepees stretched almost entirely around the perimeter of the town, but there were a few breaks where someone could slip by if they moved as quickly as a vampire.

Buddy, on the other hand, went straight to the loudest, busiest area. The population had swelled considerably in the last few weeks. The chickens that came out of the dust were nowhere near enough to feed everyone. The bones strewn across the plains showed that they had taken to eating pigs, despite the agreement not to. A steer came through the dust just then, but the chief must have told the braves to let it pass, probably on account of he didn't want to fight both us and the wolves at the same time.

I crouched behind a broken barrel to watch as Buddy approached the circle of teepees. There was some kind of powwow going on, with drums pounding and an old fella yodeling with a voice as high as a girl's. When the warriors noticed that a tubby white man had moseyed up into the middle of their shindig, they gaped at him silently.

It turned out that Buddy didn't have to do anything to start a fight. The big buck whose sister Red had sent to hell came forward and stuck out his arm. Buddy laughed drunkenly as he tumbled backward and fell on the ground. While he was down, a couple of little fellas plucked the guns out of his holsters.

A half dozen men circled around Buddy and started kicking him. Their bare feet smacked against his ribs, and his face got cut up pretty good from their toenails. I hadn't seen anyone take such a walloping in a long time. Buddy didn't curl up and surrender like most would have. He egged them on with taunts. "Is that all ya got?"

He was trying to hold their attention as long as possible so Nigel could rescue Ms. Parker. After a few minutes, he managed to get to his feet, but only stayed upright because the blows were coming from every direction. Every time he started to fall, a punch sent him the other direction.

Eventually, the big buck parted the crowd and raised a long knife. Buddy's eyes were swollen shut, but he could feel the steel on his neck. Not being close enough to hear, we could only guess that he was inquiring about his sister's whereabouts again. He did not look pleased with the response. The buck backhanded Buddy's cheek.

Buddy finally got fed up with being an Apache punching bag. "Ah, fuck y'all!" he shouted and reached behind his back where a Colt was hidden in his waistband beneath his coattails. He pulled it out and fired before they realized he was heeled. The blast knocked the buck clear off his feet. Couldn't tell where he was struck since he already had so many bullet holes in him.

None of the nearby Indians were armed, on account of them being in the middle of their powwow. Buddy managed to drop five more as they fled for cover. He turned to retreat himself, but an arrow sailed through the gun smoke and struck his back. Then something unusual happened. The big brave who Buddy had shot rose and moseyed over, not seeming too bothered by the bullet in his chest.

"How many times you think that Injun can die?" I asked in disbelief.

"If he stood for a dozen rounds of a Gatling gun, ain't no measly Colt gonna keep him down," the scalped soldier answered.

Buddy lay facedown with the arrow still in his back, unable to move. It looked to be stuck in his shoulder blade. The brave clenched a fistful of Buddy's curly hair to lift his head. As the knife blade began sawing through Buddy's scalp, blood spilled over his forehead and into his eyes.

A commotion erupted on the other end of the camp that gave the buck pause midway through the task. Luther was coming up the rear, chucking warriors like they were bales of hay. The Indians swung their tomahawks and lunged their spears at the yellow-haired giant, but he hadn't been without warm blood for very long and was still real strong.

Luther couldn't dodge every arrow, though, and for each Indian he trampled, five more followed in his place. There were too many for him to hold off, so he made a beeline for the cover of the saloon. On the way, he knocked aside the big shot-up buck before he could finish scalping Buddy.

"Give Luther some cover!" Sal shouted to the soldiers on each side of the road, and they fired at the charging braves. The Indian forces were divided and they seemed unsure who to attack. Meanwhile, a couple of husky cowboys hustled out and dragged Buddy back to the saloon. So many arrows struck the front door that it looked like a scared porcupine. Nigel came out from the backroom carrying Ms. Parker, who looked faint and paler than usual.

"I hope she was worth it," Luther said plucking arrows from his back. Nigel hadn't had an easy time of it either. After he set the lady down, he collapsed in exhaustion.

Buddy peered out from swollen eyelids. His face was striped red from the blood that ran from his forehead and a large flap of his scalp was bent backwards, showing the top of his skull. "She okay?" he asked.

"The lady will be just dandy," Nigel answered cheerily. "Some food and water might liven her spirits, though."

After Ms. Parker roused, she saw Luther and immediately tried to get up so she could hide Martin, who Mabel was attending to upstairs.

"Settle down, ma'am," I told her. "No need to worry. Luther already knows about the child."

"So he's not going to try to eat him?" she asked.

"Apparently, vampires don't eat their own kind, even if they're starving," I told her.

"So it's true?" Ms. Parker said. "Martin is a vampire?"

"Seems like he ain't entirely a vampire till he drinks some warm blood," I explained.

"And there ain't no warm blood in Damnation, unless that egg hatches a chick," Whiny Pete pointed out, a little too loudly.

"I beg your pardon," Nigel called out from the other side of the room where he was resting. "To what egg are you referring, chap?"

"The one that Sal found beneath a chicken that had come out of the dust. It's still warm. Farmer Jake says it might even hatch."

Buddy managed to get to his feet while Pete was spilling the beans. He came over and whispered in my ear, "Better hand 'er over now, Tom." I slipped the bundle of hay into his hand and he pocketed it.

Nigel rose, but he was too tired to race across the room. Also, Buddy already had a pistol in hand with the hammer cocked, which made Nigel halt in his tracks. It seemed a worn-out vampire was slower than a beat-up gunslinger. "Simmer down," Buddy told him. "You're just gonna have to wait for the next warm egg, because this one's spoken for."

Nigel glared at Buddy, but he didn't want to press the issue in his weakened state, so he just sat back down. Nigel must have reckoned he had plenty of time to rest up before the egg hatched anything with warm blood. In the meantime, having the fastest gunslinger in town look after the egg wasn't a bad idea. And it might be weeks before Nigel was strong enough to take on Buddy.

Luckily, the braves out in the road weren't keen on trying to rush the saloon. We couldn't have put up much of a fight with a wounded gunslinger and two tuckered-out vampires.

"They don't fight with fear!" Luther remarked. "That is for certain, and the big one does not show a weakness. The bullet did not stop him."

"Great! Now, we got an unkillable Indian sore at us," Sal complained.

"How can he be unkillable if he's already dead?" Jarvis asked.

"Well, it sounds better than an *unsendable-to-hell* Indian," Sal argued.

"Fair point," Jarvis agreed.

It seemed to me that we had bigger problems now than thinking up a snappy nickname for the angry fella who couldn't be sent to hell. "Now that we've stirred up the pot with our neighbors out there," I said, "do y'all think they're still gonna let livestock get through to us? After all, they're sitting between us and the dust wall."

"That's a good point, too," Jarvis smiled with no small satisfaction. The boy seemed more keen on noting good arguments than anything else. You'd have thought he ate speeches for dinner.

"Just how many pigs are left in that pigpen?" Farmer Jake asked.

"Two or three, not counting that big red one the Chinaman calls Mei."

"Prolly have to shoot the Chinaman before you butcher her," Jake noted. "He's pretty attached. I think he sleeps with her."

"Well then I'll have pork chops with a side of Chinaman!" Kenny laughed. "Throw 'em both in a frying pan together." Rodeo Bo found the remark in poor taste, and he shot the redneck a glance that made him quiet.

"Anyway, it should be enough to last a month or so," Sal said, "but they don't give offspring, so folks are gonna go hungry after that."

Chapter 14

The Old-Timer's Balls

Early one morning, before anyone was up, the walls of the rooming house began to tremble like there was an earthquake. I had a look out the window at the road that led to the dust cloud, and nothing seemed amiss. Then, moments later, a giant creature covered in thick brown fur came charging out of the dust.

The large curved bones on its shoulders looked ready to ram anything in its path. Powerful front legs pulled it forward while the smaller legs in the back struggled to keep up. From tail to nose, it measured as long as a wagon, and stood as tall as a man from the hooves to the top of its horns. The all-black hide on its massive head was bushier than the rest. It swayed in the breeze as the beast galloped in broad circles between the town and the teepees. Every footstep sounded louder than tom-tom drums.

"What in Sam Hill is that?" Whiny Pete asked. "Some kind of devil cow?"

"What ya mean?" Old Moe cried. "Ain't ya never seen a bison before? There's millions of them on the Great Plains, stretching from Texas clear to Canada."

"Not anymore," I told him sadly. "They slaughtered most of 'em for their hides years back. Only a few hundred left now, I hear."

After the bison knocked down a teepee, the Indians didn't waste any time in getting after it. They launched a dozen arrows into its haunches, but it kept galloping in circles. Finally, two horseback riders corralled it into a circle of braves who clobbered it with their tomahawks.

They quickly butchered the animal, then cooked the meat. The organs were strewn across a line and dried for later. Even the bones were smashed and the marrow sucked out. In under two hours, there was hardly any sign of the animal, aside from a fluffy new rug that was probably decorating the chief's teepee.

"Them Indians don't waste much," Jarvis remarked.

"Maybe they'll let a few pigs get through to us since they have plenty to eat now," Whiny Pete suggested.

"I don't see any hogs coming out of the dust, but who's that fella hobbling down the road?" the scalped soldier asked.

"Hey, Tom, he a relation of yours?" Kenny joked. "He sure walks like you."

The Indians were busy eating the bison, so they didn't pay any mind to the old fella as he went past their camp into town. He had a long silver beard and thinning gray hair parted over his crown. He walked with a bit of a limp, though not quite as bad as mine. More like a shuffle step from achy feet than a wound.

"He's a little long in the teeth," Farmer Jake remarked as the fella entered the Foggy Dew. The old man wore his best bib and tucker, as if he had dressed up to croak. Sal placed a whiskey in front of him and broke the news about his passing.

"Thank God!" he said, then downed the glass. "Hey mister, since I ain't gotta worry about getting the beer shits no more, how about you pour me a draft?"

Sal splashed some suds in a mug for the man, and he drank it slowly, pausing to sigh after every sip.

"I ain't seen a man enjoy a beer that much since that fella came in with a chubby liver," Moe remarked. "Doctors had him on nothin' but prune juice for a year. He called it the longest decade he never lived."

The boys at the bar wrote up their wagers on the man's cause of death and pushed the scraps of paper to the center. A miner named Liam thought it must've been a robbery on account of his swell-looking clothes. "The old-timer was prolly too slow in handing over his banknotes, so a bandit shot 'im at close range."

"I don't see no bullet holes," Jarvis pointed out. "Could've been some sort of disease inside him that kilt him."

"Probably just croaked of old age," a cowboy said.

"I'm with buckshot-face on this one," Red called up from below. "That kid's never wrong. Five dollars says it was a disease."

"Go ask 'im," Whiny Pete said to me.

"You ask 'im," I replied.

"Wanna know what kilt me?" the old-timer spoke up. "I ain't so old that I lost my hearing."

"No offense, mister. Wagering is just somethin' we do to pass the time," I explained.

The old-timer looked at me for a moment. Seemed confused, like he was wondering if he knew me from somewhere else. Then he probably decided it was old age playing tricks on him. "I got the cancer," he said.

"Anyone pick that?" I asked.

Sal looked through the scraps of paper.

"Jake guessed lung cancer."

"Mine was in the ass," the old-timer said.

"Ain't the same," Sal declared.

"My pa had lung cancer," Liam offered. "It's much worse. Left him gasping for air for weeks till he passed."

"I don't know about all that," the old-timer said. "Ever try riding a horse while you're sitting on a tumor the size of a sheep's balls? I haven't had a proper shit in months. Finally got so backed up my plumbing burst!"

"That's a horrible way to go. Prolly the worst I ever heard," Whiny Pete remarked.

"Doc called it sepsis. Said I'd welcome death when it came, and he was right."

"I tol' ya a disease had done him in," Red hollered underfoot. "That's my money!"

"Ain't specific enough," Jarvis pointed out. "Like saying someone died by accident or on account of bad luck."

"Ain't nobody ever died of good luck," Rodeo Bo added with a laugh. "'Less maybe they were gettin' a poke at the time."

"Ah, give Red the money," I said. "It's better than listening to him piss and moan all day. 'Sides, he'll probably never get a chance to spend it."

"It can go toward his bar tab," Sal decided, and collected the money.

"What's the fella doing in the cellar?" the old-timer asked.

"He shot a squaw," Whiny Pete explained.

"I see." The fella nodded patiently, though clearly a few blanks could be filled in.

Jarvis explained, "Not supposed to shoot nobody for no good reason, according to the rules up on the wall. In this case, it's kinda complicated by the fact that she was trying to stab him at the time."

Whiny Pete added, "Also, he was giving her a poke, and no one can say for certain if she wanted to since she weren't fully awake."

"I see," the old-timer said again without any surprise.

"Then her brother came in looking for her," Pete continued. "Wants to scalp whoever's holding her. The sheriff found out and said to throw Red in the cellar on account of there ain't no jail—rules bein' new'n all."

"I see," the old-timer said a third time, looking as if he had inquired about the weather and been told it was cloudy with a chance of showers.

A lot of folks in Damnation had been dead twenty or thirty years, but most were under forty-five years old when they arrived, and so that's how they looked. The old-timer stuck out with his silver beard and wrinkled face. His cancer didn't bother him no more, but he had sagging muscles and aching bones like any other man over sixty. The fellas could spot his weakness a mile off. It didn't take long for a roomful of bored men to figure out who they could pick on.

Lefty, the one-handed fur trapper, got it in his mind to give the old-timer a ribbing. Since the day he'd arrived, the boys teased him to no end about his trapping skills. As soon as he walked in the door each day, someone asked if he had caught anything good lately—*like his foot*. Now that there was an older, weaker man in town, Lefty saw his opportunity to get out from being the low man on the totem pole.

"Hey, ass rot!" Lefty called out, reckoning the others would laugh. The room remained silent. Some folks thought it was rude to pick on a fella before he'd had a chance to mourn his life properly with a drink. Others were still gun-shy about teasing newbies after watching Blind Sal shoot Amos the pickpocket. The old-timer didn't respond, so Lefty walked over and got right in his face. "I'm talking to you, ass rot. Ain't nobody else here with a rotten ass!"

The old-timer responded in a slow measured tone. "I ain't too particular about nicknames, but that's not one I care to be called by. I suppose I gotta whoop you now, or I'll have to listen to everyone call me that for however long I'm here."

Lefty chuckled nervously. "I don't know how you plan on whooping me. For one, you're old as dirt. For two, you ain't even heeled."

"A man with one hand ought to be more careful about where he stands," the old-timer told him.

"How's that?"

"You only got two options: draw or punch. You can't do both with one hand." The old-timer leaned over and let some of his beer splash on Lefty's holstered gun. Lefty jumped back with a start, but the hammer and cylinder were already drenched.

"What the hell you doing, geezer?"

The old-timer smiled with amusement. "That pistol might still fire, but it might not. You got a fifty-fifty chance, if you draw."

"If it don't fire, I'll smash you across the face with my gun," Lefty said mustering some venom.

"You might," he replied. "But by the time your gun misfires, it could be too late."

Lefty looked down at his wet sidearm and back up at the old-timer, weighing his chances of winning a fistfight with one arm. The old man was gnarled like a stump with roots clear to hell. Lefty probably reckoned that he'd catch even more slack if he got out-boxed by someone's grandpa. There was no turning back now, though.

The one-armed trapper dipped his shoulder to pluck up his pistol as quickly as he could. He was pretty darn fast, too. The old-timer just kept gulping down his beer. He emptied the entire stein so that he was left clutching the hunk of solid glass. Whatever his fate, he seemed appreciative of those last few swallows of beer. For some years, he'd endured a swelling in his backside that made sitting or visiting the latrine unbearable. If he was going to get sent to hell on his first day in Damnation, at least he had one carefree drink.

Lefty steadied the pistol at the old man's nose. It was his only chance of improving his position in the saloon. Sending someone to hell might scare off a few upstarts. Otherwise, he wouldn't last the month with one hand. He squeezed the trigger. A soggy click sounded. He squeezed it again, only to hear the same useless noise.

In that moment, the old fella came alive with the spark of youth. He swung the thick-bottomed stein with a broad smile on his face. As it crashed against Lefty's chin, slivers of broken glass sprayed across the bar. He had hit Lefty so hard that there was nothing left to the mug but the handle. The unfortunate trapper dropped to the floor, trying to pull the shards from his cheek with red fingers. The old-timer picked up Lefty's gun in no particular hurry, opened the cylinder, then gave it a blow and a spin. With the steady hand of someone who'd murdered before, he shot Lefty in the forehead.

"Whatta we call you, friend?" Sal asked afterward.

"Vernon Jackson Walker is my given name," he replied.

"Pretty fancy duds you got on. You don't fight like a rich dandy, but you sure do dress like one."

"Been scratchin' a poor man's balls all my life," he said.

"What's that?" Sal cupped his ear. "Whose balls you been scratchin'?"

"What I mean to say is, I ain't never had a pot to piss in. Took these clothes off a banker I kilt for gloatin'."

"Then why didn't ya just say so instead of goin' on about scratchin' another man's privates?" Sal walked off in a huff. "I just don't understand the old folks of today!"

The Crapper

Comings: *Judging by the number of teepees being raised outside of town, a whole lot more Indians have arrived in the last few weeks. Also, an old fella in a sharp suit named Vernon Jackson Walker came to town after cancer of the ass did him in.*

Goings: *A dozen or so Indians got sent to hell by Buddy and Luther while Nigel was rescuing Ms. Parker. One of them, I've been told, was a great warrior who'd been at the Battle of Little Bighorn, or Greasy Grass, as the Indians refer to it. They say he was one of the men who killed Custer. Also, Lefty, the one-armed fur trapper, got brained with a beer stein, then shot for trying to bully the new old-timer Vernon.*

Chapter 15

Election Day

Just as I had feared, the Indians road-blocked all livestock from getting through to town. As rations grew slim, folks started to grumble. Dead men couldn't starve to death, but they sure as hell could complain all day about having an empty stomach. Three square meals broke up the day and gave you something to look forward to. It also freshened up your mouth for drinking. An Irishman started putting ketchup on scraps of leather just to have something to chew on while he drank his beer.

"The suds are still flat," he complained. "And now I got the taste of a horse's arsehole in me mouth!"

Folks quickly began to resent the position they'd been put in because of the squabble with the Indians. All they wanted to do was eat pork chops, get drunk, and play cards till they got sent to hell. Most didn't give a lick about Ms. Parker or Red, and they were sick of all the decisions being made by others without asking their opinion. Buddy was laid up in the hotel, mending from the arrow in his back, so he couldn't speak on his own behalf. And both vampires were too tuckered out to leave their rooms for some weeks. The hungry outlaws grew more bold in their complaints.

"Sheriffs are just supposed to uphold the rules," a bank robber complained. "Not start wars with Injuns!"

"I hear ya!" Rodeo Bo agreed. "I'm a quarter Cherokee myself, so I ain't got no business fightin' my people."

"The Buffalo Soldier's right!" one of the Confederates added. "It ain't our battle. Far as I'm concerned, the war ended back on Earth! 'Sides, Red kilt that squaw. I bet if we hand him over, they'll let us have the pigs again."

"It ain't my fault!" Red hollered from below. "It weren't my idea to attack the red bellies. It was Buddy and that flannel-mouthed blood-drinker that wanted to rescue the lady."

"Red's got a point there," the scalped soldier pointed out.

"Yeah, it's true," Farmer Jake added. "I don't recall voting on any plan that'd get the savages riled up."

Everyone was complaining at once, so nobody could be heard above the bickering. Finally, someone tapped a spoon against a glass to get folks' attention. "Sounds like y'all need representation!" said Vernon, the new old-timer. "There should be someone to see that the common man's voice is heard, instead of just the law and commerce doing whatever's best for them."

"Commerce?" a cowhand scratched his head.

"Folks running this establishment," Jake explained.

"Leave me outta this!" Sal ordered.

"No, he's right!" the scalped soldier said to Sal.

"Every man should be heard," Vernon continued. "Even if he can't speak as loud as the supernaturals."

"Huh?" the cowhand asked.

"He means the vampires," Jake explained.

"Y'all need someone to stick up for your interests."

"Yeah!" the scalped soldier cheered.

"A democratically elected leader!"

"Huh?" the cowhand asked.

"You need a mayor," Vernon put it plainly.

"You think a real mayor will come to Damnation?" the cowhand asked.

"No, fool!" Jake scolded. "He's saying we should elect one of us."

"Oh, how do we go about that?"

"First, the candidates give speeches," the scalped soldier explained. "Don't ya know nothing?"

"Well, shit!" the cowhand declared. "We ain't got nothin' better to do. Might as well hear some fancy speeches while we ain't eatin' nothin'."

A spot on the floor was cleared, and anyone who wanted to could say their piece on why they should be mayor. At first, nobody seemed much inclined to take on the responsibility, since it might entail standing up to the vampires. That was one surefire way of getting sent to hell in a hurry, maybe even before the Indians attacked. Finally, Vernon stood up. He was pretty well at ease in front of a crowd, like he'd made a speech or two in his day.

"My name is Vernon Jackson Walker. I know that's a mouthful, but if you elect me, you can just call me Mayor Vern. I'd like to tell you a little bit about myself, and how I ended up here. I was born to one of the poorest families in Lincoln, Nebraska."

As he spoke, his voice sounded kind of familiar, but I couldn't recall ever meeting any really old men who could lay it on as thick as him. He knew how to pause at just the right time to give his words weight, but never waited so long that anyone could interrupt.

"As a young whippersnapper, I took to thieving to feed myself. We'd wait on the outskirts of town and hold up farmers on their way to buy seeds. One day, we stuck up a fella who didn't have anything on him except for a five-dollar watch. Said it had sentimental value 'cause his grandpappy gave it to him, but he'd gladly give us the worth of it many times over if he could keep it. I asked how he intended to do that since he was without a dime. He told me that he would send it to me."

There were quite a few thieves in the crowd, and they laughed as if they'd heard similar bargains before.

"Not only that," Vern continued, "but the man said he'd send me a five-dollar bill every year for the rest of his life. I told him I wasn't born yesterday, and asked him what was to stop him from sending the Pinkertons after me. His answer was *trust*. My partner said, 'Don't be a fool, Vernon!' We got into an argument on account of him revealing my name in front of the stranger. Then a train came by and the man with the watch slipped into the brush. We shot at him, but he was a slippery fella and we couldn't catch him."

"One year later, the postman told me there was an envelope at the main station addressed to Vernon, the Thief. He knew of my reputation and asked if I wanted to claim it. So I went down there, and sure enough there was a five-dollar bill in it. The following year, another one came. I wasn't so keen on going down to the post office and admitting I was a thief, so I decided to invest in farming equipment. I'll be damned if I wasn't half bad at it. Unfortunately, a drought came and I didn't make enough money to buy seeds for the following season. Sure enough, the five dollars came and I made it another year without robbing anyone. Things went pretty well after that. I bought more land, and I was considered successful, if I do say so myself. Eventually, I got married and had youngins who looked up to me.

"Every year, the five-dollar bill still arrived, reminding me that I was nothing more than a thief. I decided not to pick it up anymore, but the postman would chase me down on the street. I was too ashamed to tell my wife, so every year I put those envelopes in a box. Fifteen years went by, and they were still coming. Added up to seventy-five dollars.

"Finally, I decided to find the man. Hired a Pinkerton who located him from the postmark, in a town about thirty miles north. I expected him to live in a fancy house, but it was just a small shack. I knocked on the door and the fella answered. He was a little older than me and all alone. Probably had to scrape by just to send the five bucks each year. He still wore his grandpappy's watch, though."

"Did you give him back the money he sent you?" Jarvis asked.

"Hell no!" Vern said. "I shot that uppity bastard for addressing me as a thief all those years. Who was he to rub it in my face from up on his high horse?"

The men all laughed.

"And when you elect Mayor Vern to office, that's the sort of man you get. You don't have to worry about being pushed around by Indians or wolves, or even vampires! Because I reckon to make Damnation better'n ever with *good ol' American grit!*"

"Hooray!" the men cheered.

"'Cause now's the time to put us dead outlaws first," he continued. "Ahead of the wolves and the Indians and even the dang vampires!"

The men cheered even louder. Vernon took a bow and sat down. Then Sal asked if anyone else wanted to give a speech.

Sneaky Jim stood up and said, "I'd like to be mayor, too. That blind son of a bitch stole my gun, and it ain't fair, dang it all!"

"Ah, siddown!" a soldier hollered, and threw the last swallow in his beer stein on Jim.

No one else wanted to make a speech, so scraps of paper were handed out and everyone wrote down who they thought should be mayor. When Sal counted them up, it wasn't even close. Folks might have voted for Vern because he looked older and wiser, or just because they despised Sneaky Jim's backwashing ways. As for myself, I voted for Vern because of his clean shirt and jacket. He just looked the part. We couldn't have a mayor walking around town in the ragged old clothes that most everyone else wore. It just wouldn't be proper.

"A toast!" Sal called out. "To our new mayor. May he be better than no mayor at all!"

"Hear, hear!" the scalped soldier declared.

While we were clinking glasses, Mabel and Annabelle came into the saloon and asked what was going on.

"I didn't know we were electing a mayor," Mabel said. "I'd like to run for the position."

"Ah, it's too late now," Sal said. "The men already gave their speeches, honey."

"Now hold on," I said. "Mabel's got a good head on her shoulders. I'm sure she'd make a fine mayor. And we don't know much about this Vern fella, except that he used to be a thief."

"Don't be silly, Tom. The men don't wanna listen to speeches from a gal," Sal said with a laugh. "It'd be like hearin' a lecture from their momma."

Mabel just shook her head. She was accustomed to dealing with narrow-minded men and still getting what she wanted in the end. Anabelle's hide wasn't quite as thick yet. The young lady glared at the old booze clerk like she was scheming to send his ass to hell.

Chapter 16

Shithouse Crops

We now had a mayor, but food was scarce, which put folks in bad humor. The pigs had all been slaughtered, except for Mei, the big red boar that the Chinaman was fond of. A couple of the sodbusters went down to the pigpen to get her, but she was gone.

"Whattaya mean *gone?*" Sal's voice cracked.

"The Chinaman's gone, too."

"He musta took the sow with him over to the featherheads' camp," Sal decided.

"Can't say I blame 'im," the scalped soldier put in. "He prolly reckoned our days were numbered. Wanted to get on the winning side while he still had something to bargain with."

Another far greater problem loomed over the saloon, though. Nobody had given it much thought before, but it threatened our whole way of life.

"Hey, Sal," Jarvis asked. "With the Indians blocking supplies from coming in, how long will it be before y'all run out of whiskey?"

The room silenced. I had never seen thirty drunk men look so worried before. They could hardly breathe.

"Ah, I got loads of corn juice." Sal tried to put everyone at ease.

"Where at?"

"Down in the cellar. Mind your business, buckshot face."

"Down in the cellar *with Red?*" I asked.

It dawned on me then why Red had sounded so strange lately, and why he hadn't said anything at all for several hours. Sal opened up the hatch in the floor and went down to investigate. Sure enough, Red was passed out cold. He'd been steadily working his way through Sal's booze for weeks. He had spilt a mess of it, too. A couple of the boys went down and dragged up what was left, which amounted to a case and a half of whiskey and a couple bottles of gin. The beer barrels had gotten knocked over and spilled. We might've smelled it if the whole damn town didn't reek of festering wounds.

"What should we do with Red?"

"Leave 'im be," Sal said. "He can rot down there for all I care."

When everyone saw what was left of the prairie dew, I feared war might break out among us. Damnation wasn't the sort of place where most folks could just hang out without drinking some. They needed the occasional dust cutter to numb them from the horror of being dead and seeing so many gruesome wounds every day. Others wanted to forget all the bad stuff they'd done or the loved ones they weren't ever going to see again. Some drank to keep up their nerve and steady their hands for gunfights. Or they just wanted to forget they might end up somewhere worse. For whatever the reason, just about everyone drank, except Jarvis.

"Why y'all so serious all of a sudden?" the kid grinned from the side of his face that hadn't been shot up. Nobody could tell if he was teasing.

"I can have words with the Iroquois fella that I'm friendly with," I told the boys. "We do a bit of trading from time to time. Maybe he can clue us in on the chief's intentions."

That was enough to soothe things over for the night. Everyone just wanted to hear that they could keep on drinking and gambling and not have to think about how they were still hungry and bored and dead.

"All right, Tom. You can go and speak with your red friend about the gut-warmer situation," Mayor Vern spoke up. "As the highest elected official, I authorize it. While you're at it, see what's holding up the meat that these fine gentlemen are entitled to."

The next day, I went over to the well outside of town where I usually found Little Bear. There was no water in the well, but the old squaws still went there to beat the dust out of their rugs on the stone casing. Since the Iroquois people didn't get much say in things, Little Bear wasn't a fan of the chief and didn't mind gossiping.

"Some tribes want to attack white men," he told me, "but they afraid of Long Tooth with hair like wheat."

"You mean Luther, the vampire?"

"Navajo say he skin-shifter. Lakota say he mosquito man. Everyone have different name, but everyone fear his magic. Some say we should make peace with Long Tooth."

"What about the Apache brave with the shot-up chest, the one looking for his sister?"

"You mean Black Moon." He nodded. "Black Moon has big medicine. He get up after fat man shoot him. Now, some think he has bigger medicine than Long Tooth. Black Moon want to make war on all white men."

"Will the other tribes follow him?"

"Apache, Cherokee, and Sioux follow whoever have biggest medicine. And Black Moon have bigger medicine than chief. He may have biggest medicine of all warriors ever."

"Okay, I get it. He's a strong fella. So is this Black Moon in control of the whole nation now?"

"Chief still chief," he said. "Some tribes no want to fight for Black Moon's sister, Running Horse. Lakota and Cheyenne say she drink too much fire water and lie in too many teepees."

"What's your opinion on the matter?" I asked.

"Don't matter," he answered sullenly. "Nobody care what Iroquois people think."

"But what do you reckon are the chances of us getting any livestock or whiskey in the future?" I asked.

Little Bear shrugged. "Ask chief."

I went back to the Foggy Dew and told the others about the division among the tribes.

"We should negotiate directly with the chief," Mabel suggested.

"Hell no!" Mayor Vern declared. "Not while we have their backs to the wall!"

"We ain't got no advantage," I said. "Luther and Nigel are both spent. They haven't gotten out of bed for a week. And who knows if they'd even wanna fight on our side again."

"The teepee creepers don't know that," the mayor said. "I say we wait 'em out, then press for demands. Not just the pork, but eggs, too."

"And if they say no?" a soldier asked. "We ain't gonna charge out there and attack a whole nation with a few dozen hungry men."

From the back of the room, Farmer Jake spoke up. "I found something that might be of interest concerning the food situation." He wouldn't say no more and insisted we all follow him across the road to the alley behind Mabel's new saloon. "Lookie there." He pointed to the ground beside the latrine.

"What?" the major squinted.

"Don't you see the green leaves growin'?"

"What is it?"

"Moss," he said. "When it rained during the wolf attack, the runoff must've collected here. The silt's more fertile on account of it being next to the water closet. It acts like compost. Then the sunshine that broke up the vampires' fight must've triggered spores to grow."

"Can we eat it?" I asked.

"I don't reckon it's the sort you can eat."

"You dragged us out here to see some shithouse weeds ya can't even eat?" the mayor scolded.

"It's good for dressing wounds," Jake defended. "And water won't pass through it, so you can keep stuff dry beneath it."

"Great," Vern teased. "It'll protect us from the rain we don't have!"

"Don't ya see? If moss can grow here, then other stuff can, too—under the right conditions."

"What kind of conditions?" Mayor Vern asked.

"Like if it rains again and there's more sunshine."

"Ain't no way of knowing if that'll ever happen again," Sal said.

"But if it does, we could collect the rainwater in buckets."

"I got a mess of seeds that came in the wagons over the years," Sal offered. "You can plant them in that shithouse dirt, if you like."

"It could be years before anything grows—if ever!" Mayor Vern screeched. "In the meantime, I'll devise a battle plan. For the approval of the constituents, of course."

"Huh?" Whiny Pete asked.

"He means we're gonna vote on whether it's a good plan or not," Jarvis explained.

"Hey Jake, lemme know when you grow us a cow!" Vern said with a laugh, and headed back into the saloon.

"Don't listen to him," I told Jake. "It's real good what you discovered. And I think it's a fine plan to set up buckets in case it does rain again. Who knows? Someday, there could be a whole field of crops growing next to this shithouse. Better yet, plant those seeds beside Sal's commode. He pinches more loaves than anyone."

Chapter 17

The Rusty Nail

While the mayor was devising his battle plan, Mabel worked out a truce with the chief. Nobody was sure how she had managed it. It might've helped matters that Nigel was standing beside her while she negotiated. Some folks claimed she had to let the chief give Annabelle a poke to seal the deal, but that was just mean-spirited gossip.

The chief probably hadn't had the upper hand since steel was brought to the New World. He was practically bursting with giddiness to be the one declaring terms. His normally stoic hook-nosed face nearly cracked a smile. Mabel didn't get any pigs or chicken or whiskey, but the chief offered her first dibs on the smaller game animals that wandered out of the dust. There were also several cases of "rotten grape juice," as they called it. The Indians wouldn't touch the stuff because it looked like blood.

On opening day of the new saloon, Mabel prepared quail with opossum bacon and fancy French wine that had been on its way to San Francisco. The Rusty Nail was a half story higher than the Foggy Dew with a pitched roof. The red nails in the new timber had a nice look to it. When you walked in the front door, it opened up to a great hall that made it feel like a church where souls were lifted to the sky. It had a second-story catwalk just like the Foggy Dew, but this one had more rooms. The walls of the barroom were covered in fancy colored paper and red felt tapestries.

"It's so dang clean," one sodbuster remarked. "I feel like I ain't clean enough to get shitfaced here!"

"It'll get soiled soon enough," Sal said, peering in to check out the competition.

"You sure outdone yourself in gussying up the place real nice," I told Mabel.

"Alls it took was a little taste," she said. "Lots of this stuff was just collecting dust in the back of those old wagons. I don't know why someone would leave these wonderful fabrics lying around while they spend all day in a dank saloon with bare wood walls."

Sal snorted at the slight. "I barely had the time to patch up the giant hole the vampires put in my wall. When would I get around to hanging fancy sheets?"

"Looks like you'll have plenty of time now." Rodeo Bo snorted. "I don't expect you'll be getting many customers."

Mayor Vern wasn't too pleased since Mabel had gone over his head in negotiating with the chief. He didn't want to be outshone, though, so he congratulated her on the peace she had achieved, as if it was his own personal victory.

"Like I always say," he told her, "you can accomplish anything with *good ol' American grit*—when you put your faith in your democratically elected leader. I dare say I set the groundwork for the deal with the chief by holding my ground. He sensed the mayor was gonna put the squeeze on him, I bet."

Mabel just smiled graciously, even though the chief didn't know we had a mayor. Annabelle stood behind the bar, filling glasses and collecting a nickel apiece. The men guzzled down the wine, and it soon went to their heads. It wasn't long before one of the soldiers asked her how much she charged for a poke.

Being a polite southern girl, she tried to discourage the fella without causing a fuss. "You ain't got that kind of money." His friends laughed, but the soldier wouldn't be put off.

"I got as much coin as any man in the room," he insisted. His sleeve showed he had died just short of lieutenant colonel, so he'd always be a major and, judging by his tone, a major shit heel. "So what is it? Either my money ain't good enough, or you only sling that cunt to red bellies."

Annabelle wasn't accustomed to such language. She turned white as a sheet. The arrow wound in Buddy's back had just healed, and he was sitting within earshot. Judging by the sour puss on his face, he didn't much care for the disrespecting of women, and it didn't matter whether they were sporting ladies or a southern belle with a burnt-up back. He rose from his stool to put the man in his place.

Mabel caught him by the sleeve. "The girl can handle herself, deputy," she said with a wink, and topped off his glass.

Annabelle quickly regained her composure and turned to the major with a polite smile. "Sorry to say, sir, but this is not that kinda place and I definitely ain't that kinda girl. If you're real lonesome, maybe one of the squaws in the flatlands will welcome you into her teepee. That, or you can try the wolves' saloon—that is if you don't mind a furry backside."

More of the men laughed this time. The major couldn't think of a proper response, so he just sat there quietly. As a consolation, Annabelle poured some wine into his glass to let him know there were no hard feelings.

"See," Mabel told Buddy, "that gal's got gumption!"

Everyone's bellies were soon full of hearty game meat and their teeth stained purple from fine French wine. After going without food and drink for a spell, it was easy to get stinking drunk. Also, most folks weren't accustomed to the "rotten grape juice." Since it wasn't as strong as whiskey, they considered it red beer. And not being acquainted with its strength, they drank it at the same pace as plain old beer.

Eventually, the rude major became unsteady on his feet. He was leering at Annabelle from across the bar like a dog at dinner scraps. Finally, he leaned over and said something nasty to her that I couldn't hear. Annabelle ignored him while she collected glasses. Soon, he got fed up and threw a coin at her, which bounced off her charred back. She might not have even felt it.

"My money ain't good enough for ya, huh? Well then I'll take that cunt for free!" he hollered, then reached over to grab her between the legs. His drooling lip met with an empty bottle of wine. Shattered glass rained across the bar. He fell to the ground, but the little lady wasn't done yet. She walked around and gouged his throat with the end of the broken bottle till blood gurgled from the rim.

"See that!" one of the soldiers squawked. "She broke one of the rules. Number five on the list is *no killin' over dumb shit*. And she did it right in front of the sheriff and the deputy. Ain't y'all gonna do somethin'?"

Nigel had just arrived after spending several weeks in bed. He didn't look entirely mended, but he was enjoying a glass of decent red wine for a change. Judging by his expression, he wasn't in any mood to meddle in any human quarrels. Luther hadn't surfaced yet. Since he wasn't as accustomed to going without warm blood, his recovery took longer.

"I wouldn't say that qualifies as dumb shit," Mabel argued with the soldier. "If a man grabbed you between the legs, you wouldn't be in the wrong to shoot him, now would ya?" She stared down the soldier, not willing to budge an inch.

"That's different," he backpedalled. "She was leading him on. Anyways, if a man grabbed my privates, I'd challenge him to a draw out in the road. I wouldn't cold-cock him with a bottle."

Nigel glared at the soldier. Then he looked over at his deputy. The two had not spoken since their falling out over the egg. Buddy clearly didn't want to interrupt his drinking for the likes of some creepy soldier.

"Them rules is hanging in the Foggy Dew," Buddy pointed out. The ends of his mustache were dripping with wine. "They don't apply here."

The hint of a smile showed on Nigel's face. "Right-o! As the deputy attests, the matter is out of our jurisdiction." He lifted his goblet.

"Tol' ya," Sal remarked as he headed for the door. "This place won't be clean for long!"

The Crapper

Comings: *Seems like there's more Indians than ever, but no new soldiers or anyone else have arrived in town.*

Goings: *During the grand opening of the Rusty Nail, Major Edward McGarry got knocked over the head with a wine bottle, then gouged in the neck by sweet little Annabelle because he manhandled her. The major was from New York and very proud of his war record. He often bragged of having fought at the Bear River Massacre, in which I'm told about two hundred and fifty starving Shoshone men, women, and children were killed.*

The tribe's land was in a fertile valley in the Washington Territory, and it had been taken over by Mormon farmers, leaving them little choice but to raid the settlers for food. The army's attack was in part retribution for the Shoshone skirmishes and also to assure future safe passage to the gold mines in the Northwest. After the Mexican-American War was over, Ed got reassigned to San Francisco, where he became involved in politics, drank too much, and eventually cut his own throat with a pen knife in a fancy hotel. It seems the ladies there didn't like him much either.

Also, in case you didn't hear, Buddy and Nigel have agreed that the rules on the wall of the Foggy Dew don't apply in the new saloon. That should make things interesting!

Chapter 18

The Woman Who Died of Good Luck

Out of loyalty to Regular Sal, I split my time between the Rusty Nail and the Foggy Dew. Most folks favored the new saloon on account of the wine and the grub and the lack of dust, so it was usually just me, Sal, and Red underfoot. Red didn't say much after we took all of the nose paint out the cellar, except for his pissing and moaning about how he was hungry and thirsty while everyone else was having a grand old time eating pheasant and getting sloshed at the Rusty Nail.

One afternoon while Red was asleep, a woman wandered in, probably on account of it being the first saloon she came to and she didn't want to catch a chill. The lady wasn't flashy like Mabel, or real pretty like Ms. Parker, or young like Annabelle. She was on the plain-looking side, and you might not have taken notice of her in a crowd, that is, except for the fact that she was buck naked. Sal quickly fetched a blanket and draped it over her shoulders. Then he found some old bloomers and showed her to the washroom where she might tidy up.

"I didn't notice any wounds on her," I said. "Did you?"

"Can't say I did," Sal replied.

"It's too bad there's no one else around to wager on what kilt her," I said.

"We can wager!" Sal tried to muster some enthusiasm. "Five bucks says it was ammonia."

"The stuff that you clean floors with?" I asked.

"No, the lung fever!"

"You mean *new-moan-ya?*"

"Whatever."

When the lady returned to the bar, she said shyly, "Pardon me, sirs, could you tell me where I might find the closest parlor house?"

Sal was shocked. "Dear, you don't mean to tell me you're a soiled dove?"

She looked at Sal crossly with her arms folded tightly in front of her. Finally she replied, "I don't see how that's any of your business." Her indignation might have been warranted if she hadn't arrived in her birthday suit.

"I beg your pardon, ma'am," Sal apologized. "It's just that you ain't gussied up like no painted lady. I woulda sooner took you for a schoolmarm— if you had on some proper clothing."

"What's your name, ma'am?" I asked.

"Mollie," she replied.

"What's the last thing you remember, Mollie?"

"I was with a man in Tombstone," she blushed. "And we were having relations. Then I fell from the bed." She rubbed her hand over the back of her head, and when she took it away it was streaked red. "I reckon he must've cleared me out and dumped me outside of this two-bit town. Are we still in Arizona?"

"We definitely ain't in Arizona," Sal told her.

Mollie didn't want us to take her for a country bumpkin. She might have feared we'd try to put one over on her, so she went on boasting like a sharpie from the big city. "Y'all should get yourselves to Tombstone. There's four churches and over a hundred saloons. We even got a bowling alley and an icehouse!"

"That blow to your head was a mortal one, ma'am," I informed her.

She chuckled like we were just pulling her leg, but she could tell something wasn't quite right. The hollow feeling made it easier to realize. Being alive can be confusing since your mind might say one thing while your body says another. One consolation of being dead was that there was no more tug of war. The body hardly said a peep, except that it was empty—*all the time*. Some folks reckoned it gave them a sense of clarity about their lives. On the other hand, most people who ended up in Damnation had mucked up their lives so badly they didn't want to see it clearly. Sal placed a glass in front of the lady.

"So where am I?" she asked timidly.

"It ain't heaven," I told her, "and it likely ain't hell neither. Might be somewhere in between. I can't say for sure. Folks call it Damnation. The man behind the bar has been here longer than most, but he's just as likely to tell you a pack of lies. You may want to avoid getting shot, in case you end up somewhere worse. You won't starve, but you are going to feel hungry, and drinking helps fill up that awful emptiness you're feeling. But if you drink too much, it'll feel a whole lot worse afterward."

Sal poured three fingers of whiskey into the glass. "The first one's on the house. And here's ten bucks to get you started. You can try to win more in cards." Sal shrugged. "If anyone ever shows up to play."

"One more thing," I added. "It's been said that if you can refrain from killing anyone for one year, you can get into heaven. It probably ain't true, but it gives some of us hope."

"How do you kill a dead person?" she asked.

"Shoot 'em... choke 'em... stab 'em..." Sal answered. "Same as the living."

"Are we the only ones here, aside from all those Indians out there?" she asked.

"Nah, there's vampires and werewolves, and a mess of other folks at the saloon across the way."

Mollie lifted one eyebrow doubtfully. Then she gulped down her drink and got up.

"Where you going?" Sal asked.

"You said that only the first one's on the house. A girl's gotta earn a living, don't she?"

As the door closed behind her, Red woke from his nap beneath us and wanted to know what all the racket was about.

"A naked lady just left the saloon," I told him.

"I ain't fallin' for none of your tall tales, pencil pusher," he said. "Who was it that just walked out, Sal?"

"Tom ain't lyin' to ya," Sal griped. "I can't even get a plain-looking harlot with no shirt on her back to drink in this saloon!"

Mabel wasn't the sort of proprietor to force a girl to turn tricks, but she also wasn't the sort to discourage it. She offered Mollie a room and protection in exchange for a percentage of her earnings. Mollie might have been the plainest looking strumpet in Tombstone, but she was the only strumpet in Damnation. The men liked to flirt with Annabelle while she refilled their glasses. She was younger and prettier, but if they had any money left at the end of the night, they'd go upstairs with Mollie.

Whiny Pete was the first to question me about her. "Hey, Tom, I thought you said all whores go to heaven?" he asked, trying not to accuse me of lying.

"We don't usually get the professional sort of saddle tramp 'round here," I told him. "I expect she must've done something pretty bad."

"Why's that?"

"She gave comfort to lots of lonesome men who wouldn't otherwise get it. If anyone's balancing the scales, I reckon that should've made up for most of the run-of-the-mill bad things she could have done."

Chapter 19

The Hundred-Dollar Corpse

About a week after Mollie arrived, a wagon came out of the dust with no driver. Two braves in war bonnets rode by and gave it a look, but they got spooked and rode off. After seeing Blind Sal's eyes gobbled up by the turkey vulture, I expected whatever was in the wagon to be a gruesome sight, especially since it scared a couple of tough-looking warriors.

A dead mule pulled the wagon all the way to the center of town, where it stopped in front of the dry trough. A body was laid out in the back with silver dollars over his eyelids. A small crowd gathered around. We expected the man would wake up with a start, still harboring surprise for whatever had killed him. Several minutes passed, though, and he didn't budge.

"I thought in Damnation the dead were supposed to get up and start talking," Jarvis said.

"Me, too."

"Seems like this one ain't."

"Seems."

"Maybe he saw all them Injuns out there and died a second time of fright," Whiny Pete proposed.

"I ain't seen that happen before," Old Moe said. "Suppose it's possible, though."

"Nah," I said. "If that were possible, lots of folks woulda been scared straight to hell as soon as they found out where they were. Yourself included, Pete."

"It's true," Moe agreed. "Nobody made a bigger fuss about being dead than you did after you caused a stampede that kilt all them children."

"Maybe this fella just had a bad ticker is all," Whiny Pete said, now looking worried that his own worry could do him in.

As the town's new self-elected historian, Jarvis had to put in his two cents on the matter. "In an old issue of *The Crapper*, I read that a man named Fat Wally came to Damnation after his heart gave out in a brothel. If the numbers are correct—and I can't say for certain that they are—he was here for five years without his heart giving out again from fright. Then Whiny Pete shot him during some sort of wrestling match. The description was kinda vague."

"It wasn't vague if you were there!" I defended. "The paper's supposed to sum stuff up for folks who were around and maybe drank too much to recall or passed out early—not for newbies to study like some sort of almanac."

"Simmer down there." Gut-Shot Granny put her hand on my shoulder, which surprised me since it wasn't often she saw fit to leave off on her knitting in the middle of the day.

"I beg your pardon, ma'am." I removed my hat, not wanting to get on her bad side.

"Ain't no use in getting all worked up about it," she said. "Fat Wally never could have died of worry. That child didn't fret about a damn thing, except maybe losing in cards to Red. And that didn't happen very often."

"That's true, too," Old Moe said. Agreeing with folks was how he came to be the oldest man in town.

"Enough of this lollygagging," Sal interrupted. "Let's get this dead fella out of the wagon before he turns. Check to see if there's anything worth salvaging while you're at it."

The coins were wedged into his sockets pretty good. When Sneaky Jim took them off, his eyelids popped open and he stared up at us like a ghost, which was peculiar considering we were all ghosts in the strict sense of the word. The sip stealer jumped back in surprise, but the dead man remained dead. They lifted him onto the road, and rope marks showed around his neck.

"Hey," Sal scolded Sneaky Jim. "I saw you pocket them coins. Them's supposed to go to the undertaker, as payment for burying the body."

"We ain't got no undertaker here," Jim argued. "Ain't even got no more pigs to chew up the bodies."

"He's right," I said. "Without any pigs, the bodies are gonna pile up pretty quickly."

"Could bury 'im," Liam the miner suggested.

"That dry silt is too fine for diggin'," Farmer Jake argued. "As soon as you lift a spade from it, the hole fills right back in from the sides."

"It might be too fine for an amateur," Liam boasted. "Not a professional. Just needs the proper technique. I'll have you know, I'm the only miner in this town who didn't die in a collapsed tunnel."

"So then you can dig a hole for the body," Jake suggested.

"I ain't sayin' I'm gonna do it," Liam balked. "Just that I could if I was so inclined. I didn't even know the fella. I ain't gonna break a sweat over some stranger for two measly silver dollars."

"Hey, lookie here. He's a wanted man!" Jarvis held up a poster he had found on the floor of the wagon. It showed the dead man's picture and offered a hundred-dollar reward, caught dead or alive.

"I guess someone earned a hundred dollars for the man," Sal said. "What'd he do?"

"It says: *Vernon Jackson Walker... wanted for armed robbery in Lincoln, Nebraska.* Hey, that's the mayor's name!"

"It sure is," I said.

"You suppose there's two of 'em?" Jarvis asked.

"Kind of an unusual name," I said. "And Lincoln ain't that big of a town neither."

"I've never been," Jarvis said regretfully.

"You ain't missing much," I told him.

"That dead man staring up at us certainly matches the picture on that wanted poster," Gut-Shot Granny interrupted.

"Know what I was wondering?" Sal said.

"What's that?" I asked.

"If this wide-eyed thief is Vernon Jackson Walker, then who's the dead man in the fancy shirt who's been mayoring us all?"

"Good question," I said. "Seems there's only one person who can answer it—if he's inclined to."

"I reckon so," Sal agreed. "Petey, go and fetch the mayor. Let's see what he has to say about this."

Chapter 20

The Straight Shooter

Mayor Vern spent most of his time at the Rusty Nail enjoying the free wine that Mabel permitted him on account of his position, as well as the attention of Annabelle, whom he was wise enough not to try manhandling. He definitely wasn't happy to be pulled from the saloon where he'd been flirting with a barmaid young enough to be his granddaughter.

As Vern stood over the body of the wanted man, he shook his head in disbelief. A large crowd had now collected in the road to see what all the hoopla was about. Sal handed Vern the poster with the man's picture and name.

"Mighty strange, this fella having your name and being from the same town as you," Sal smirked.

"Okay, I admit it," he confessed. "He's Vernon Jackson Walker, and I ain't."

"So was all of it a hoax?" Whiny Pete asked. "Even the part about you shooting a man with a five-dollar watch?"

"No, not all of it," the mayor replied. "You see, I was the one with the watch. It was my grandpappy's, and this here thief wanted to take it from me. I pleaded with him. Told him I'd send him five dollars every year till the day I died if only he'd let me keep it. And you know what? I did. And you wanna know why? 'Cause I'm a man of my word."

"Then why'd you tell us a pack of lies?" Jake asked.

"Yeah!" the scalped soldier said angrily. "A man of his word wouldn't have no cause for fibbing."

"What I don't get is it weren't even nothin' important," Kenny added. "Not like anyone expected you to be some kinda big-time watch thief."

"You wanna know why I done it?" the mayor's voice grew louder. "I'll tell you why. 'Cause I'm a straight shooter, and a straight shooter gives it to you straight. I lied to ya. Sure! I admit it here and now, right to your faces. All of ya! And I'd do it again next time."

"I done it 'cause it was what you wanted to hear. Y'all wanted someone with *good ol' American grit* to represent ya. Someone who'd lie for ya." He hocked up some phlegm and spat on the ground. "Someone who'd cheat for ya if he had to. Someone who'd do whatever needs doin'! And that's exactly what I done. 'Cause this ain't Lincoln, Nebraska, or Kansas City, Missouri, or even Tombstone, Arizona, for that matter. This here's Damnation! And in Damnation you need a lyin' cheatin' mayor to get things done, and to keep you safe from them Injuns!"

The mayor paused to look a few of the fellas in the eye. He seemed to be weighing the effect of his words, like a grocer with a jilted scale.

"Now any man who thinks differently can just march right out there into the plains and try having words with the savages. You'd be lucky to keep your scalp! Just ask the deputy about that one. He's the quickest gunslinger in town, and he barely escaped with half a mop on his crown."

The crowd seemed to be of two minds. Some reckoned the mayor was plain old full of shit, and he should be shot on the spot. The fear of an Indian attack was a sore spot for a lot of the others, though. They'd follow anyone who claimed to know a way they could keep their scalps.

"If y'all like," he offered as if he was being charitable, "we can all go back to the Rusty Nail and grease our hollers with some of Mabel's red beers. Let's hash this thing out like gentlemen. I'll hear every single man's grievances, even if it takes me all night! Now I don't promise I can fix everything, mind you, but I'll do my damnedest for each last man with *good ol' American grit*—because I'm straight shooter!"

A few of the boys got fired up by the speech and saw fit to applaud. Then the buzzard swooped down and landed on top of the wagon. Since no one bothered to shoo it away, it hopped over onto the chest of the real Vernon Jackson Walker. The first few pecks at his eyeballs sprayed blood onto the thief's chest. Then the ghost buzzard pecked deeper into his head and pulled out a long red vein, like it was digging a worm out of the earth. After that, no one saw much use in standing around watching the thief's eyes get gobbled up, so they followed the mayor back to the Rusty Nail.

Gut-Shot Granny wasn't won over by what she heard. "I noticed he didn't say anything about hearing womenfolk's grievances," she said.

"That's a fair point, ma'am," I agreed. "And if you had run for mayor, you would have had my vote."

"Ha!" she laughed. "If you'd a voted for me, they woulda sent you to hell and I'd be stuck with nothing to read in the commode!"

Whiny Pete lingered behind. He liked how the mayor made him feel safe, but he also wanted the people he'd known the longest to be on board. "Mayor Vern *is* a straight shooter, I'll give him that," he remarked. "And that's better'n not knowing who you're dealing with."

"Yeah, but when's he shootin' straight?" I asked. "Before, when he told us what we wanted to hear, or now, when he's saying he lied to us just to get elected?"

The question made Pete confused and he didn't want to harp on the matter any longer. "Ah, I don't know, but he's the only one who can bargain with the Indians," he argued.

"The Injuns don't even know we have a mayor," I pointed out. "Mabel's the one who struck a truce with the chief."

"Yeah, but the mayor laid the groundwork. I heard him say so," Whiny Pete defended. "If it weren't for him, the vampires might start another war."

"I ain't sure about all that," Sal said. "There could be a war with the Indians any day now, whether the vampires start one or not. I will say this, though: The mayor makes a fine speech. I'll give him that."

"Sure, it was fine as far as speeches go," I said. "But did y'all notice he still didn't bother telling us who he *really* is?"

Chapter 21

Sergeant Silence

Buddy sat at the end of the bar in the Rusty Nail with his flap of severed scalp swaying with the breeze that came through an open window. He was sipping a glass of wine and watching the ponies ride around in circles out in the plains. The once-chubby gunslinger had slimmed down quite a bit, on account of he didn't care much for smaller game animals like opossums. He said that he felt like a bully eating tiny critters, even if they were twice dead.

When Annabelle put some roasted squirrel skewers in front of him, he winced and pushed it away. "This red beer is all I need. It makes my belly so warm, I don't need no food."

Buddy's face was still black and blue from the beating the Indians had given him during Ms. Parker's rescue, but he didn't complain. He was tougher than an old boot. Then Ms. Parker came along and sat beside him. Buddy fidgeted nervously, trying to flatten his upturned flap of scalp like it was misplaced hair. When he remembered it wasn't ever going to lay properly again, he started to get up in embarrassment.

"Don't go." She grabbed his sleeve. "I just wanted to thank you for what you did. It was very courageous of you to face all those Indians just to provide a distraction."

"Ah, it weren't nothin', ma'am." He blushed.

"It was indeed," she said. "You don't have any special abilities like the vampires or the wolves, and for you to go out there all by yourself—well, that's about the bravest thing I can imagine."

"Let's not make a big thing of it, ma'am. I'm sure you woulda done the same."

"That's what I'm saying!" Her eyes moistened. "I don't think *anyone* would do that. Not even a vampire would walk straight into a camp with hundreds of angry Indians—and they nearly *scalped* you! You poor thing."

"What I mean to say is you woulda helped me in your own way," Buddy told her. "Same as I done for you."

Buddy kept covering his head wound, not wanting the lady to rest her eyes on it for long, but his futzing only drew her attention to it. And whenever her eyes lifted, he got more uncomfortable. Finally, Ms. Parker pulled his hands from his head, then pressed her lips against his forehead.

"Oh, Buddy, I think you look handsome exactly the way you are!" she announced loudly.

A soldier was walking by just then, and he whistled. "Lookie here, fellas. Baldie's got a girlfriend!" he teased. Being new to town, the soldier was not aware of Buddy's talents with a pistol.

"Don't mind him," Ms. Parker said.

The soldier sat down at a table with a few other army boys who were playing poker. He'd already run out of money, so he couldn't play. After a minute, he grew bored and called out to Buddy, "Hey, your wig's slippin' off!"

"That ain't no wig," Whiny Pete informed him. "He was half-scalped while saving the lady from the redskins."

"He knows it ain't no wig," Jarvis told Pete.

"Lemme get this straight," the soldier heckled. "You got an Indian haircut for that hussy—"

He barely got the word out before a gunshot sounded. At first, it was hard to tell where the soldier had been hit since he showed no wounds. Then he started gagging loudly. The bullet had gone through his open mouth into his tongue, and he was choking on the blood and tissue that had slipped down his throat.

Buddy walked over, cupping his hand behind one ear, and taunted the man. "Sorry, friend. I didn't hear that! Can you speak up, pal? Awful noisy in here!"

The soldier spat out some shattered teeth and a hunk of his own tongue with the bullet in it. Then he sat back gasping for air. He had to ball up a rag and stuff it in his mouth in order to soak up the blood.

"What's the matter?" Buddy kept on him. "Cat got your tongue? Don't be shy now! What's your name, soldier boy? Tell you what. I'm gonna call you Sergeant Silence because I think that's all we're gonna get from you from now on."

Ms. Parker was too horrified to watch any more. She quickly headed for the door. Buddy called after her. "Sorry, ma'am. I just couldn't sit there and let the man insult you like that."

The tongueless man's friends looked more put out by the interruption of their card game than anything else, but it wouldn't look good for them to let their comrade go unavenged. The rest of the soldiers would give them a hard time over it. Then the bronc busters would call them yellow. Next, the miners would cut ahead of them in the chow line. Eventually some alfalfa desperado might stab one of them for a second helping of raccoon steak.

Two of Sergeant Silence's friends decided to take a stand. They pulled their guns, but before their wrists rose above their hips, Buddy shot them both in the face. Ms. Parker hadn't crossed the threshold yet, and she spun around in fear, thinking Buddy might've gotten hit.

"I'm real sorry about this, ma'am," he told her. Then another soldier drew. Buddy sent a bullet into his gut. Ms. Parker stormed out while he reached for his other gun. The last soldier got off a shot, but his aim wasn't very good, and he hit a sodbuster in the back before Buddy returned fire.

"Stop it!" Mabel screeched as her chandelier nearly got hit in the crossfire. "This ain't no place for gunfightin'!"

"If I may offer a bit of friendly advice," I told Mabel. "Sal always kept an eight-gauge behind the bar. Firing a round into the ceiling, accompanied by a few harsh words, usually breaks things up. Nobody likes a spray of buckshot in the face—no offense Jarvis," I added.

"None taken." The kid waved.

"As I said, ma'am, it's a pretty good incentive for folks to take their grievances outside. Just be sure there ain't no one in the room above, of course."

By then, more soldiers decided to join in on the fight. Buddy ducked behind a beam to reload. He was outnumbered ten to one, and the sheriff was nowhere to be seen. It looked like he might need to find a new deputy soon. It was a good thing Buddy had lost some weight because their bullets were chipping away at the post he was hiding behind. Finally, a blast sounded from the catwalk above. Mollie, the quiet harlot, was standing up there in nothing but her bloomers with a rifle in her hands.

"The lady said take yer shenanigans outside!" she hollered in a voice much louder than anyone thought her capable of. "And what the lady says goes!" She fired a warning shot at the boot of a soldier. The man fell to the ground with a scream.

She wasn't so plain-looking up there in her lingerie with a gun in her hands. The soldiers quickly lost interest in avenging their tongueless friend. Buddy sat back down on his stool to watch the ponies run across the plains as he drank wine. Those who had the means lined up for a roll in the hay with Mollie. Her dance card was full for the rest of the week.

"I don't get it," Old Moe pondered aloud. "Why would she wanna lay with so many smelly men? Being a sporting lady is hard enough when you're alive, but these men reek of the grave. And what's there to do with her earnings? Ain't like she's sending it back home to youngins or buyin' fancy clothes from a shop."

"Maybe she's saving for a farm," a cowhand suggested. "Gonna retire and live the good life."

"What farm?" Mayor Vern squawked. "You gotta grow more'n moss to have a farm. All them buckets that Jake set up don't mean shit if there ain't no rain. It's a good thing I made a deal with the Indians through Mabel, so y'all have a steady supply of meat. Meat'll keep your bellies full. You can count on that, not some flavorless weeds that sprout from the dust!"

The Chinaman was no longer around to haul bodies to the pigpen. And even if he had been, there weren't any more pigs left to eat the bodies anyway. The soldiers that Buddy had shot stayed piled up on the floor. Eventually, a couple of husky cowboys dragged them to the boardwalk in exchange for free wine, but they wouldn't take them any farther than that.

Eventually, the buzzard pecked out their eyeballs. Seemed to be its favorite part to eat. There were far too many bodies for the vulture to pick all the bones clean, but every single one of them had their sockets emptied. A desert bird normally wouldn't come across so many carcasses all at once, and it was getting chubby on account of it. The Indians still couldn't manage to put an arrow in the buzzard, and nobody wanted to waste a bullet for fear that a war might start at any moment.

Chapter 22

The Red-Beer Poets

After Mollie broke up the ruckus between Buddy and the soldiers, Mabel gave everyone a glass of wine on the house to settle folks down. One good thing about the red beer was that outlaws didn't get as angry as they did when they drank regular yellow beer or whiskey. Some liked to reminisce about their old sweethearts or boast about the big heists they had pulled off when they were still alive.

Since the round was free, Jarvis tried a few sips just to see what the rotten grape juice tasted like, and it got him all worked up. Right away, he started praising Buddy for how he took out five soldiers all by himself. He was so excited you'd have thought he'd just seen Buffalo Bill's Wild West Show.

"Tell me something," he prattled worshipfully. "When you pull your gun that quick, is it practice that takes over or is it just, like… instinct?"

"Hmm." Buddy thought on it a spell. "Suppose I learnt it in the orphanage."

"They taught you how to quick-draw in an orphanage?" There was no putting off Jarvis when he wanted to get the full story, so Buddy had no choice but to oblige him.

"Can't say they taught it, exactly. It's just where I learnt it. See, the orphanage was right next to some railroad tracks, and trains used to pass at all hours. It was so loud, you couldn't hear nothing else. The older boys took advantage of the noise. Since the nuns in charge couldn't hear no yellin' above the clatter, they'd put a beating on the younger boys, like myself. They picked on me on account of I wasn't so slim—even as a child. They called me *fatso* and such.

"So one night just after lights out, the building began to shake like it always did when a train approached. The biggest and meanest of the bullies pinned down a pimply redhead kid whose daddy had dumped him there that afternoon. While he was beating on the kid, I got fed up and started wailing on the bully. Alls I could hear was the clatter of the train going by: *thump-thump, thump-thump!* I reckoned if I let up and gave the bully a chance, he would've clobbered me, so I just kept going. When the train finished passing, he had a bloody lip and never bullied no one again.

"Ever since then, whenever someone tries bullying me, something takes over and I can hear that same thumping in my head. I supposed it helps me focus. Sure, I've shot my share of tin cans while practicing to be Wild Bill Hickok. Can't say for certain whether it's made me any quicker. I'll tell you this, though: As the years pass, seems like everything's gotten a lot quieter, aside from that same thumping I hear whenever a bully draws."

"Ah, what a load of horseshit!" Sal said from the doorway. He'd come with his scattergun to see what all the gunfire was about.

"What the hell's a train again?" Old Moe asked.

"Don't ya 'member?" Sal told him. "It's what dandies ride nowadays instead of horses, so they can bullshit all day instead of watching the trail."

Seemed like Regular Sal was lonesome all by himself, so I followed him back across the road to the Foggy Dew to keep him company. Ms. Parker was sitting at the bar when we arrived. Sal poured us two whiskeys from his dwindling stash. No one else was around except Red beneath the floorboards, and he hadn't said much in days, aside from the occasional curse. You'd hardly know he was there if not for the snoring.

"Buddy's just like the rest of them," Ms. Parker complained. "A no-good thug!"

"It ain't his fault," I told her. "It's hard to behave in this godforsaken place. Least when we were all alive, there was scripture to follow. That's all hogwash in this sunless world of vampires and werewolves. Can't be sure of a damn thing here. You wake up in a hopeless cloud of doubt and drink just to forget about it!"

"I wake up in the same cloud of doubt," she argued. "You don't see me starting gunfights for no good reason!"

"Ah, it's different for men," I said. "We get hassled if we look soft. Everything a fella does is just to prove he's worth a damn! All he can do is shoot before he gets shot. And now that there ain't no rules in the Rusty Nail, everyone's back to killin' each other over dumb shit again!" My speech was slurring a bit. "Pardon my language, ma'am. The whiskey and wine must have gone to my head, 'cause my tongue's slipp'ry-er than a snake."

"I'd say it's that dang wine," Sal grumbled.

"Course it is," Red erupted from below. "Got 'em all thinking they're Walt fucking Whitman!" he shouted.

"You'll have to pardon his language, ma'am," I said. "The Irish are a talkative people, and it seems Red's solitary confinement has made him a bit odd of late."

"Well, wine and solitude doesn't excuse *all* bad behavior!" Ms. Parker fumed and stormed out the door.

Chapter 23

Vern's Gambit

After Ms. Parker left, I sat at the bar sipping my whiskey and writing up the next issue of *The Crapper*. Sal went into the kitchen. Through the doorway, I could see him rifling through a salvaged trunk of fabrics. He hoped he might win back some customers if he fancied up the walls, like Mabel had done.

Red had passed out cold, so it was nice to have some quiet time to myself without any bickering or gunfights. There weren't many places in Damnation where a man could find some peace, but the least popular saloon was one of them—for a few minutes anyway. Then a flaming arrow sailed through the broken window and struck the bar just beside my elbow. The burning rag wrapped around the shaft smelt as if it had been dipped in kerosene.

"Duck!" Sal yelled.

I tumbled off my stool and hit the ground just in time. A second arrow followed right after. It wasn't on fire, but the point sunk into the bar where I'd been sitting.

"They're gonna burn down the dang saloon!" Sal hollered. "We better skedaddle!"

All the commotion woke up Red, who yelled for us to let him out. "I smell smoke up there. B'Jesus, don't lemme burn for what I done!"

The hatch to the cellar was on the other side of the room, and we couldn't get to it without crossing in front of the window where the arrows were coming from.

"C'mon, boys!" Red pleaded. "If I didn't kill that squaw, she'd a kilt me for certain. You know it your damn selves! It don't warrant no death sentence."

"Ah, hell!" Sal huffed and grabbed his scattergun. "Tom, you try'n put out those flames. I'll give you some cover."

"What'll I use?" I asked. "There ain't no water."

He dragged the chest of fancy fabrics from the kitchen. "Smother 'em with these. Ain't no use in dressing this place up anyways. It'd be like putting lipstick on a pig."

Two riders were circling by, one after the other. Black Moon came first, launching a flaming arrow into the wall. Then another rider followed and took aim at whoever tried to put out the fire. After a couple of passes, Sal had their timing figured. As soon as a flaming arrow struck the mantel, he emptied both barrels. The whole window frame splintered apart as the spray of buckshot hit the horse and the rider. After they toppled over, Black Moon reared back on his pony, letting out an angry holler before riding off.

Sal and I did our best to put out the flames. They were spreading up the walls, and we didn't have enough hands to smother them quick enough. Luckily, some men from the Rusty Nail turned up. They'd heard the gunshot and were hoping to find something worth wagering on, but they pitched in all the same. If we didn't smother the fire quick enough, the building would surely burn to ashes.

"Hey, Regular Sal, toss me some more of them pretty rags!" a cowhand called out with a laugh. "Ooh, red lace! Was you fixin' to make this place into a cathouse?"

By the time the trunk was empty, the blaze was nearly out. Just a few cinders remained. The Foggy Dew was in no great shape. Some of the walls were charred worse than Annabelle's back or Luther's cheek. But it was still standing, and Red was still beneath it.

"Can I get out now?" he begged.

"I'm afraid that's under the sheriff's jurisdiction," I told him. "The rules are still on the wall. That part didn't catch fire."

After all the heavy lifting was done, the mayor showed up on the scene. He put on a good show of being outraged. He had a knack for complaining about how something shouldn't have happened after the thing was done.

"Them double-crossing bow-benders!" he griped. "What happened to the dang truce they agreed on with Mabel?"

"They didn't attack *my* saloon," Mabel said. "Maybe the treaty wasn't meant to include mean old men."

"Well, I guess I couldn't expect much, sending a woman to do men's work."

The scalped soldier wanted to put in his two cents, as he usually did when strategy was involved. "It prolly didn't matter what the agreement was. Injuns were likely trying to torch this saloon just to get us all in one place when they attack," he said. "It's what I'd do. Hell, it's what we done with the plains Injuns. After we burnt their teepees, they all ran to the river where they was easy pickins' with nowhere to hide."

"Hey, Tom, maybe you could have words with that Iroquois fella you're friendly with," Sal suggested. "See if you can find out what their intentions might be."

"Yeah, Tom," the mayor ordered. "Ask your red friend what gives."

The Crapper

Comings: *Mollie Mangrove was a sporting girl to the hardscrabble miners of Tombstone, Arizona. She had been there during the shootout at the O.K. Corral, though she was taking a bath at the time. She heard a bunch of gunshots, but didn't think nothing of it since it was a regular occurrence in Tombstone. Mollie died of a head wound during vigorous relations that caused her to fall from bed. It might not have been a fortunate event for her, but you could say someone was getting lucky at the time. She ain't quite sure why she didn't make it into heaven, but we ain't quite sure there is one, so I didn't press her on the matter.*

Goings: *Buddy shot a soldier in the mouth for disrespecting Ms. Parker. It seems like the fella might not bleed out as long as he keeps that rag in his mouth. Sergeant Silence, as he's come to be called, has been unable to provide me with any details about his life, nor any of his friends who didn't fare as well. Buddy sent four of them to hell before Mollie broke the matter up with a rifle in her skivvies, proving to be a better shot than most soldiers.*

Also, Sal shot an Apache warrior off his horse because he was trying to burn down the Foggy Dew. Since then, the mayor has ordered me to inquire about the Indians' intentions. So if I don't return, you can likely assume they intend on doing us harm, and this would therefore be the last issue of the paper.

Chapter 24

The Indians' Intentions

Little Bear wasn't at the dry well when I got there, but we had a system where I could signal to him. I'd wave a dirty sheet like I was shaking the dust from it. He must've had a view of the well from his teepee because it wasn't long before he moseyed down the path in no particular hurry. Seemed like he enjoyed the breeze and wasn't bothered by all the dust blowing around.

It was hard to tell his age. He'd been in town about as long as me and might've made it about twenty-five years before the bullet hole in his breast had sent him to Damnation. He looked a lot younger on account of how small he was, but he carried himself like an old chief who'd fought in countless battles. Never seemed surprised by anything. As if he'd seen it all before, and whatever you told him just confirmed it was a bunch of horseshit.

As soon as he sat down, he removed his moccasins to rub the bottom of his feet. There was no use in interrogating him since he knew what I was after, and if he was inclined to oblige me, he wouldn't be rushed, no matter what I said.

After some minutes, he finally began speaking as if we were already in the middle of a conversation instead of just starting one. For him, the typical exchanging of pleasantries was done with a simple nod or just by sharing the same space for a spell.

"Some tribes fear Long Tooth," he said then paused. "Others think Black Moon has bigger medicine. Everyone agree on one thing: Never trust white man again. He break too many treaty with every tribe. No one want to make same mistake. Now, when white man ask for treaty, we attack before you do."

"Ain't there nothing we can do to smooth things over?" I asked. "There's gotta be some way for us all to get along."

"Your great-grandfather make many promise to our people. He only keep one."

"You mean the president?" I said. "What was it?"

"If we go to white man school and talk like you and live in box, then we get food."

"Are you talkin' about *assimilation?*" I asked.

"You do same. If live like Indian, get treated like Indian."

"Does the chief feel this way?" I asked.

"*Un-un,*" he affirmed with a solemn bow.

I went back to the others and told them what Little Bear had proposed.

"*Assimilate!?*" the mayor screeched. "They reckon we're gonna strip down to our britches and sleep in teepees like a buncha savages?"

"To the Indians, it don't matter if you had white parents and spent the last fifty years in a saloon. For them, alls you gotta do is follow their ways. Then you're an Indian, same as the rest."

"Same as the rest, hell!" a soldier swore. "We won't be breaking bread at the chief's table where the best cuts of meat are served, that's for sure! They'd prolly give us dead squirrel."

"It ain't like that with Indians," I tried to explain. "Everyone gets the same, and visitors get the best of all. It's a matter of pride with them."

The scalped soldier was flabbergasted by the notion. "You ain't considering becoming a prairie nigger?" he asked. "No offense, Bo."

Rodeo Bo waved it off. "None taken, you hairless hillbilly." A few of the fellas laughed.

Whiny Pete was the most worried about the threat of an attack. He clenched his fingers, working up the courage to say something. Finally, he interrupted, "Joining the redskins has gotta be better'n waitin' around to catch an arrow in the head!"

"Besides, they got all the whiskey!" a soldier added. "This dang frog juice is making folks too sappy. What you do when the candles are out is your own business, but yesterday I saw two fellas holdin' hands beneath the poker table in the middle of the day!"

"Shit, at least there's women in their camp," a cowboy argued. "And a few of them squaws is pretty decent-looking once you wipe the mud from their brow."

Whiny Pete was already sold on it. The skinny bruised-up boy stripped down to his breeches.

"What ya doin' boy?" the soldier asked. "You had too much wine?"

"I'm jumping ship!" he said and tied his long johns around a stick. Then he marched out the door waving them like a flag.

"That boy's gonna get himself a haircut," the mayor said.

The soldier wasn't so keen on Pete's odds either. "He'll prolly catch an arrow before he gets that close. Them long johns ain't been warshed in years. They were far too gray to be taken for a surrender flag. If you waved 'em in front of my house, I'd shoot you—no questions asked!"

"Ah, forget that sniveling kid," the mayor barked. "Say, Tom. I have a counteroffer for your red friend."

"They ain't bargaining," I told him. "Their whole point was that bargaining with white men got 'em all kilt to begin with. It's the only thing all of the tribes agree on."

"Can't say I blame 'em." The scalped soldier saw my point. "After what Custer done... Telling 'em they could keep their one sacred place, till he caught a whiff of gold on it."

"And at Wounded Knee!" another put in. "That sure was a slaughter!"

"Just the same," the mayor said. "Everyone has their price. Tell 'em all they can live in peace, and we won't unleash the great power of Long Tooth on them. We just want the pigs and the eggs... and also the whiskey and the beer—like how it used to be before all this hoopla started. In return, they can have the cows."

"The wolves might have something to say about that," I said. "They ain't gonna wanna give up their beef."

"Now see here. I got a plan," the mayor said. "You tell the Injuns that we'll back them up against the wolves. Say that after they attack those mangy mutts, our Long Tooth will come from the rear, like he done to them."

"Luther is still pretty worn out," I reminded him. "And there's no saying he'd agree to it even if he was well-rested. Nigel couldn't take on the whole pack neither. And the wolves would figure out real quick that there ain't no warm blood for them to feed on."

"The vampires ain't gotta actually fight," the mayor said. "Neither do the rest of you."

"You sayin' we're gonna double-cross 'em?" the scalped soldier asked.

"You goddamned right we're gonna double-cross 'em!"

"Oh goodie!" He rubbed his hands together. "So how's it gonna work?"

The other soldiers weren't as enthusiastic about the plan, but since it didn't involve them fighting anyone, they didn't object.

"The Injuns might wipe out the wolves, or the wolves might wipe out the Injuns," the mayor explained. "Either way, it don't make much difference to us. Whoever wins, there will be a lot less of them afterward. Then we can set whatever terms we like."

Sal shrugged. "It might work."

"There ain't no way that it could possibly fail," the mayor said.

The next day, I went out to the dry well and waved a tattered sheet. Before long, Little Bear moseyed on out, and I told him the offer that the mayor had proposed. He said he would present it the chief. Then he moseyed back to camp just as slowly as he had come.

About an hour later, he returned. "Okay," he told me. "Chief say we attack tomorrow after *Poltach* feast."

"Pol-what?" I asked.

"We have ceremony where we give gift."

"Like Santa Claus?" I asked.

"Who?" he asked back.

"Santa Claus is an old white-haired man with a beard who gives presents to children during the wintertime."

"Ah, you mean great-grandfather of your country!" he nodded excitedly. "He give many land in winter, but then take all back in spring."

"Nah." I grimaced. "Different guy."

"Oh." Little Bear looked disappointed. "We still attack tomorrow after feast."

Chapter 25

The Double-Cross

Everyone gathered to watch from the Foggy Dew. Sal's burnt-up and broken-down saloon wasn't as comfortable, but the angle from the window had a better view than the Rusty Nail. Mabel reluctantly came across the road for the event. Even Luther finally roused from his bed. On account of him being on his back for so many weeks, all the blood had left his toes, and he had to limp around on two dead legs, barely able to stay upright. He sat in a chair by the back wall, trying to keep his eyes open long enough to see the Indians attack the wolves.

"You can't sleep your whole death away, old chap!" Nigel teased him. "I spent much of my first year in bed. When I finally got up, I could barely dodge a bullet. It's not the sort of town where you want to let them catch you at half strength."

All afternoon, there had been a thunder of tom-toms coming from the Indian camp. It was growing louder with each passing hour. They had roasted a couple of pigs, and the smell of it was driving everyone mad with hunger. The mayor assured everyone that after the Indians attacked the wolves, we'd be having steak for dinner.

"Hear that?" Sal said. "The drumming has finally stopped!"

"The dirt worshipers must've finished their powwow," the mayor announced. "The show should be starting any minute now."

"Good, I can't wait to see them featherheads get ate up," a cowboy said.

"Five bucks says the savages make dog stew out of the wolves," a soldier countered. Money started flying across the bar in a frenzy. There hadn't been so much action in the Foggy Dew for months. "Just like old times," Sal said as he scribbled down a list of the wagers.

"For tonight it is." Mabel smiled and filled Sal's goblet up with the wine she had brought over. It was from some place called Burgundy, and must've cost someone a pretty penny.

About a hundred braves gathered out in the road, with bows and arrows and a few rifles. We all stared out the window, giddy with anticipation to see a battle we didn't have to fight in. Then a wolf suddenly crashed through the back door. Two more followed right behind it. A high-pitched holler came from the road out front. Then Black Moon appeared at the same broken window that Sal had blown the frame off while shooting his friend. The angry unkillable Indian launched an arrow. It struck Luther in the gut. The sleepy yellow-haired giant toppled out of his chair onto the floor.

"We've been double-crossed!" Sal yelled.

The soldier boys weren't much use in an ambush, particularly in a saloon. Half of them were drunk, and the rest didn't know where they had left their guns. The carpenters who had built Mabel's saloon were still in good fighting condition. One pulled a hammer from his work belt and chucked it at a wolf's snout. A couple of the others were heeled, and they got off some shots till the wolves fell on them. Rather than take the time to finish off each man, the wolves just mangled their hands so they couldn't pull a trigger.

The mayor dove behind the bar and curled up at Sal's feet while he unloaded his scattergun. Nigel might have been some help, but as soon as the action started he grabbed little Martin from Ms. Parker and bolted up the stairs to the store room. The lady was left to fend for herself, until Buddy stepped in front of her with a pistol in each hand and got busy making holes in mutts. Unfortunately, they were coming in too fast to fight off.

A giant wolf, nearly the size of a bear, jumped on Buddy's back and tore into his shoulder. He yelled out in pain, but instead of trying to shoot the beast he dropped his gun so that he could reach into his pocket. He was leaking a lot of blood, but his last thought had been to keep the egg he'd been carrying around from being crushed. As Buddy collapsed, it slipped from his hand and rolled across the floor.

The wolves had taken down every man who was heeled. All that could be heard were the sounds of jaws tearing into flesh. I went for the pistol that Buddy had dropped, but a wolf had my bad leg in its jaws and was chewing it like a milk bone. The egg wobbled over the uneven floor, which sloped to the back of the room. Finally, it tapped against the far wall beside Luther. He was slumped over with Black Moon's arrow still sticking from his gut, barely clinging to the afterlife. When the egg knocked against the wainscoting, he looked over.

A crack splintered down the length of the shell. Then a few seconds later, a tiny claw pushed through the top. Luther sat bleeding out on the threshold to hell, but he was still curious about it. Maybe the smell got his attention. Since the creature was upside down, it took some time before a small soggy head finally surfaced from the hole. Nobody noticed it except me and Luther. It let out a chirp, which was a lot louder than you might've expected from a tiny chick.

When the wolves looked over, the chick had already scampered off out of Luther's reach. He had the empty shell in his hand. There was a gooey mess inside that likely contained some drops of warm blood. Luther slurped it down, and his eyes instantly glowed yellow. He plucked the arrow from his gut without so much as a wince.

As he stood, two wolves jumped for him. He caught them both by their necks, one in each of his giant hands, and smashed them together like cymbals in a marching band. Four more wolves came for him at once, but it was no use. He punched and kicked too quickly for them to get him. After they were laid out, the rest didn't see any use in attacking a freshly fed vampire, particularly one as big as Luther. Argus, the pack leader, howled and all of the wolves retreated at once.

The mayor saw his opportunity. He crawled out from behind the bar and grabbed the baby chick while Luther was still chasing down stray wolves. The task tuckered Luther out, and he wanted to renew his strength with some of the chick's blood. The mayor was already clutching the bird tightly against his chest, petting its tiny head with an evil smile.

"Easy there, big fella," he told Luther. "You take another step and I'll twist this little chick's neck. You might get a mouthful of blood, but after that it'll run cold, and you'll never feed again. Just take 'er easy and I'll ration you a drop at a time when you need it."

"That's my chick!" Buddy moaned from the ground.

"That goes for you too, slim. I got my thumb on its neck. You may get off a bullet, but I'll make sure the last thing I do is squeeze."

The mayor pricked the chick with a safety pin and squeezed out a drop of blood on the bar. After Luther licked it, he was good as new. When Nigel came back downstairs, he was given the same deal as Luther. No one could blame him for accepting. A century is long time to go without feeding. The mayor now had two healthy vampires protecting him. Of course, that didn't keep folks from criticizing him.

Sal was the first to remark on how the mayor's plan had backfired. "Seems like the teepee creepers took your idea," he pointed out. "Clearly, they set the wolves against us."

"I'd say the plan worked perfectly," the mayor argued. "Ain't nobody gonna attack me now that I got a steady supply of warm blood."

"Don't you mean *us?*" I asked.

"Huh?" the mayor gaped blankly.

"You said ain't nobody gonna attack *me*. Don't you mean ain't nobody gonna attack *us?*

"Oh, right." He smiled. "Hey Sal, pour some of your stash of whiskey you got hiding back there. Ain't no reason to be rationing it no more. Tomorrow, I'll have words with the Indians about who gets what."

The Crapper

Goings: *By my count, five soldiers were sent to hell when the wolves attacked, after the mayor's plan to double-cross the Indians backfired. The carpenters who built the Rusty Nail all got their hands mangled, so if you're looking to have something fixed, it might be awhile. I'm not sure why Mayor Vern keeps going around saying it was the "most successful plan in the entire history of Damnation." The only upside was that a baby chick hatched in the middle of it, and now he's got a steady supply of warm blood to ration to the vampires for protection.*

Chapter 26

Little Bear and the King

The mayor didn't waste any time in informing the chief of the new pecking order. He marched straight into the camp with Nigel on one side and Luther on the other. A brave let an arrow fly at the mayor's head, but Nigel caught it midair. Then Luther dashed forward and swept the legs out from under the bow shooter. The other warriors reached for their weapons, but the chief signaled for the visitors to be heard.

"See here, Squanto," the mayor barked. "I'm here to tell you maize-munchers there's gonna be some changes. I got two well-fed Long Teeth here. Just one of 'em was enough to send them wolves packing, so a bunch of you spear-chuckers wouldn't stand no chance against them. From now on, all the whiskey, wine, and beer that comes out of the dust goes straight to me. You hear? Also, we get the cows, too."

Even from the edge of town, we could hear the mayor yelling loud and clear. The chief didn't say a peep back. His eyes fell on the mayor's breast pocket. He seemed mighty curious why a baby chick's head was sticking out of our leader's coat. When the mayor finished talking, Luther filled a wheelbarrow with booze, and Nigel led a steer back to town.

"Steaks for all my boys!" the mayor announced when he walked into the Rusty Nail. Everyone cheered. When Mabel reached for some liquor, he stopped her. "Not so fast, little lady. If you want to sell my hooch, you'll be giving me a percentage."

Mabel didn't have any other choice but to agree. Her stock of wine was running low, and the chief would be giving all supplies straight to the mayor. Those who had thought he was acting too big for his britches before were bowled over by Vern's uppityness now. He sat at the end of the bar, barking orders like a king on a throne. Annabelle kept his glass full, and the vampires kept him safe. Since there was only one sporting woman in town, he pretty much had dibs on her around the clock.

"Get on over here, you strumpet!" The mayor yanked Mollie by the arm. The poor girl accepted her lot uncomplainingly. Her life had no doubt been filled with toil, and she didn't expect much more in death. She had been having words with Luther, and he didn't look too pleased about the interruption.

"Up those stairs, harlot. I'm in the mood for a poke. *Now march!*" The mayor gave the little lady a shove, and she fell while mounting the steps. Luther's eyes glowed yellow with anger. He began to go after the mayor, but Nigel stopped him.

"You might endanger the fowl, old boy. Think of the warm blood."

"I don't care if I never drink blood again," Luther replied angrily. "That cretin infuriates me."

"We'll need it if we are to summon the dark one."

Luther hesitated a moment, then gave up on the idea. Instead, he reached behind the bar for a bottle of gin and poured a tall glass to calm himself. He emptied it with two gulps. It wasn't five minutes later when the mayor returned, sweaty and disheveled, with Mollie following behind him, still adjusting her dress.

"It sure is a shame we ain't got no water for those seeds," Farmer Jake remarked.

"What the hell we need seeds for?" the mayor asked. "We're on the top of the food chain now. I say who gets what, and I've already told the chief we get the cows!"

"Ain't no predicting when cows'll come through the dust, though," Jake said.

"It's true," Old Moe agreed. "Pigs can be scarce some weeks, too. That's why Sal kept a pigpen, and there's more mouths to feed nowadays."

"If folks don't eat, they get irritable," I added. "They might even wanna elect a new mayor. One who does what he says, and is who he claims."

"Not with two vampires guarding me they won't."

The mayor pulled me aside when no one was within earshot, and leaned in so that I could see the rotten teeth in the back of his mouth. His breath was worse than a dead mule's. It was a mystery to me how Mollie could bear to be beneath such a man.

"Don't go saying no more nonsense about me in that shithouse paper of yours," he warned.

"Shithouse paper?"

"Yeah, the one everyone reads in the shithouse. I won't have you slandering me in it."

"It ain't that sort of publication," I told him. "Mostly, it just records who comes and goes."

"Don't give me that," he snarled. "I know how you like to slip in your take on current events, like how you said my plan to double-cross the Indians had backfired."

"Well it did."

"As far as I can see, everything worked out perfectly. End of story. And that cow-pie gossip rag shouldn't say otherwise."

"What do ya mean?" I asked. "The wolves mauled five men. Four others got their hands mangled so bad that they can't shoot a gun. The only successful thing was you happened to get your hands on that chick, which gives you power over the vampires."

"It was the most successful plan in the history of Damnation. Period."

"You've only been here a few months. How would you know anything about the history of Damnation?"

Vern's face reddened. "There ain't no use in you writing up nothing about that other dead guy named Vern, 'cause there ain't no story there neither," he ordered. Then he stormed off.

The next day, I ran into Little Bear while I was stretching my legs out by the dry well. He smiled at me innocently, as if there were no hard feelings between us. I gave him the stink eye, but he wasn't put off and came over to pester me.

"You ain't gonna pretend like you didn't lie right to my face, are ya?" I asked.

"Little Bear no lie. I say we attack after feast. I didn't say *who* we attack." He giggled with no small amusement.

"That ain't honest!" I scolded, but could do little more than pout about it.

"I told you. We never trust white man again. Whatever you say, we do opposite."

"So there ain't no chance of us *ever* having a real treaty?"

Little Bear thought on it a moment before answering. "When I was boy, white man make treaty with my chief so that we don't attack. They offer small piece of land. Afterward, they say we can't hunt or fish or graze animal on land. That winter, many of my people get sick from not eating.

Then they catch white man sickness and need medicine. Chief sold some of land back, but white man say agent decide when we get money and what can use for. By spring, most of my people dead. Then white man took rest of land and gave nothing in return."

"Look, I'm sorry for your people's sufferings," I said in earnest. "If there was something I could've done about it, I would've, but I wasn't *even there!*"

Little Bear shrugged as if that wasn't relevant. "After white man shoot me, I come here and talk to others," he continued. "Same thing happen to every tribe. Now, I ask you: If happen over again, would white man still kill my people and take land? Tell me *the really!*" he ordered.

"Yeah," I confessed. "The land's just too damn valuable. If it weren't for gold or timber, it'd be for farming or something else. There's a whole mess of people going to America every day from all over the world, and they all want a place to live. I suppose my kind is like a sickness to your kind. I wish it weren't so, but it is."

"Now, *we are sickness!*" Little Bear said. "And white man just want to be left alone." He laughed loudly.

"I guess it's a good thing we got two Long Teeth and a baby chick with warm blood to keep them strong." As soon as I said it, I realized I shouldn't have.

"Long Teeth like warm blood?" he asked innocently.

"Among other things," I added, but the clever Iroquois didn't seem like he was buying it. He just nodded.

Those who hated us the most now knew our weakness. If they captured the chick, we'd be at their mercy. Little Bear went on his way. Then some yards down the path, he paused for a moment and looked up at the sky. I couldn't tell exactly what he was looking at, but it made him smile.

Back at the Rusty Nail, most folks were in fine spirits since there was plenty of whiskey to drink and meat to eat. No one had much to complain about. Those with enough money might even get a roll in the hay with Mollie, if the mayor wasn't already occupying her. But since there were no rules posted on the wall, no one gave much consideration to common courtesies. Vern was the rudest of all.

"Get over here, harlot!" he ordered Mollie, and when she didn't move fast enough he backhanded her. "When I say come, don't dally with them soldier boys!"

"But I was just—"

"Don't sass me!" He tried to strike her again, but before he could, Luther grabbed his wrist. His eyes glowed yellow with a flash of anger. Slowly, he lifted the mayor a foot off the ground just by raising his arm in the air.

"You want your damn poultry blood, don't ya?" Vern threatened, then pulled the chick from his pocket and held his thumb on the bird's throat. "With just the teensiest bit of pressure, I could crack its backbone!"

Nigel appeared beside Luther and placed a hand on his shoulder with a nod. Luther could've torn the mayor's head off and gotten a few sips of warm blood from the chick. But after that, he'd have to face an eternity of hunger. Not to mention there'd be no chance of feeding little Martin any warm blood. The giant vampire put the mayor back down on the ground and headed for the door.

"That's more like it," Vern scolded. "Listen to your limey friend here."

Nigel must have taken exception to the term because he gave Vern a quick jab to the face. It wasn't hard enough to knock him down, but it let the mayor know he should watch his lip.

The Crapper

Comings: *Seeing as how I forgot to mention it in the last edition, I would like to inform everyone that a corpse with rope marks around his neck came to town a few weeks back. This corpse didn't mosey up to the bar for a drink like the rest of us did. It stayed dead. I reckoned I shouldn't deprive the fella of a proper announcement just because he ain't moving around—or because some people don't want you hearing about it.*

A wanted poster in the wagon identified the man as Vernon Jackson Walker—the very same name our mayor has been going by. Mayor Vern still hasn't said who he really is, since he definitely ain't the dead fella from the wagon. He has also repeatedly ordered me to tell you that his plan of double-crossing the Indians was the "most successful plan in the history of the Damnation," even though he's only been here a few months and several men got sent to hell on account of it. The only success that I can see is he now has a baby chick full of warm blood, which he can use to get the vampires to do whatever he wants.

There might not be another issue of this paper since the mayor is threatening to have the vampires send me to hell if I say anything bad about him, but he can kiss my ass.

Chapter 27

A Change in the Weather

I woke up one morning to find the rooming house was darker than normal. I reckoned my eyes were finally giving out, till I craned my neck out the window. The streaks of violet and yellow had vanished from the sky, and a plain gray blanket hung over the town. It offered so little light that you could hardly see across the road.

"Ya think it's the end of the Earth?" Kenny asked.

"Hmm." Jarvis scratched his head. "Why is it that you think we're still on Earth? Not that I'm sayin' you're wrong or anything. I was just wondering is all."

"The end of the Damnation then," Kenny corrected himself.

"It could be the end of us all," I said. "But I don't reckon Damnation is going nowhere."

By midday, large raindrops began to fall from the storm clouds, and the dusty ground thickened into mud cakes. You couldn't walk ten feet without slipping and falling. Luckily, there was still some boardwalk in front of the more well-traveled storefronts, even if half the boards were missing. Everyone gathered in the Rusty Nail, except Sal and Red.

"You reckon it must have rained here before?" Kenny asked. "Maybe that's why they built the boardwalk."

"Can't rightly say," Moe answered. "I been here the longest but I ain't never met nobody who was around when it was built. When I first arrived, folks usually didn't last more'n a couple months. Even the fella who told me the town was called Damnation got sent to hell a day later."

"Maybe all of this happened before," Jarvis suggested. "Not just the rain, but every bit of it, from the Indians taking Ms. Parker to the vampires getting her back, and that little chick coming out of its shell just in time for Luther to have some of its blood and save us all!"

"Let me get this straight," Bo said with smirk. "You're sayin' we all been here before... Like we all got sent to hell, then somehow got reborn and done every bit of it again exactly the same way?"

"Could be." Jarvis shrugged. "Mighta all happened more'n once!"

"So even the mayor was an asshole before?" I asked.

"Course he was an arsehole," the Irish fella answered. "What else would he be?"

"So how many times you think this all happened before?" Bo asked.

"Who knows?" Annabelle said with shrug. "The mayor might've been an asshole countless times before."

"Enough of this past lives nonsense!" the mayor barked from the corner of the bar where he'd been dozing until he heard his name. "Fill up my glass, girl! And the rest of you better stop bad-mouthing me if you want any more of my holler juice. I swear there ain't ever been a mayor in this town who got treated worse than me."

"Just how would you know that?" I asked, unable to stop myself. "You only been here a few months. We don't even know who built the boardwalk. There could've been a hundred mayors that got treated worse."

"Well if there were, they certainly weren't as *generous* as me!" Vern shouted. "And I blame it all on that lying shithouse rag of yours. You printed a bunch of lies about me, and it's got everyone against me!"

The one upside of the rain was that folks got their first baths in years. For some of them, it'd been decades since they had any water to wash up with. They finally got to clean their filthy wounds and rinse the bloodstains from their clothing. While the wet garments dried by the fire, the men sat around in their skivvies playing cards. The rain didn't let up. It kept lashing down so hard that it leaked from the ceiling onto the barstools.

"My beer tastes watered down," Blind Sal complained.

"It should!" Mayor Vern told him. "Rainwater's been dripping into your glass for half an hour. Can't anyone fix that roof?"

"All the carpenters got their hands mangled when the wolves attacked," Mabel reminded him.

"As I recall, that happened during the most successful plan in the history of Damnation," I teased.

"Oh, was that the most successful plan?" Annabelle joined in. "That one where a mess of men got sent to hell?"

"Quit your jawing!" Vern said with no small satisfaction. "That plan caused this little chick to be hatched, which is the reason why you're having steak for dinner instead of sawdust."

"The chick would've hatched eventually," I argued. "We prolly wouldn't have been fighting off the Indians at the time. They only attacked because of your plan to double-cross them first."

"Enough of you and your lying shithouse rag!" Vern scolded. "Ain't nobody else in this town handy with a hammer?"

One of the carpenters with a mangled hand spoke up, "Even if they were, there's no roofing material. It would all leak."

"Tear the roof off the other saloon," the mayor suggested.

"Sal ain't gonna like that plan," I said. "'Sides, his roof leaks worse than this one."

"I got an idea," Farmer Jake said.

"What's that? You gonna grow us a new roof?" the mayor snickered.

"I already did," Jake replied. "Remember that peat moss beside the latrine that you said was useless?"

"Yeah."

"I tol' ya it won't let no water through, didn't I? With the help of a few men, I could dig some of it up and sling it over the holes up there. Should keep us dry awhile longer."

"Well, what you waitin' for?" the mayor barked. "You sodbusters go help the man. I gotta do everything round here?" Vern polished off his drink, then rose from his stool. "Come on, Mollie. Time for a poke." He grabbed her by the arm and yanked her away from her conversation with Luther.

The giant vampire stood and glared at the mayor. You could tell it was taking all of his willpower to keep from tearing the little bully into a hundred pieces.

Chapter 28

The Huckleberry Bible

Once they had the peat moss in place, the roof didn't leak a drop and the stools were as dry as a bone. It was a good thing, too, because the rain didn't let up for several weeks. During that time, nothing came out of the dust—not people or wolves or vampires. But most importantly, no animals.

"Ain't even a teensy chipmunk come through?" Kenny asked.

"Nah," I told him. "There's a few scouts out there watching, and they ain't seen nothing."

"You kiddin' me, Kenny?" Liam the Miner said. "The wolves or the Indians will grab whatever comes through the dust. They ain't gonna abide by the mayor's terms while they're half starved."

"How about any elk?" Kenny persisted.

"What's wrong with you, boy?" Liam said. "Didn't you hear what I said? They certainly ain't gonna let no elk get through. Not when they ain't getting no chickens or pigs of their own to eat."

"What if no animals ever come through the dust again?" Bo asked. "That mean we just gotta starve for eternity?"

"I don't think you'd starve for eternity," Jarvis pointed out. "The wolves'd prolly come and eat us eventually. They'd be starving, too. If not them, then the Indians would."

"This happened before, as I recall," Moe said looking a little foggy about the details.

"Everything!" Jarvis got real excited. "Are you sayin' you're just rememberin' it all happened like this before?"

"Nah." Moe laughed. "I was just rememberin' that no animals came through the dust for a spell. Musta been fifty years ago. You 'member, Gut-Shot Granny?"

"Oh yeah," she said. Then she turned to me and whispered, "Not really."

"What did y'all do?" Kenny asked.

"Nothing!" Moe laughed. "Sal always had a pen full of pigs in case of lean times. Nothing came out of the dust for six months, but we ate heaps of bacon every day. By the time we were down to the last pig, more animals started coming again. You telling me you didn't keep a few steer on the side?"

"The mayor told me to slaughter 'em all for the contest," Mabel said. "He wanted to see who could tell a rib eye from a prime rib. 'Member? A lot of the meat just went to waste. Whatever the buzzard didn't eat is long spoiled by now."

"Ah, enough of your sass mouth!" the mayor complained. "Ain't you got nothin' left in that kitchen of yours, Mabel?"

"It'd be putrid by now if it wasn't cured," she replied. "And nobody thought to cure anything."

"Sal always cured some pork for a rainy day," I told them. As soon as I said it, I regretted it.

"I thought it didn't usually rain here," Jarvis questioned. "Until that time when the wolves attacked the Foggy Dew with a battle ram."

"It was just a manner of speaking," I said.

"Hold on second!" the mayor interrupted. "Did I hear you say somethin' about cured meat?"

"Um, I don't recall," I tried to backpedal.

"Don't give me that!" the mayor ordered. "I can sic one of these vampires after you if you ain't inclined to talk!"

"Well," I explained. "Sal wasn't the sort to look on the brighter side of things. He always fretted over what might go wrong down the road. So he cured a bunch of pork just in case a situation like this arose. But I don't expect he'd be much inclined to share it with any of us after how he's been treated lately."

Mayor Vern gave Luther a silent nod, and they both headed across the road to the Foggy Dew. Nigel stayed behind at the bar. They must not have considered shaking down a skinny old bartender to be a two-man job. Also, Nigel could make sure they didn't get ambushed when they returned.

"I don't expect that'll end well for Sal," the scalped soldier predicted.

"That's the second time I should've kept my mouth shut," I admitted.

"When was the first?" Jarvis asked.

"Mind your damn business."

Jarvis didn't say a peep for nearly a full minute, but when he got in a speculating mood, there was no keeping the boy quiet. "If the last time it rained was when wolves were attacked," he said. "Do y'all think it was the Lord using rain to protect ya?"

"I can't say for sure," I told the boy. His questioning was already testing my patience. "Seems like a pretty big coincidence to me, though. One minute it was dry as a desert. The next, it was coming down in buckets, just when they were charging the door."

"So if the Lord was protecting you from the wolves then, who do you think he's protecting us from now?" Jarvis asked. He wore a blank expression that made it hard to tell if he was teasing or being sincere.

"Maybe it ain't us he's protecting," Jake suggested.

"Who's he protecting then?" Liam asked.

"He might be protecting the Indians from *us*," Bo suggested. "We got the Long Teeth on our side. If it wasn't raining out, we might raid their camp for whatever meat they got left."

Nigel spoke up, giving some weight to Bo's theory. "I certainly do not intend to get soaking wet just so you chaps can consume cold dead animals."

"See? Maybe the Lord is protecting my people after all," Bo said. "Remember, I'm a quarter Cherokee."

When the debate died down, it was Annabelle's turn to stir the pot. "Why's it gotta be a *he* anyway?" she asked.

"Huh?" Kenny shrugged. "Who ya mean?"

"The Lord!" Annabelle said. "Why's the Lord gotta be a man? Maybe the Lord's a woman!"

The men at the bar all laughed loudly at the notion.

"Don't be silly, little lady," Kenny told her. "Course the Lord's a man. It says so right there in the Bible."

This time, it was Annabelle's turn to laugh. "I had a proper southern upbringing and went to Sunday school once a week. I've read that book from cover to cover. Nowhere does it say I might end up in a saloon full of complaining outlaws—even if I am a sinner."

"You telling me the Bible is wrong?" Kenny pressed her.

"Does the Bible mention anything about wolves that stand up like men and vampires who drink blood?" Annabelle asked.

"A course not!"

"Then as far as I'm concerned, the Bible ain't no truer than the *Adventures of Huckleberry Finn*."

Chapter 29

Armed to the Fangs

Vern and Luther returned with Sal's stash of cured pork packed in a barrel with saltpeter. It wasn't enough meat to feed everyone, but it was enough to keep the mayor from going hungry awhile longer. He wasn't shy about making Annabelle serve him big juicy pork chops right there at the bar in front of forty famished men whose bellies hadn't seen anything but rotgut whiskey for weeks.

One evening, a half-starved snake oil salesman yelled, "I can't take it no more!" Then he lunged for the mayor's dinner plate while he was flirting with Annabelle.

Even though Luther had been across the room talking to Mollie at the time, he suddenly appeared from behind the man. His large hand clenched the fella's shoulder tightly before he could take a bite. The joint crumbled and there was nothing left to hold the arm in place. It drooped down like a wet noodle, so low that his hand nearly touched the ground. The salesman screamed to high heaven.

"Quiet him down!" the mayor ordered.

Nigel stepped up and punched a hole clear through the pork chop thief's throat. His fingers pushed through the other side, along with broken bits of spine and neck muscle. Seeing a man in such pain but unable to call out really spooked the rest of the fellas. No one thought about going against the mayor after that—at least not for a few days.

Things got really bad when the liquor finally ran out. Some of the men were accustomed to going to bed drunk and waking up to have a beer first thing for breakfast. They hadn't been entirely sober for years. After two days, they were so desperate for a drink that a few reckoned they could get the drop on two unarmed vampires now that they weren't seeing double.

"Hell's gotta be better than sitting around starving and watching the mayor shove food down his gullet all day," a horse thief complained.

"That chicken blood might make 'em fast, but they can't dodge every bullet," a sodbuster added. "Not if a bunch of us shoot at 'em at once."

"I say we ambush 'em while they're dillydallying at the bar."

"You gonna break the rattlesnake code?" I asked.

"That don't apply to demons."

Four men volunteered to draw on the vampires at the same time. As far as plans go, it wasn't the worst one ever hatched in Damnation.

Luther was beside Mollie when the first shot sounded. Nigel shielded the mayor with his arm, and the bullet pierced his left elbow. As Luther turned to protect Mollie, the second bullet nicked the side of his face. It wasn't the handsome side, so you couldn't really tell if the melted cheek was wounded. The other two bullets struck the bar.

Before they could get off another shot, Luther quickly bolted around the room, knocking all four gunmen to the floor. Once they were down, he circled back and kicked each of them in the neck to break their spines. After that, none of them could move, let alone lift a gun. They just lay there whimpering until some soldiers dragged their bodies out to the road. Not long after, the buzzard pecked their eyes out.

It had been a close call—too close for the mayor's liking. If there'd been a few more men willing to draw, the outcome might have been different. From then on, Vern insisted that both vampires wore sidearms.

"I feel ridiculous with this thing on," Luther complained as he practiced pulling the pistol from his holster. "Ooh, look at *me*. I'm a cowboy!"

"I never had cause to carry one myself," Nigel said. "But it is far better than plucking lead from your body."

The drops of chicken blood had healed up Nigel's elbow good as new, but Luther's face remained half melted. When he spoke with Mollie, he pointed his handsome side toward her and put his hand over the ugly half. Even though he was nearly seven feet tall and a few hundred years old, he was still just as bashful about his looks as Jarvis was with the buckshot in his face. The wound didn't bother Mollie, though. She kept pulling Luther's hand away from it and ran her fingers along the edge of his charred jawbone.

The mayor didn't much care for the way Mollie fawned over Luther. To show his displeasure, he pinched her behind then pulled her onto his lap. It certainly put Luther in a pickle. On the one hand, he could take out the whole town without breaking a sweat. But if he killed the mayor, he'd go hungry for eternity. All in all, it was a mighty dangerous game to be pitting a vampire's hunger against his feelings.

Vern wasn't too popular with the outlaws either. One day a bank robber challenged him directly. "It ain't fair, you gettin' all the food and us gettin' none," he argued.

The mayor must have been feeling generous, because he didn't have the man shot on the spot. "Tell you what. We can draw for it," he suggested.

"Sure thing, old-timer." The bank robber smiled.

"Luther here will act as my proxy."

"I ain't sure what that means."

"Means he'll stand in for me."

"But he ain't human. It ain't fair putting a man against some kinda demon." Luther glared at the man.

"All right," the mayor said. "Let's even the odds then. Any ten men in the room versus both Luther and Nigel."

"I'd take them odds," shouted a man from the crowd.

"Me too," shouted another.

Hunger and sobriety inspired a number of men to step forward. When ten of the fastest were decided upon, they headed out to the road. A few of them were professional card sharks who had cause to pull a weapon with some frequency. Of course, no one had ever seen a vampire draw a gun before, so there was no way of knowing how quick they were.

Mabel had been standing beside Nigel when he shot John Wesley Hardin, and all that she could see was the cloud of gun smoke before he slipped a pistol back in his pocket. His hand must have been moving real fast, but that didn't mean his trigger finger could keep up with practiced gunslingers.

The fight would define the balance of power in town. If the men won, they'd get what remained of the mayor's meat, but without vampires to defend against the Indians and the wolves, we might not last very long. Going without food and drink had made the men desperate, and they no longer cared about their long-term survival prospects. As everyone headed out to the road to watch, the only one who remained in the saloon was Sneaky Jim. There were no sips to be stolen, but he took the opportunity to have a few nibbles of the mayor's cold pork chop.

The rain had let up some, though it was still sprinkling. The puddles were all dark red from the runoff of the piles of leaking bodies. The water pooled in a shallow ravine at the edge of town, and it resembled a river of blood separating the camps on the plains. The scaffoldings in the distance that held the Indian corpses dripped scarlet.

The road going through the center of town was muddier than a bog. When you lifted your foot, loud sucking noises announced your every move. The ten men lined up with their backs to the two vampires. Sal started counting, and they began walking. As all of their boots pulled from the mud, twelve tiny shrieks sounded. It was nearly loud enough to drown out Sal's voice. Seemed more than likely that someone would lose a boot before they reached ten paces.

Finally, the men all turned around at once, but not one of them managed to clear leather. The vampires proved to have a knack for the quick-draw. They pulled and fired faster than any bona fide gunslinger I had ever seen, and they kept on firing, so rapidly you couldn't see nothing but a cloud of gun smoke getting thicker. All ten men fell with bullet holes in the center of their foreheads.

"What the hell happened?" Blind Sal asked.

"Vampires won," Regular Sal told him. "Shot 'em all before they even dusted a handle."

"Hmm, serves 'em right," Blind Sal said. "Damn foolish plan, not waitin' till they grow weak again."

The Crapper

Comings: *No animals have arrived in over a month, and I'm so hungry I can barely write. As we've all come to realize, knowing a lack of food can't kill you don't make it any easier to bear. Hungry is still hungry, whether you're dead or not! No new people have come to town either, though if you ask the mayor, a thousand head of cattle will arrive in Damnation any day now and this paper is all just "hogwash gossip" meant to besmirch his good name.*

Goings: *Four foolish fellas drew on the mayor, and Luther broke their necks. Ten additional men drew against both vampires and were decorated with holes in the head. They were all pretty rotten bastards. Maybe I'll say a word or two about the interesting ones if I ever get something to eat.*

Chapter 30

Another Change in the Weather

One morning, Vern came into the Rusty Nail with just Nigel guarding him. Luther must've slept in. No one ever mentioned it in front of the mayor, but it was common knowledge that Mollie typically spent the night in his room. Vern had likely heard the ruckus they made. She was not a quiet woman—nor a delicate one, from the sound of it. Sometimes, her screeches could be heard as far away as the rooming house. If Vern was the jealous sort, he didn't make a fuss over it, so long as he still had protection from the riffraff and could still give Mollie a poke from time to time when he wanted to.

"Why you suppose Mollie still bothers to sell herself to dead men?" I asked Mabel. "Her beau is bigger'n stronger than anyone else in town."

"Maybe she don't like depending on anyone," she guessed. "Likes her independence."

"But there ain't even no food or drink to buy with her earnings."

"Old habits die hard." She sighed. "How am I supposed to know?"

As soon as the mayor sat down at the bar, Mabel went to the kitchen to fetch him a cup of coffee. She even brought him a saucer of real milk that Sal had kept sealed in a jar. It had soured some time ago, but could still lighten up his Arbuckle's. The mayor offered a few spoonfuls of it to the little chick in his breast pocket, so as to replenish those drops of blood he was rationing to the vampires.

The sections of the roof that hadn't been covered with moss and sod clattered with the endless rainfall. It had been going on for so long that folks were accustomed to speaking in a half shout just to be heard over it. The pitter-patter always made me yawn. There wasn't any use in stretching your legs since you'd end up drenched. All you could do was sit around and watch the mayor eat.

From time to time, the rain let up to a light drizzle, but it had been coming down pretty much constantly for weeks. The only thing smellier than a room full of dead men is a room full of dead men in damp clothing. It was hard to find anywhere that was entirely dry. Seemed like every inch of town had either been rained on or sat on by someone who'd gotten rained on. The driest place was probably the pissed-on seat of the commode.

"Howdy," the mayor said to me, tipping his hat. Hadn't seen him act so polite since election day. "How's it going for you, Tom?"

"Fine, mayor. Thanks for asking," I replied. "But if one more mudsill remarks on how it's still coming down like cats and dogs out there, I'll gladly forfeit any hope of getting into heaven just to shoot the soggy bastard."

"Fair enough," he replied. The complaints about my "hogwash news" usually didn't begin till midday. The mayor wasn't much of a talker before he had his coffee.

Suddenly, without any gradual tapering off, the noise on the roof stopped altogether. The silence was odd on account of how loud everything else now sounded, like the mayor's slurping of his coffee and the snoring coming from the back of the room.

"Is Farmer Jake puttin' more weeds up on that roof?" I asked.

"Nope," Mabel answered.

"You sure? I can't hear nothin' above us."

"Farmer Jake is asleep in the corner," she said. "So either the rain has finally stopped or some other overall-wearing corn-husker is decorating my saloon with greenery."

We all quick-footed it outside to investigate. Sure enough, the rain had finally stopped. The gray clouds above were brightening with the normal streaks of violet and yellow that had been there before the storm.

"Never thought I'd be grateful to see that gloomy old dusk again," I said. "Or dawn, if that boy Jarvis is right."

"It's a miracle!" Nigel pronounced in jest, then stood in the center of the road with his arms stretched like Christ almighty. He smiled mockingly at the Bible-thumpers. Just then, the clouds above parted and blinding rays of light broke through.

"Seems Jarvis was right," Farmer Jake remarked. "It can't be dusk if the sun's coming out."

"Reckon so," I agreed.

The light shining down wasn't like last time, when a single beam was focused just on Luther and Nigel as they fought in the road. This time, it was everywhere at once. Nigel took off running as flames appeared on his arms and face. The doorway to the hotel had the closest cover, so he dove through it in a hurry, then rolled over, patting out the flames on his cheek before it melted away.

The mayor was still standing by the doorway of the Rusty Nail. A crowd gathered in the street, which he would've had to pass through in order to follow Nigel into the hotel. A few of the fellas noticed that the mayor was now without protection. Vern hustled back into the Rusty Nail and locked himself in the kitchen, where all his meat was stored.

Just a few minutes after their eyes adjusted to the light, the men remembered the awful hollowness in their stomachs. "The English blood-sucker is caught in the hotel. I say we string up that hoarding mayor while he can't stop us," a cowboy suggested. "He's still got cured meat left, and I ain't ate in weeks."

"The big sandy-haired one is caught in the hotel, too," a soldier added. "Ain't no telling how long that sun'll be up in the sky, so we better get at it!"

The bloodthirsty mob of outlaws headed toward the saloon, but Buddy jumped in their path with two guns drawn. "You ain't doing nothin' of the sort," he told them. "Long as Vern's got that baby chick, nobody touches him."

"Just why is it that you care so much about a teensy bird," a soldier asked. "You ain't ate in so long you startin' to look like a dang skeleton wearing a skin-colored blanket."

It was true. Even when the Indians were giving Mabel smaller game animals Buddy'd hardly had any. Now, he was lean and sober. Some folks used to believe it was the beer and whiskey that made him fast, but it was probably just slowing down what he was really capable of. Not only was he a lot faster now, but more alert.

"That teensy bird is the only living thing in this town—aside from Martin," Buddy added. "We may not be sure if that kid's a vampire, or if he might become one someday, but we are sure that the little critter in the mayor's pocket has got a heartbeat. Now, I ain't sayin' old Vern is in the right, but we ain't gotta destroy every damn thing in this town just 'cause we're hungry. Think about it from the little chick's point of view. It was born from a momma that was already dead! Now, it's got nobody to raise it... Nobody to teach it right from wrong... It prolly won't ever lay eyes on another living chicken. Hell, it's the sorriest dang orphan there ever was!" Buddy started to get choked up as he said it. Seemed like he realized just then why he felt so protective of the little chick. It was an orphan, same as him.

He dried a bit of mist from his eye and he continued, "Can't we just have one dang thing that's innocent in this town without everyone tryin' to tear it to pieces?" Buddy held his head high, trying his damndest not to let any tears roll down his cheeks.

The speech fell on deaf ears. A hundred hardened men looked at him without so much as a blink. The hollowness inside them ran too deep. It needed to be filled.

"I'm starved!" a cowhand shouted. "I don't give a damn if that chick ain't got no momma. You ain't stopping me from eating whatever grub the mayor's got left. And when I'm done, I'll make chicken stew of that bird, too."

He reached for his pistol, but as soon as he touched the handle, a bullet tore through his side. Another man tried to take advantage of the distraction and rush the saloon door. Buddy shot him in the back and he fell before he reached the doorway.

"You back-shootin' bastard!" a soldier called out. "What about them rules?"

"I wrote 'em," Buddy said. "And I'm breaking 'em!"

"C'mon, boys!" the soldier called out. "He can't take us all on. He ain't no vampire. He's just a man like the rest of us."

Buddy was a man, but certainly not like the rest of us. Maybe he was just cut from a different cloth, or maybe he was shaped by what he'd been through. Whatever the reason, that dead gunslinger had skills we'd never learn, no matter how hard we tried.

As the soldier tried to draw, he got shot in the bicep of his shooting arm. He was a stubborn fool and tried to draw again with his other arm, but Buddy's next bullet shattered his collarbone. His friend beside him pulled a sidearm and took a bullet in the thigh. That didn't put him off either, so he received another one in the hip. Buddy was just trying to wound the pigheaded fools instead of sending them all to hell, but some men are magnets for lead. Buddy ducked behind a barrel, giving them a chance to come to their senses.

The mob now seemed divided over the matter. Some were too hungry to give up. Others reckoned Buddy had the same quick-firing speed as the vampires. The skinny man who had once been fat was outshooting an entire crowd. A couple of soldiers dropped to one knee behind a stack of corpses on the side of the road and used the bodies as a barricade to rest their barrels on. It seemed to be a stalemate. Nobody knew how many bullets Buddy carried with him, so they didn't want to join a losing side against him.

Farmer Jake suddenly shouted, "Lookie over there!" He was pointing toward the lot behind the Foggy Dew, at something peculiar enough to make the men leave off on their gunfighting. It was an even stranger sight than the sun above our heads.

A field of leafy green sprouts about three inches high stretched all the way to the end of town. It was much thicker and greener than the patch of moss surrounding the outhouse behind the Rusty Nail. The oddest thing was that this field looked like it was actually *growing before our eyes*. Seemed like the seedlings were reaching out from the ground for more sunshine, almost twitching in place. I knew flowers opened their petals and plants leaned toward the light over time, but these dancing weeds were moving as quickly as worms wiggled.

"What's going on?" Blind Sal asked.

"Seedlings are sprouting where I laid the seeds that Sal gave me," Jake told him.

"I didn't give you no dang seeds," Blind Sal argued.

"Not you! *Old* Sal—the bartender from the saloon."

One of the newer boys was confused. "What ya mean? Annabelle's the bartender."

"No, the bartender at the other saloon, the Foggy Dew." Jake pointed.

"You kiddin' me?" he said. "That half-burnt shithole with the smashed windows is a saloon?"

"Damn straight!" Regular Sal called out from the back of the crowd. "Least it ain't got a dang salad on the roof!"

"All right. No need to fuss over it," I broke the matter up. "Tell me something, Jake. What did ya plant over there?"

"Corn, mostly," Jake replied. "Mighta been some other stuff mixed in, but I expect the husks'll likely overtake it."

"If it's growing that fast," I said, "maybe we needn't fight over the mayor's stash of meat."

"Like hell," a cowboy said. "I ain't no maize-munching bow-bender. I gotta have meat!"

"Well, you can wait around till the corn grows or you can get yourself shot tryin' to eat that little bird," Buddy said as he stood from behind the barrel. The cowboy saw his opportunity and raised his rifle. Buddy shot out his right eye as if he was just pausing to tip his hat. "That goes for the rest of you, too."

Another fella standing behind Buddy lifted a pistol. There was no way of knowing how Buddy even saw the man draw. Maybe the sun brightened on the barrel, which reflected in a window. Maybe Buddy just had quicker reflexes than a vampire, and it had only been the booze and the heft of his gut that'd been slowing him down. He spun around and shot that fella in the face, too. After that, most folks reckoned it wasn't worth it to go up against Buddy, no matter how hungry they were.

The Crapper

I wasn't expecting to write another edition so soon, but the bodies are piling up, and while we're waiting for the corn to grow I ain't got much else to do.

Comings: *Not a soul or beast.*

Goings: *I discovered some interesting news about one of the soldiers the vampires shot up before the sun appeared. Most of them were named either Sam or some variation of William, and they'd been pitching hay before they joined the army. I won't tell you about all of them, because their stories bored me to tears.*

There was one fella, named Herman Ziegner, who had a pretty interesting life. He was born in Germany and came to America as a child. He had been in the Battle of Wounded Knee, which wasn't so much a battle as massacre. According to what he told some others, they'd been sent into Lakota Territory to disarm the natives. One of the tribesmen was deaf and couldn't understand the orders. They tried to get his rifle from him but he didn't want to surrender it since he had paid a pretty penny for it. A scuffle broke out, during which the rifle discharged. A few Indians shot at the soldiers, so naturally they opened fire. About one hundred and fifty Lakota men, women, and children were killed.

Herman confessed to killing a few himself and was given a medal for "conspicuous bravery." He returned to New York City, where he was a night watchman in a building that they called a "skyscraper" because it was over ten stories tall. The guilt of what he'd done to the Lakota people ate at him, so eventually he returned to their territory to beg for forgiveness. The Lakota took him in as one of their own. Herman married a squaw and they had a child.

Then one day the army came back to attack the Lakota again. After the battle started, Herman slipped into a dead soldier's uniform, aiming to get his wife and child to safety. When he entered his teepee, his wife speared him while trying to protect her child. Ain't that a sumbitch?

Herman's family was killed by the troops, but he managed to survive. They even pinned another medal on him. This time in the name of the man whose clothes he had borrowed. Herman couldn't tell them who he really was, so after he healed up they dispatched him to the island of Cuba to fight the Spanish forces. He starved to death, along with many others, at the Battle of San Juan Hill.

Herman only took up arms against the vampires because he was sick of being bossed around. He reckoned most wars happened on account of two men didn't get along, and they made everyone else part of their bickering. So when there was a call to stand up against a couple of demons protecting a mayor who thought he was better than everyone else, he volunteered.

In other news, after the sun came out, Nigel fled to the hotel where Luther was already fast asleep. Buddy then took up the job of protecting the mayor, on account of he's still holding that little chick. Buddy doesn't want to see it butchered because it's an orphan, same as himself. Buddy then shot a bunch of men who weren't as sympathetic to the motherless bird. I haven't sorted out all their stories yet, but they were hungry fools aching for the mayor's stash of food.

Chapter 31

Rosalie

We expected that the sun, or whatever it was shining above us, would soon get covered over by clouds, or that it might set each day on a regular basis like it did on Earth. Neither of them happened. The bright circle hovered directly above Damnation in the same spot, not budging an inch. It burned with the heat of high noon all night and day. Made the temperature hotter than summer in Arizona without the relief of an evening breeze. You couldn't wear a duster walking down the road or you'd bake like a turkey in an oven. All those years of darkness had made most folks as pale as Irishmen—even the ones who were half Italian. By the second day, just about everyone had sunburn. You could hardly tell the cowboys from the Indians—except the cowboys remained overdressed.

The one good thing about all the rainfall was that it had filled up the dry well. And with water in the well, you could finally wash your stinking clothes of dirt and sweat on a regular basis. Most of the men weren't too particular about how they smelled. It was usually just me there every couple days, and some squaws.

One evening a woman came beside me as I was scrubbing my socks on a washboard. She was on the husky side, nearly as curvy as Mabel, and pretty in her own way, with black curly hair and soft round cheeks. Her skin was darker than the squaws' but not quite as dark as Bo's. She also had bright blue eyes, which seemed to leap from her face. It was hard to say what her roots might have been. My curiosity got the better of me, and she soon caught me hawk-eying her.

"Ain't you never seen a Creole lady before, *monsieur?*" she said in a loud challenging voice.

"No, ma'am." I hung my head low in shame. "I apologize for my rudeness. I'm afraid I ain't ever heard of it before. Is it the name of an island?"

"No, silly! Creole ain't no place," she laughed. "It's in the soul. I was born in *Looosiana!* My momma was a slave in Haiti before the revolution, and my pa was a French soldier. Creole just means I'm a mix of people who wasn't a 'pposed to be mixin'. But I'm one hundred percent werewolf!" she added proudly.

"Oh, I ain't seen much of your kind around since the sun came out," I said.

"*My kind?*" she was taken aback. "Whatchoo mean *my kind?*"

"No offense intended, ma'am. It's just that wolves seem scarce as of late. To tell you the truth, I didn't even know there were any lady werewolves, especially none as pretty as you."

"Oh, you're a little charmer, ain't ya?" She blushed. "Well, I guess I'll forgive you this time. It's true. We used to hunt by the moonlight. Dem old habits die hard, guess you could say."

"So it ain't like with the vampires?" I asked. "They caught on fire when the clouds parted."

"Oh, no." She laughed. "Though not many would venture out in dis heat wearing a thick coat."

"Where are my manners? I never introduced myself. My name's Thomas, ma'am." I stood and wiped off the suds to take her hand. "Pleased to make your acquaintance."

"Rosalie." She smiled as I held her fingertips, then said with a bow, "*Enchanté.*"

"So you must be as hungry as us?" I asked. "Seeing as how nothing's come through the dust of late."

"That's another reason why the wolves sleep all day, but I can't get no rest in such a stinky den. Ain't nobody had a *bat* in years. Even when it was raining, they all hid inside."

"I hear ya!" I said. "The rooming house is filled with shot-up soldiers covered in festering wounds. I don't see how they can bear it. I must be the only one whose sense of smell didn't die with him."

"Oh, you're a hoot!" She laughed again. "At least you don't have a wolf's nose. I can smell those cowboys from a hundred yards away, and I have to be in the same room as the dirtiest dogs you ever seen!"

"So why do you do it?" I asked.

"Where else would I go? Ain't like the Indians will have me. Nor would your kind take a shine to me."

"*My kind?*" I pretended to be offended.

"Oh, you know what I mean." She smiled.

"So it ain't no great shakes over on your side of town neither?"

"If you're a male wolf, it ain't so bad. Females don't get much say, especially since we can't have any pups here."

"We have the same problem."

"How's that?"

"When we were electing a mayor, they wouldn't even let Mabel speak. They said folks didn't wanna be bossed by a woman—though I think she would have done a much better job than the fella who won. So Mabel opened her own place, where she has the final word."

"Smart lady. How'd she do it?"

"With the backing of one of the vampires."

"There's more than one now?"

"Oh, yeah. Luther's even stronger than Nigel. They're both hiding out in the hotel on account of the sun. I expect they're pretty tuckered out since they ain't fed in a spell."

"You don't say."

I wondered if maybe I had already said too much. Rosalie was easy to talk to, though, and I couldn't see her using my words to do us any harm.

"Guess I need me a vampire to help me open my own place." She chuckled.

"It might not be a bad idea. In my opinion, men waste too much time thinking about fighting one another to run anything properly. Mabel negotiated peace with the chief, and her saloon was doing better'n Sal's ever did—till livestock stopped coming from the dust," I added. "She's even got a soiled dove working for her."

"You have prostitution!" Rosalie gasped. "It don't sound like ladies are any better off on your side of town."

"Just the one," I said. "Nobody forced her into it. There's also Annabelle, who tends bar."

"So you got a saloon owner, a booze clerk, and a soiled dove. Is that about the size of it?"

"Gut-Shot Granny's a woman, too. She ain't got no job to speak of, except playing cards and shooting folks on occasion."

"Seems like I got a better situation where I'm at," Rosalie decided. "Alls I have to do is smell a bunch of dirty dogs and wash my own clothes."

I could have sat chewing the fat with her all day, but I didn't want to overstay my welcome so I bid her a nice evening.

"*Au revoir*, Thomas," she said with a smile.

Chapter 32

The Unsetting Sun

Early the next morning, the mayor came into the Rusty Nail with just Buddy guarding him. Buddy wasn't drinking, so it wasn't hard for him to get up first thing. Most folks tried to sleep as long as possible since there wasn't any breakfast to miss. When they did wake up, there was nothing to do anyway but sit around and think about how hungry they were. The only reason why Annabelle roused to open the saloon was to pour the mayor some coffee. Then she went into the kitchen to take a nap.

"I gotta use the commode," Buddy informed the mayor.

"Well, use it," Vern replied. "I ain't gonna sit on your lap in the shithouse!"

"You might at least wait by the door, so I can get to ya sooner—in case somethin' happens."

"Just go," the mayor told him. "I don't need protecting this early in the morning. Tom ain't heeled. He's still trying to get into heaven, 'member? And no one else is up yet."

"What about him?" Buddy looked toward Blind Sal, who was sitting in the corner, nodding his head to the sound of dust hitting the window.

"He can't see! You worried a blind man's gonna take a shot at me?"

Buddy shrugged and went off to relieve himself. The mayor sat petting the tiny chick in his lap as he drank his coffee. I went back to scribbling some notes for the paper.

"What hogwash news are you scribbling now?" the mayor asked me. "More lies about me, no doubt!"

"Afraid not," I told him without looking up. "The fact is, unless you leave town in a hurry, I ain't got much else to say about you."

Vern liked to see his name in print, even if the news wasn't very flattering. To him, not being spoken about was even worse than being slandered. He went on pestering me. "I bet you'd really like to know why I took that thief's name, huh?"

I was still kind of curious, but lots of folks had secrets, and I didn't chase them down. Also, I reckoned that if I let on that I wanted to know, he'd lord it over me and probably never spill the beans.

"If I told ya, you'd probably sell more papers than you ever did," he boasted. "It'd be the most popular issue in the history of *The Crapper!*"

My silence was getting under his skin. One thing the mayor couldn't stand was being ignored.

"Fact is, I was once a very esteemed person. Way more important than the mayor of some shitty town short of hell. I'll have you know that the only reason why I chose the name Vernon Jackson Walker is because I signed the order for his bounty right before I died. How was I to know he'd turn up here?"

I lifted my face just long enough to give the mayor the stink eye. "If you don't mind, I'm a little busy right now," I told him.

"You still don't remember me, do you?" He sounded a little offended. "I dare say you were a lot more helpful the last time we met in the Dakota Territory, before it became a state. I guess I can't blame you for not recognizing me. I was a lot younger then, and you always did have trouble looking me in the eye when you were working for me."

"Hearst?" I said in disbelief.

"So you do remember! As you can imagine, I've made a lot of enemies during my lifetime, so I figured I should keep my real name a secret. You never know when a jilted miner is gonna come after you for not getting paid. Of course, none of that matters now that I have the fastest gunslinger in town protecting me. Besides, it seems like the only person in Damnation who suffered on my account was a spineless journalist I bullied into writing some articles."

"But you can't be George Hearst!" I said. "Ms. Parker said you went on to become a senator."

"I sure did, among many other notable accomplishments. I also married a girl over two decades my junior. When I died at the ripe old age of seventy, I was one of the richest men in the country!"

I could see some resemblance between the old man and the much younger shit heel who I had worked for. It didn't add up, though. "From what I heard, George Hearst died some five years back," I said. "I reckon he went straight to hell."

Looking closer now, the pointy nose and wide eyes were a dead match. It was hard to believe I had overlooked it.

"Let's just say this wasn't my first stop," he said.

Right in front of me was the man who had ruined my life. He had those families in the Black Hills killed, and he forced me to print the lies that I was killed for. I scanned the room for a weapon. He had to pay, but there wasn't anything within reach. Then I noticed that Mabel had put a scattergun in the umbrella stand behind the bar, just like I had advised her to. Even with my bad leg, I could probably reach it and blast a hole in the bastard before Buddy came back from the commode.

I can't say for sure exactly what happened next. I rose to get the eight-gauge and send Hearst's ass to hell, but before I reached it, a gunshot sounded. I looked up and there was blood spurting from a bullet hole in his fancy shirt. Blind Sal was still sitting in the corner. Only now there was a gun on the table in front of him. A wisp of gray smoke drifted from its barrel. I didn't hear any footsteps.

"Did you shoot him?" I asked.

"Shoot who?" Blind Sal asked back.

"The mayor."

His only reply was, "I didn't see a thing."

"I guess I can't argue with that."

The mayor slouched forward with a creak of his chair. The chick leapt out of his hands and tumbled onto the floor. Then it flapped its little wings furiously, managing to flutter several feet through the air. I got up and chased after it, but the wound on my bad leg slowed me. When I reached out to grasp it, the chick scurried beneath the swinging doors onto the boardwalk. It tried to fly once more. This time it rose several feet above the road. The sun blinded me for a moment.

The next thing I saw was the silhouette of a giant wing swooping down from above. The dead turkey buzzard grabbed the tiny chick in its talons and took off without touching down. The Indians must have been stalking the bird, because a mess of arrows sailed up at it, but they all missed. The buzzard flew straight up until it was out of range, then circled above the plains. It finally set down near the edge of the dust cloud on one of the funeral platforms. Then it tore the little chick apart. The only source of warm blood in Damnation was gone.

The gunshot brought a small crowd out into the road. Buddy ran out from behind the saloon, still buckling his belt. "What the hell happened?"

"The mayor got shot, and the chick got ate by the buzzard," I told him.

"Who shot the mayor?" he snapped angrily.

"Can't say for certain, but the smoking gun was sitting in front of Blind Sal."

"Damn it all!" he cursed. I expected that would be the end of Blind Sal, but Buddy didn't bother shooting him. Seemed like he was more upset about how he couldn't keep anything innocent alive for long. Once again, Buddy was the only orphan in Damnation. Maybe having another motherless creature around made him feel less lonesome. He broke down and started weeping right there on the boardwalk.

The men all looked away, not wanting to be witness to another man's weakness. Ms. Parker came to his side, though. She put her arm around Buddy, and the two of them wept together.

"A couple of softies," a soldier remarked.

They might have been softies, but Buddy was still the fastest gun in town, and Ms. Parker was the mother of a tot who might someday destroy us all.

Chapter 33

Scrawny Will

It didn't take long after the mayor's body hit the ground for the men to raid the kitchen of the remaining cured meat. What was left wasn't nearly enough to go around. Divided evenly, each person might've only gotten a single bite. Not that it occurred to anyone to divide it equally.

A half-starved lumberjack ripped a sodbuster's tongue out while trying to pull the pork from his mouth before he swallowed it. A bronc buster managed to chew and swallow a few mouthfuls, but he got shot before it hit his stomach. They debated on cutting him open for the meat, then decided it would be easier to cook the man whole. The smell of burnt cowboy turned folks' stomachs, though, so they didn't bother eating him. They reckoned it was more civilized to wait until the corn could be harvested.

"If I'm gonna eat someone, I'd rather it be a woman anyways," Rodeo Bo remarked.

"Why?" a soldier asked. "Ain't like you're makin' love to the fella 'fore you eat 'im."

"It ain't that exactly. Women are more tender. They ain't got big muscles'n hair all over 'em."

"You got a point there. How about children then?" the soldier pressed. "They ain't hairy nor muscular."

Bo weighed the matter delicately. "If they was already dead, and I didn't have to kill 'em? Sure! They'd prolly be tastier than a woman on account of them being younger'n fresher, like veal."

"Only one child in Damnation, though," the soldier added.

"Ain't nobody eatin' Martin!" Buddy said from the doorway. His eyes were still red from weeping over the chick. He wasn't about to see the boy get butchered, too.

"We ain't saying that, Buddy." The soldier tried to backpedal. "Just speculatin' on who you'd eat if you had to, and they was already dead."

"Ah, ain't none of y'all got the stomach to eat a man," Liam the Miner insisted.

A grave voice from the corner of the room announced, "I've eaten human flesh." Everyone turned to lay eyes on a bearded man who folks called Scrawny Will. He'd been in town longer than me by some years, so I had never interviewed him. I wasn't sure if his nickname referred to how skinny he was or his lack of grit.

"We were crossing the Sierra Nevada Mountains on our way to California," he recollected grimly. "There were nearly ninety of us when we started out. George Donner, the fool leading us, insisted we take a shortcut, but it ended up taking even longer. We arrived at the pass late in the season and an early blizzard trapped us near Truckee Lake. We had to spend the whole winter there, with only enough rations for a few weeks.

"When things got dire, we decided to make snowshoes out of the oxbows and hides. A dozen of us who still had the strength set out for help. The snow was over twelve feet high, and you couldn't see more than a foot or two in front of you. A man soon starved. We carved out his thigh meat and cooked it on skewers. We wept as we ate it, trying not to look each other in the eye. But it gave us the strength to go on for a few more days. I took apart my snowshoes and ate the ox hide. More people froze or went mad. We stripped the dead of their muscles and organs, then dried them to carry with us. It was nearly a month before we found the footprints of a Miwok tribe, who led us out of the mountains."

Jarvis couldn't keep himself quiet any longer and had to question the man. "What happened to the others back at the lake?"

"After I recovered some," he went on, "I returned to Truckee Lake with one of the rescue parties. When we got there, I found out my two-year-old son had starved and been eaten. About half of the original party survived, but only those who'd eaten human flesh. That fool Donner was still alive, but I used my pocketknife to make sure he never got off the mountain. That's probably why I ended up here."

"Did you have to kill the people that you ate?" Jarvis asked.

"Nah, they were already dead, except for two Indian guides I shot."

"The Lord forbids eating folks," Gut-Shot Granny said. "But I suppose killing savages for food ain't so bad. They're more animal than people anyway—unless they're baptized, of course."

Jarvis took exception. Being the son of a preacher, he had strong feelings on the matter. "You're telling me it's okay to kill and eat a person, unless you dunk 'em in water first and recite a bunch of mumbo jumbo?"

"It ain't mumbo jumbo!" Gut-Shot Granny got offended. She was so worked up she put down her knitting needles, which wasn't a good sign. "The Bible is the word of the Lord!" she thundered.

I pulled the boy away just in time, saying, "He didn't mean no disrespect, Granny." It was a good thing I interrupted because the old lady already had the barrel of a pistol aimed at him from beneath the yarn in her lap.

"Listen here, sonny," I told him. "I know you got it in for me and my facts, but this ain't like saying how I wrote up something wrong in *The Crapper*. That old lady has shot a hundred men bigger'n stronger than you for saying a lot less about a dusty old book that she has no cause to believe in. You ain't changing her mind about it no matter what you say."

"Why do you care?" His voice cracked. Seemed like he never had anyone look after him before without giving him a beating. "What's it matter to you if that old lady shoots me anyhow?"

"I dunno." I shrugged at a loss. "Guess I'm just accustomed to seeing you around is all. You're the only one who questions stuff 'round here. And if I let you get shot, we might go on believing a bunch of nonsense that prolly ain't true, like how we used to think that it's dusk instead of dawn."

As we reached an understanding, I noticed that Gut-Shot Granny's words had gotten under Scrawny Will's skin. He began arguing loudly.

"That Bible of yours says we shouldn't eat folks," he scolded. "But where was your Lord when my family was starving in the mountains? Where was he when I had to cook up my friends to live another day? Where was he when my little boy starved, then got ate?"

A gunshot sounded and the crochet in granny's lap hopped in the air. Will slumped over and fell to the floor.

"The Lord was just testing you, sonny, and you failed!" Granny hollered at his corpse with no remorse. "You done failed!"

A lumberjack dragged away the skinny corpse, and Gut-Shot Granny quietly returned to her knitting with a cheerful smile.

The Crapper

Goings: The man we've come to know as Mayor Vern finally got sent to hell. The smoking gun was in front of Blind Sal, though nobody can honestly say that they saw him pull the trigger, not even Blind Sal. Just before the mayor got shot, he told me that he was really Senator George Hearst, a wealthy mine owner and greedy scoundrel from Missouri. For what it's worth, Hearst also said that Damnation had not been the first place he went to after dying. Unfortunately, he didn't have the time to say anything more.

The little chick that Hearst was holding hostage got ate by the turkey vulture, so there's no more warm blood to keep the vampires strong enough to protect the town, if it ever gets dark enough for them to leave the hotel again.

Lastly, William Foster, a carpenter from Pennsylvania who went by Scrawny Will, got sent to hell by Gut-Shot Granny after a heated theological debate. Will was a part of the Donner Party that got stuck in the mountains on their way to California. Half of the group survived by eating the other half. Foster admitted to killing two Indians, but said that the rest of the people he ate were already dead. He survived the ordeal and went on to have six more children before dying of cancer in San Francisco.

Chapter 34

The Idea of a Century

As the days wore on, the muddy ground grew dry and cracked beneath the unmoving sun. Luckily, Farmer Jake had set up every pot and pan in town to capture the rain while it was still falling. There was no way to know if it would ever rain again, so he rationed drops to each of the cornstalks instead of drenching the whole field. The corn was growing faster than he had expected. After just a few weeks, it was already waist high.

"How long till we can harvest it?" I asked.

"Usually it takes two, three months at the soonest," Jake replied. "But at the rate it's growing now, it could be ready in half that time."

"Why's it growin' so quick?" Kenny said.

"Can't say. Could be on account of how drenched the ground got from raining nonstop all that time. And now there's sunshine around the clock! I ain't never growed nothing in conditions like this before."

"Maybe because it's the dang afterlife," Bo remarked with a laugh. "Hey, Moe, you ever seen anything grow in Damnation before?"

"Just those withered cacti you see out there in the plains," Moe answered. "We ain't never had the rain to support nothing else."

"Hmm, that gives me an idea," Jake said. "Cacti can grow in sandy grit without much nutrients, but there must be coarser clay and other stuff below that silt."

"Say it plain," Moe told him.

"The roots from the corn have to be feeding from a different type of dirt, and that dirt might be easier to dig through."

Jarvis let out a loud curious sigh and scratched his buckshot-riddled chin.
"What is it, boy?" I asked.

"Ah, nothing."

"Don't give me that. Just tell us what you're thinking about already instead of sighing in the corner like Socrates has come into the saloon."

"I was just wondering," he spoke up, "if we dug down far enough, maybe we'd come out the other side, like how they say if you dug through the Earth, you'd end up in China."

"Yeah, maybe we'd come out in a town filled with dead Chinamen," Bo added, and everyone laughed.

"That's ridiculous!" a soldier argued.

"Why?" Jarvis said. "Dead Chinamen gotta go somewheres, and we only got the one Chinaman here. Where the rest of 'em go?"

"Y'all sound crazier than Spiffy did when he'd ramble on about dead souls being kept on Jupiter," I said.

"I don't know about no dead Chinamen in Jupiter, but that gives me an idea," Liam the Miner said. Since he liked to boast that he was the only miner in town who hadn't died in a collapsed tunnel, his thoughts on the matter were worth a listen. "Maybe we could tunnel underneath that dang wall of dust, and see what's on the other side!"

Everyone silenced. Seemed odd that no one had thought of it before. Countless miners had come and gone, and all they ever did was drink and play cards.

"That's the best darn idea I heard in a hundred years," Old Moe announced.

Gut-Shot Granny was inclined to agree, but not without commenting. "Too bad you didn't come up with it twenty years sooner!" she heckled. Of course, Granny wasn't going to knit us out of Damnation, so folks sided with the wiry miner.

Liam had arrived in town before me, so I never interviewed him for *The Crapper*. I still had no idea how he died, and it occurred to me then to ask him.

"Not in a collapsed mine, I'll tell you that," he reminded me once more. "I built my walls too sturdy for that. Didn't cut no corners, no matter what the bosses tried to tell me. Safety first!"

"I don't doubt it," I told him. "Just curious about how you got here is all."

"What done me in was the torches blew out. Sometimes, you get a windblast in a mine, and all of a sudden it's pitch black. The fool behind me kept swinging his pickax in the dark, and he hit me in the back." Liam turned to show the gash between his shoulder blades. "If you look real close, you can see bits of gold dust in that wound. That's the real shame of it. We finally found some color in that mountain, and I died before I could cash in!"

* * * *

The next time I went to the well, it was nearly dry again. I pulled out a final bucketful of water and stripped down to wash my skivvies with it. As I was lathering up my washboard with soap, Rosalie came along with a load of clothes to wash, which caused me no small amount of embarrassment. Luckily, I had tied a sheet over my privates.

"*Excusez moi, monsieur*," she said with a blush.

"Sorry, ma'am. Seems the well has run dry. This here bucket is about the last of it. You can have it, though."

"Darlin', I won't hear of it!" she insisted. "How could I deny a man with dirty underwear the last bucket of water?"

Now I was the one blushing. "They ain't *that* dirty, ma'am."

"How about we share the water then," she suggested. "We'll just wash what's most important, is all."

I turned my back as she removed her dress and put her bloomers in the bucket. She wrapped herself in the sheet she had been intending to wash. We sat on a stone with our undergarments soaking together in the bucket.

"I sure hope it rains again," I remarked.

She shot me a scolding look. "I hope you ain't too put out by having my brassiere brush up against your drawers!"

"It ain't that at all, ma'am," I said. "It's just that I was kinda hopin' we'd still have occasion to meet again in the future."

"Oh, you salty dog!" she slapped my wrist playfully.

We sat silently for a moment. Then she reached over and threaded her fingers between mine. Nothing untoward happened. We just sat in the sunshine holding hands, a werewolf and a reporter, as our undergarments soaked in the last bucket of water. Damnation didn't get any better than that.

Chapter 35

Private Gash

Early one morning, the walls of the rooming house began to tremble. I looked out the window, expecting maybe another bison would come charging out of the dust. There was a thunder of footsteps, just like last time. Only these were closer together, like whatever it was had already reached top speed. A loud groan bellowed in the distance, then a huge black animal tore out of the dust faster than any bison could move. Its head was tilted downward and a large hump swelled over its shoulders. Short curved horns pointed outward, aiming to gore something. Somebody must have done something awful to him, because he was the angriest beast I had ever seen.

"What the hell is that?" a soldier asked.

"Looks like a mean-ass bull!" Jake said.

"It's a Brahman," Rodeo Bo informed us. "And a big one at that. Mighta been crossbred with a longhorn, even though his horns are short and tight."

Once the bull reached the middle of the open plains, he stopped running. The turkey buzzard was curious about the new arrival. He swooped down and landed on the tired beast's back. The bull didn't like that at all. He reared up and began bucking his hindquarters while he thrashed around in a circle.

"You ride them suckers?" the soldier asked.

"Not that one, I wouldn't. If you managed to cover him with your hide, he'd throw you in about a second, then trample you. He's a real stomper!"

"At least maybe his meat will keep the Indians fed a while longer," Jake said. "Could give us time to harvest the corn."

Sure enough, it wasn't long before a couple of horseback riders appeared at the edge of the Indian camp, racing straight toward the bull with bows drawn. They rode up real close and launched a mess of arrows into his side, but it didn't have any effect.

"His hide must be made of the same stuff as that unkillable Indian!" Buddy declared.

An arrow finally pierced the bull's ear, and that got his attention. He turned and charged the riders in a hurry. They weren't ready for it and couldn't get out of the way fast enough. Their little geldings got knocked down like bowling pins. One of the riders caught a hoof in the face.

"I expect he won't have much to say after that." Bo was downcast since he was a quarter Cherokee, and they might have been distant relations.

"I expect not," the scalped soldier agreed, but he was smiling about it.

A couple more braves came out to help their fallen brothers. The fella who caught the hoof in the kisser had ridden his last pony. They laid his body over the back of a horse and took him out to the funeral platforms. The other man just had a bit of a limp, no worse than mine. The bull was calmer when nobody was pestering it. He moseyed around the plains at a leisurely pace, snorting at the ground in search of something to chew.

"I bet it wouldn't be so hard to ride that bull," one of the soldiers said. He was a young private who had gotten killed in the very first charge of his very first battle. He had tripped and smashed his face on a rock, so they called him Private Gash. The other soldiers teased him to no end, so he was constantly trying to show his mettle. "It's ain't nothing but a cow with horns and a set of balls! Alls you gotta do is creep up on 'im while he's sleeping, then hold on real tight till he tires out. I could ride that sumbitch, I tell ya!"

"That's something I'd like to see." Bo smiled. "I don't reckon you'd last ten seconds. That might seem like a short time, but it ain't when you're on the back of an angry bull. It's about the most dangerous ten seconds there is. Too many damn ways to get hurt." Bo rubbed his head. "Trust me."

Private Gash wasn't about to be talked down to. "Ah, whatta you know, you damn Buffalo Soldier!" he said. Bo just nodded with a smile.

Oddly, the Indians didn't send any more riders out to try taking down the bull. He kept wandering around the flatlands looking for grass to graze on, but it was all dry dirt with a few stubborn cacti. There wasn't a single weed out there for him to chomp on.

Eventually he made his way back to town, where he found the patch of moss beside the latrine. Luckily, that satisfied his appetite, and he didn't wander over to the corn field on the other side of the road behind the Foggy

Dew. The bull stayed put. When he wasn't munching on the moss, he slept in the shade cast by the shitbox, which was a pretty good incentive for folks to do their business elsewhere.

* * * *

Even though there wasn't any more water in it, I still went by the well each day hoping to see Rosalie. She never showed up while I was around. One time, I came across Little Bear as he was knocking the dust out of a rug. He was in his usual good spirits. If being dead and starving couldn't sour his mood, then surely nothing could. I reckoned I'd try to take him down a notch or two by teasing him about their failure to slaughter the bull.

"Ah, we no touch black bull." He shook his head as if that were unthinkable.

"Well, y'all certainly tried to, least those two fellas who got mowed down did."

"That was before." He acted like I was some kind of simpleton and should know as much already.

I asked slowly, "You mean before you found out your arrows don't have no effect on him?"

He wasn't put off and kept up his belittling tone. "Chief say bull has spirit of great Lakota holy man. Agency police break many promise to him. Then they shoot him because they afraid he join Ghost Dance rebellion against white men. Now, Sitting Bull too angry to stay in shape of man."

It was becoming clearer to me now. "Lemme make sure I got this straight," I told him. "You think that Chief Sitting Bull is over there eating the weeds beside our shithouse?"

"Could be." Little Bear shrugged with his playful smile. "I don't hear him say he not."

A lot of the fellas were hoping the Indians would slaughter that bull pretty quickly, and not just so they wouldn't hanker after our corn. The bull's grazing patch blocked the path to the outhouse closest to the Rusty Nail. The next closest one was all the way down the road, and most folks didn't plan their business too well. They often waited until the last minute, then dashed out the back and wet their pants when they remembered an angry two-ton animal was in the way.

"I got good news and bad news," I announced when I returned to the Rusty Nail. "It looks like we're stuck with that bull."

"What's the good news?"

"So are the Indians."

"How's that good news?" Jarvis asked.

"They think that bull has the spirit of the Lakota holy man Sitting Bull in it."

"I don't care if Jesus Christ is in that bull," a cowpuncher said. "I'm fixin' to put some lead in him so I can piss sooner. I can't be walkin' halfway across Damnation every time I gotta take a leak."

"What about the latrine behind the Foggy Dew?" Jarvis suggested.

"Sal only lets paying customers use it," Mabel said bitterly.

"Who'd pay to sit in that half-burned saloon?" the scalped soldier argued. "There ain't even no whiskey to buy."

"Yeah," Kenny added. "Least this place don't smell like a fireplace and have a loudmouthed redhead below the floorboards."

"Hold on there a moment," I interrupted. "You fellas are missing the point. Think about it. If the Indians believe Sitting Bull's spirit is hanging out beside our latrine, they might be less inclined to attack us."

"Ah, I gotta take a piss," Kenny said. "And that means I still gotta walk way down the road. I say we shoot 'im anyway."

The men began to squabble. They were divided over what should be done. There was an even split between those in favor of taking a leak sooner and those who wanted to keep their scalps.

"Simmer down, y'all!" I said. "If arrows can't take down that bull, then bullets probably won't work either, so there ain't no use in frettin' over it."

"Bullets may not be able to penetrate his hide," Kenny said, "but vampire teeth prolly could."

"Bulls are good eating!" Rodeo Bo added, patting his belly.

"Is their meat tougher than reg'lar steer?" Liam the Miner asked.

"Nah." Bo shook his head assuredly. "A bit leaner, but it ain't no tougher. Some say it's even tastier than steer. You just gotta cook it right. There's less fat, so you don't wanna overcook it or it'll dry out on ya."

"I'm sure you got a mess of recipes, but unless you're gonna take down that bull yourself, none of them matter," I reminded him. "Vampires can't come out while the sun's still shining. Besides, there's another reason why we shouldn't slaughter that bull. If the Indians believe the holiest Lakota warrior is in that bull, what do you think they'd do if you slaughtered it?"

"They'd prolly storm this place in a hurry," the scalped soldier said. "And not just to take some corn. They'll scalp every one of y'all! Just like they done to me."

"So what do we do?" Mabel asked.

"I say we bide our time without causing a fuss," I answered. "In the meantime, the corn's still growing, and maybe Liam's onto something with his hole-digging plan."

Chapter 36

The Hole-Digging Plan

The Indian camp now stretched around the entire perimeter of Damnation. There weren't any breaks where the miners could start digging right in front of the dust wall. They'd have to ask the chief to clear away some teepees first—and nobody was keen on doing that.

"What the hell'd be the use of tunneling out of here if a bunch of prairie coons followed right behind us anyway?" Liam asked.

"Might be plenty of animals on the other side," Jarvis suggested. "Maybe we could all get along over there—if there was nothing for us to fight over."

"I ain't digging outta here just to get a hatchet in my back when I reach the other side," Liam said. "I already took a pickax in the spine for not being choosy enough about who I dig with. You can't trust no red men."

"Liam's right," the scalped soldier said. "We gotta play our hand close to our chest. There could be another town on the other side of that dust wall, and it might be much better than this one. We wouldn't have to share it with no bow-benders or wolves—just us men. We could fill in the tunnel once we get there and never have to see any of them again."

I wasn't too keen on the idea of never seeing Rosalie again, but I reckoned the mob wouldn't make an exception for a Creole werewolf just because I was sweet on her.

"What about the vampires?" Jarvis asked. "Do they come to the other side?"

"I don't see any need for that," the scalped soldier replied. "It'd be a good chance to get free of their kind. They prolly wouldn't even wanna go unless there's warm-blooded animals over there."

"They'd probably be glad to see us go!" Farmer Jake put in. "Except maybe Ms. Parker and Martin. Nigel might put up a fuss if we take them."

"Well, it ain't up to him," Buddy sneered, then pulled out his pistol and gave the cylinder a spin to show he meant business.

"Luther's pretty sweet on Mollie, too," I added. "He might wanna follow her if she goes—that is, if it ever gets dark enough for him to leave the hotel again."

"That's between them." Buddy shrugged. "Ain't no use in us talking about it anyway while there's still sunshine. Both of 'em could be trapped in the hotel for a hundred years."

The fellas were getting too carried away, wasting breath on things we couldn't control. "Let's get back to the hole-digging plan," I said. "How ya gonna tunnel under that dust wall with all those Injuns in front of it?"

"We gotta start back a ways," Liam explained. "We'll just dig down deep enough so that we can tunnel under their teepees without them noticing."

"That silt's too fine to tunnel through," one of the other miners argued. "The walls would cave in."

"That's what I thought, too," Liam admitted. "But like Farmer Jake said, those crops must be getting nutrients from somewhere. Can't be from that dry topsoil. I bet if we go down a few feet, it'll thicken up nicely. Then we just gotta brace the walls every three feet or so."

The closest place for the miners to start digging without arousing any suspicion was a shack on the edge of town. During the Gold Rush, plenty of wagons had arrived in Damnation loaded with equipment, so there was no shortage of shovels. The miners worked in shifts around the clock, hauling out dirt in wheelbarrows. They were a tireless lot, and they seemed to enjoy the labor over idle hands.

In just a couple of days, they managed to clear out enough dirt to build a wall along the road. It also served as protection from the bull. We couldn't separate the beast from his favorite spot under the shade of the outhouse, but at least we didn't have to worry about him charging us every time we left the saloon.

Day after day, the sun kept shining and the corn grew taller, but nothing came out of the dust cloud. The Indians looked on our maize like youngins outside a candy store. They were just waiting for it to ripen. Their bellies were just as empty as ours, and they still outnumbered us more than four to one.

"We should just let 'em have the corn," a cowhand suggested. "Least then we won't get scalped for it."

"Ain't no red men getting my crops," Farmer Jake argued. "I growed 'em, and I plan on eating 'em."

The cowhand didn't like our odds. "You ain't gonna be able to eat nothing when you're in hell with an arrow in your throat."

A few others weren't so sure we could hold out long enough. The Indians looked to have gone through all their dried meat. Hundreds of hungry warriors surrounded us. For all they knew, we might still have canned soup and dry goods left, though we had long run out.

"Why do you suppose they ain't raided already?" Jarvis asked. "Any day now, a mess of soldiers could come through the dust and even up the odds. Or the sun could set. Seems like now's the best time for them to attack, while the vampires are still hiding in the hotel."

"Remember, the Injuns don't know Luther and Nigel can't go outside when the sun's shining," I explained. "They ain't never heard of vampires."

The scalped soldier had a theory. "We used to have a Comanche scout in our battalion," he said. "He told tales of a mosquito man, who sucked people's blood, but it didn't have to hide from sunlight. I reckon they think the Long Teeth are one of them."

"So we can bluff 'em?"

"Not exactly," I said. "When I was speaking with Little Bear, I might've let it slip that the Long Teeth got their power from the chick's blood."

"What kind of a dummy are you, Tom?" Mabel scolded.

"The Indians saw that little bird get ate by the buzzard," Jarvis said. "They must be just biding their time, knowing the vampires are getting weaker and hungrier while the corn's still growing."

I felt bad that my gabbing had put everyone in danger. I didn't want them to lose all hope on account of me. "Maybe them miners'll tunnel straight outta Damnation before they attack."

"Maybe," Mabel said. "But we don't even know where it'll lead."

"Gotta be someplace better'n here," Gut-Shot Granny put in.

"Not necessarily," Jarvis interrupted. "If that Bible of yours is right, and we're in some kind of purgatory, then those miners could be digging us a hole straight to hell."

The room silenced as everyone considered it. The prospect of hastening the trip to hell didn't seem to alarm anyone. Folks fretted more about *how* they got to hell than *when*. The idea of getting scalped or chewed up by wolves was most troubling. A quick bullet to the head wasn't a bad way to go. If they just had to walk through a tunnel into hell, that would be a piece of cake.

"I don't care if the tunnel leads to heaven or hell," Annabelle announced. "At least the digging gives those miners something to do while the corn grows. They give me the creeps sitting around all day staring at my tits. Some of them are old enough to be my grandpappy."

"The miners are a nervous lot," Mabel agreed. "Ain't doing no good having them stand around worrying us and drinking what's left of the liquor. At least lifting shovels keeps them from lifting glasses all day."

It turned out that Liam was right about the soil. A few feet below the surface, the silt was thicker and coarser. It held together in brittle chunks, unlike the fine grit on top that ran off a spade as soon as you lifted it. The entrance to the tunnel was a hole in the floor of the shack about four feet wide. You had to crouch to pass beneath support beams made from old hitching posts. As the tunnel headed toward the dust wall, it widened and sloped farther downward so that the men could stand upright. It was supposed to bottom out at fifteen feet below the surface when it passed beneath the Indian camp and, hopefully, the wall of dust. They used scrap wood from broken-up wagons to keep the walls and ceiling from caving in.

"How long you think it'll take to get past that wall?" Kenny asked one of the miners on a break.

"At this rate, we might get there in a few weeks. No telling how thick it is, though, so I can't rightly say how long it'd take to pass beneath it."

"How do you even know it's a wall?" Jarvis asked.

Everyone silenced.

"What ya mean, son? You can see the wall clear as can be surrounding the whole dang town. You must be as sightless as Blind Sal."

There was some laughter around the room.

"A wall has two sides. If you can't see the other side, then how do you know there's an end to it? If it's a wall, how come the buzzard don't just fly over it?" he asked.

That got the men's attention. Nobody had considered that before. It was too high to climb, but that bird would surely have flown over it if it was possible.

"Maybe it ain't no wall at all," Jarvis suggested. "Maybe it's just the end of Damnation, and that's all there is."

The miner sat back down with a heavy sigh. The thought of tunneling forever and never finding an end took the wind out of his sails.

"Hold on a minute," I interrupted the boy. "When you first got here, you were speculating about how there might be hundreds of towns like this one that we keep getting sent to. This fella gets off his hump and decides he's gonna start digging to find out. Now, you're gonna tell him there might not be anything in the afterlife except this crummy strip of rotted-out buildings, and there ain't no hope. I'll tell you this: It's a lot easier to go dreaming up new worlds than it is to actually look for them."

"I guess I didn't see it that way."

"I'm sure you didn't. Now, let this man enjoy his drink in peace before he goes back to hauling dirt from the ground just to try'n save your hide!"

Chapter 37

The New Richest Man in Town

Each day, the piles of dirt outside the saloon got bigger. Soon they formed a wall five feet high that encircled the bull's entire grazing area, which was good because old Sitting Bull was running out of moss to munch on, and nobody wanted to face him when he got hungry and irritable again. Not to mention it kept him from wandering off and eating the corn, which was nearly shoulder high.

"I still say I could ride that bull," Private Gash boasted.

"Ah, you couldn't even ride yourself into your first battle," another soldier teased. "You try to mount that beast, and you'll get a gash on the other side of your face."

The young private reddened and stomped his foot. "If that damn rock hadn't got in my way, I woulda killed way more men than you. And I bet I could ride that bull longer than any man here!"

Bo smiled. "I'd like to see you try. In fact, I got two bucks that says you won't last three seconds."

"I'll take some of that action," a sodbuster interrupted.

"Us army boys are made of stronger stuff than you cowpunchers," another soldier said. "Even if he didn't see no battle, a young private like Gash here has to go through rigorous training. I have five bucks on him lasting ten seconds."

"I don't know about ten," another soldier put in. "But he'll definitely make it five. Hell, I can stand anything for five seconds."

Everyone piled their money on the bar. Mabel made a list of the wagers. There hadn't been anything exciting to bet on in weeks. Cards quickly grew tiresome, especially since Mabel was rationing the last of the liquor. Nobody was permitted more than three drinks a day, so the boys had money burning holes in their pockets. Mostly, though, folks just wanted to think about anything aside from their empty stomachs and the Indians surrounding us.

"Not sure what I'll do with all my winnings," Bo said. "But it'll be nice collecting money from all you fools."

We went outside and lined up at the wall around the moss patch. Sitting Bull was fast asleep beside the latrine. They tied a rope around Private Gash. Then he climbed up on the roof of the outhouse so they could lower him down onto the bull. There was no saddle to hold on to, so Gash had to lash a rope around his neck real quickly. Sitting Bull was snoring loudly. He might have been dreaming of the old days before he became an animal, sitting around the teepee and passing the pipe among his buddies.

The private was light as a feather, and they were able to lower him down slowly without thrashing around. After gently straddling the bull's back, he slipped a rope around his thick neck. As soon as Gash tightened it, the beast woke up with a start and rose to his feet. The poor boy got tossed into the air with the first jump. Sitting Bull must've thought there was still something on his back, because he continued to buck frantically. His hind legs rose in the air, way above his head like he was doing a handstand. Then he reared up his front legs even higher. Soon the bull was spinning and twisting with all four hooves off the ground at once.

Gash wouldn't have been able to hold on even if he'd been strapped to a real saddle. The poor boy couldn't manage to crawl away fast enough. He got trampled several times. Seemed like he was still squirming around after the first few stomps, but no man could withstand two tons pouncing on him over and over. None of the men wanted to go in and drag the body out, so we left it there, which was fair warning for anyone else who might be thinking of hopping the wall.

Afterward, there was a quarrel over how long Gash had been on the bull. Some thought the counting should have started as soon as he covered the bull's back. Others thought it shouldn't have begun until the bull actually woke up.

"Normally, the ride don't start until the gate opens," Bo insisted. "You can't say you rode a bull if it wasn't awake. Hell, I could ride a sleeping bull all day if I was gentle enough."

Turned out that most of the wagers were for longer than five seconds anyway, so it didn't really matter. Mabel tallied up the bets, and Bo had won the lion's share.

"I ain't never had so much money in my life!" he remarked.

"Neither have most of these fellas," Mabel told him. "You're probably the wealthiest person in town right now."

"Never thought I'd see the day." He smiled proudly. "I finally got all the money I need, but there's nowhere to spend it. Imagine that!"

After seeing the way Private Gash got trampled, nobody else was much inclined to try riding the bull, which was a shame because there was little else in the way of entertainment.

The miners kept tunneling steadily toward the dust wall, but they eventually ran out of wagon wood to support the walls and ceiling. They started tearing the floors out from some of the unused buildings, but a lot of that wood was rotten. The only thing that could be done was to move the braces farther apart.

"I ain't cuttin' corners," Liam insisted. "Safety first!"

"I hear what you're sayin'," one of the mangled-handed carpenters replied. "It's just that there ain't much sturdy wood left. We already took what was worth salvaging—unless we tear down the saloon."

Liam weighed his options. His principles were one thing, but he didn't want to be left without a place to drink if the tunnel didn't lead anywhere. "Guess we could put braces every five feet instead of every three," he gave in. "I don't like it, though, and I wanna go on record that I'm against it. Remember, I'm the only dang miner in this town who ain't had a tunnel collapse on him."

Moving the braces farther apart seemed to hold well enough, and they pushed onward, but the tunnel was longer than they had figured, and it required even more wood. The carpenters suggested moving the braces out even farther.

Liam was unwavering. "It won't hold."

"Guess we could just rip up the saloon and drink out in the open."

It turned out that Liam's feelings about where he consumed his libations were even stronger than his feelings about how he built his tunnels. "I ain't getting sloshed under the stars like no dirty Injun! Drinking indoors is what separates man from beast."

"What else can we do?"

"Ah, shit!" Liam gave in. "I'll move 'em to eight feet apart, but that's the limit!"

Chapter 38

The Man in the Silly Hat Has a Plan

The miners expected to tunnel beneath the teepees any day now. Meanwhile, the corn shot up to full height. Then silks appeared at the top of the stalks and started to turn brown. Finally, the day came when the end of the ears peeked out from the husks.

"See that?" Farmer Jake pointed. "Soon as those ears round out some more, they'll be ready to eat."

"When will that be?" I asked.

"Some of 'em could be picked right now. The rest might need a day or two."

The Indians had been watching, and they knew they couldn't wait much longer or we'd start eating the precious maize. A raiding party assembled out in the plains. They rode up on their horses and launched a few arrows at the front of the saloon. While we were distracted, a brave snuck over and grabbed the ripest-looking corn near the edge. Our lookouts fired a few shots, but the raiding party quickly ran off.

"They're just testing us," a soldier advised. "Wanna see what kind of defenses we got in store for them."

"Prolly wanna make sure the corn's worth fighting for," Farmer Jake said, picking up one of the ears the brave had dropped. He peeled back the husk, and as he bit into it, his eyes lit up. "Not sure if it's 'cause I'm dead and ain't had none in so many years, but that's the sweetest corn I ever ate!"

I took a bite as well. Sure enough, it was sweeter than any corn I ever ate. Even dry and uncooked, I could've eaten the whole ear if Buddy hadn't ripped it from my hands. We collected the ripest ones and cooked them up in Sal's smoker. Once we all had a chance to taste it, nobody could imagine giving the crops up to the Indians while we went hungry. Every last man agreed the corn was worth fighting for.

"Prolly get sent to hell anyways," the scalped soldier declared, mustering some bravery. "Might as well go with some sweet corn in our bellies!"

The Indians must've felt the same, because the next day a much larger raiding party gathered out in the plains, wearing full war paints. A couple of drummers pounded on tom-toms to get the men riled up. They began marching straight to town.

"I guess this is it," the scalped soldier remarked.

"How far along is that tunnel?" I asked Liam.

"Thought for sure we'd have reached the dust wall by now, but it seems we still have a ways to go."

"How long?"

"Might be just a matter of feet. I can't go and pace it out above ground now. The bow-benders would shoot me down before I got ten feet. We'll just have to judge by the vibrations. We'll know when they're above us the way they're carrying on."

"Well, get back in the tunnel and keep digging!" I told him.

Even some of the experienced soldiers froze up when they saw the legion of angry braves outside. Most of them had never been in a battle where they were outnumbered. They were accustomed to having the upper hand in both artillery and men. Surprisingly, the blathering, know-it-all scalped soldier didn't want to stand up and lead the troops.

Luckily, Sal marched in from the back door. He was wearing a big floppy hat to protect his bald head from sunburn. "All hands on deck!" he called out. "Push that piano up against the front door!" he barked. "And shutter those windows!"

"Doesn't he have his own saloon to defend?" Mabel asked.

"Sal got us through this last time," I said. "He knows what he's doing. 'Sides, there ain't nothin' to defend in the Foggy Dew, except Red locked in the cellar."

"That's certainly questionable," Bo said.

I grabbed a rifle and hustled up to the second-floor window. I hadn't mentioned it to anyone lately, but once again I was getting close to making it a full year without shooting anyone. By my count, it was just a matter of days. And just like last time, when the wolves were attacking us, there didn't seem like much chance of me making it through the day. Odds were pretty good that an arrow or a tomahawk would send me to hell.

I decided I would try to wing a few Indians in the arm or the leg. Then maybe someone else would finish them off before they bled out. That way it wouldn't be me who killed them. And if they healed up, that was fine, too. I didn't have any desire to send anyone to hell. They were just trying to fill their bellies, same as us. Little Bear was probably right. The way they had been treated by white men when they were alive, they'd be in the right to attack us now. Unfortunately, I was still a white man and not too keen on getting scalped.

The one good thing about fighting Indians was that they moved a lot slower than werewolves, so it was easier to take aim. I shot the first one in the foot. He hopped around on the other foot until the fella in the next window finished him off. The next one, I caught in the thigh. He limped for cover. If he wrapped it tight, he might see another day, but the way the bullets were flying he'd likely get hit again. After that, I blasted one in the shoulder. He got up afterwards and threw a hatchet with his other arm. He had some good aim with that thing. It struck the fellow next to me in the face. Sal quickly took the man's place.

"Howdy," he said, tipping his funny hat.

"Howdy, Sal." Just then an arrow tore through my right sleeve. It left a gash in my beer-curling muscle that leaked a fair amount of cold blood. The fella who had launched it was shrieking like a banshee. His war paints weren't like the rest of them. Green and purple circles covered his cheeks and forehead.

"Hey, that ain't no Indian," I said.

"Who is he then?" Sal asked.

"It's Whiny Pete with his bruised-up face, wearing a breechcloth and headdress. That pissant nearly hit me!" It burned me up so much that I aimed right at his heart and squeezed the trigger. He dropped straight to the ground and didn't stir. Right away, I regretted it.

"Guess you ain't getting into heaven this year," Sal remarked.

"Guess not."

"Now we might never know for sure if it was possible."

"Ah, don't give me that, Sal! We already know it's just a bunch of hogwash. Moe told me how your old boss Willy made up that nonsense to keep two gunslingers from gutting him."

"I know Willy said it in a pinch," Sal admitted. "I ain't denying that. But it don't mean it ain't true," he argued. "A year after Willy got gutted, I seen one of them gunslingers get lifted up into the sky by a beam of light! I don't know if it took him to heaven or hell, but he had to go somewhere because he vanished."

The entire Indian nation now surrounded us. When they were all out of their teepees, there were a lot more of them than anyone had reckoned. They filled up the flatlands between town and their camp. Looked to be a thousand screaming warriors out there, all thirsty for revenge against those who had killed them. Black Moon, the unkillable brave, stood in the center, hooting and hollering a war cry that made the scalped soldier weep.

"I don't wanna get scalped *again*," he said. "It hurt like the dickens last time."

"Ain't nothing left for them to scalp," I told him. "They'll prolly just put an arrow through ya and be done with it."

Those who still had their hair weren't reassured. A few of them lost their nerve when they saw what we were up against. Sal threw down his gun and walked away.

"Where you going?" I asked.

"I got an idea," he said, then called out to Jarvis who was quivering in the corner. "Hey, buckshot face! Follow me!"

Chapter 39

Bo's Pickle

We were running low on bullets, and it was clear we wouldn't be able to hold off the Indians much longer. The godless soldiers knelt down on the floor and began praying like altar boys.

"Please Lord!" the scalped soldier wept. "Just let the Injuns take the crops and leave us be. I don't wanna burn in hell for no corn on the cob."

The wind suddenly picked up, sending dry tumbleweeds bouncing across the plains. It blew so hard that a sheet of dark gray clouds drifted across the sky. The sun was soon covered, and the town was darker than it had ever been. I could hardly see the road from the window.

"Maybe we'll get some help from the Long Teeth now," Jake suggested.

The scalped soldier had already lost all hope. "Why would they bother leavin' the hotel when there's a couple hundred angry Injuns at their doorstep?"

Martin started crying loudly, so Ms. Parker took him upstairs to feed.

"I reckon if it stays this dark, the Injuns wouldn't notice if we slip out the back," a lumberjack said.

"Where would we go?" I asked.

"We could go hide out in the tunnel until those miners dig us a way out of here."

The wind kicked up once more. This time, only the clouds in the corner of the sky shifted. A pale round circle shone through with just enough light to see by.

Sal turned to me. "Is that the same moon-like thing you saw last time, Tom?"

"Seems like it," I answered.

A long howl sounded in the distance, like a dog who had just woken to find he'd missed supper for an entire week. Rosalie had told me that the wolves were keen on hunting at night. Conditions seemed right for that now.

"Guess we ain't skinning out now," Kenny said.

"The Injuns might get some reinforcements, too," the scalped soldier said. He got back down on his knees to pray some more.

The braves surrounding the saloon didn't fuss much about the change in the weather. After their eyes adjusted to the dimness, they kept battering the front door. They might've reckoned some sort of storm god was rooting them on. It didn't occur to them how the absence of light might affect the other residents of Damnation.

Not long after the sun vanished and the moon rose, Luther charged out of the hotel, blowing the door clear off the hinges. His eyes were glowing yellow. Before they knew what was happening, he began throwing men around like rag dolls. Nigel followed behind him with a pistol in each hand, firing into the swarms of warriors blocking the road. They were both well-rested, so they managed to dodge the first few arrows and hatchets thrown their way.

For every man that Luther threw, there were ten more right behind him. Nigel was a quick shot. He laid out a dozen men, then ran out of bullets. While Nigel paused to reload, Black Moon rushed him with a stiff shoulder and knocked the vampire to the ground. Nigel got up, dusted his lapel in annoyance, then threw a punch at the unkillable Indian. It hardly had any effect. They traded blows back and forth, but it seemed they were evenly matched.

Finally, Luther broke up the brawl by chucking a skinny brave at Black Moon. The body knocked him off balance, allowing Nigel to slip away. The vampires were well-rested, but they hadn't had any warm blood since before the sun came out. They were running out of steam and needed to rest. We moved the piano away from the front door and they both dashed inside.

"There are too many of them," Luther admitted.

"Indeed," Nigel agreed breathlessly.

The walls shook from the Indians' charges. Nigel raced upstairs to protect little Martin. After closing the bedroom door, he smashed the support beam, causing the doorframe to collapse and making it impossible to open the door.

"Guess he ain't fixin' to lend a hand," a soldier remarked.

"The other one ain't gonna be much help neither," a cowhand noted.

Luther had collapsed at the bar, where Mollie was tending to him. She plucked a couple of arrows from his back, but there wasn't much she could do without warm blood. He needed a few weeks of bed rest.

"Ain't anybody got another baby chick with warm blood?" a sodbuster asked.

"The only warm blood left in town is in that child up there," a cowboy explained.

"Of course it is," Gut-Shot Granny said. "That's why that other vampire took him upstairs."

"I don't get it," Kenny said. "Why's he care more about protecting that child than gettin' scalped by a thousand Injuns."

"Martin's blood is poison," Luther muttered weakly. He barely had the strength to talk.

"What's that?" the cowboy asked.

"He said it's poison," I told him. "It's part of their vampire religion. They think the boy is the son of Satan or some nonsense. I overheard Nigel say they can't drink Martin's blood because it'd be poison for vampires."

"It's true," Luther said.

"How do you know?" Mollie asked.

Likely on account of it was Mollie doing the asking, he answered, "I tried it. I snuck into the baby's room after I overheard you all talking about him. I pricked him with a pin and tasted just a drop of his blood. It was indeed warm, so warm that it burnt my tongue, and I had to spit it out. No vampire could be nourished by that child. It would be like drinking boiling water."

"Lemme get this straight," Jake said. "We got the son of Satan upstairs and a thousand angry Injuns outside?"

"When you put it like that, it don't sound so good," Kenny said.

"Yup, y'all are certainly in a pickle," Bo said, not looking at all worried.

"What ya mean *y'all?*" Kenny asked. "You're in the same pickle."

"Nope." Bo chuckled. "I ain't got no skin in this game. 'Member? I'm a quarter Cherokee. I share blood with some of them."

"There's a few hundred braves out there that won't think there's any difference between you and me," Kenny argued.

"Maybe so," Bo said. "But I ain't fightin' none of my people. If I saw some wolves out there, it'd be a different story. As it stands now, it ain't my pickle."

Bo calmly moseyed up the stairs and went into the room beside the one with Nigel, Ms. Parker, and Martin.

"I told ya that dark fellow wasn't to be trusted," Kenny said.

Chapter 40

A Helluva Racket in the Road

The front door was starting to crack down the middle. The next charge would certainly split it open, so we all pointed our guns at the doorway to cut down the first man to enter.

"Aim for the legs," the scalped soldier advised. "If we stop 'em in their tracks, we can use their bodies as a barrier to block the rest from coming in."

"Fair enough," I agreed. "Hell, that's prolly the first good idea you've had all month."

While we steadied our barrels on the front door, four braves broke through the back door. They came into the barroom with their bows already drawn and launched their arrows before anyone could turn and fire. Luther leaned over to shield Mollie and caught one in the shoulder. The Indians didn't bother with the unarmed soldiers kneeling on the ground praying. They went straight for the women. Seemed like their plan was to take them as hostages.

One brave grabbed Annabelle in a bear hug. Another put Mabel in a headlock. A third went for Mollie. Luther summoned some strength to stand and protect her. The brave swung his hatchet with all his might. Luther wasn't armed, so he raised his forearm in defense. The blade wedged into the bone pretty deep, which prevented the brave from pulling it out to take another swing.

Luther was barely able to remain on his feet, but he managed to palm the warrior's head and hold him back with a straightened arm. The fella got feisty and pulled a knife from his waistband. Then he got busy slashing at the wrist above his head. Luther grimaced with each slice, but he didn't let go. His eyes glowed yellow in anger, and he squeezed the brave's head so hard that his thumb broke through his temple. When Luther pulled his finger out, it looked like he had dipped it in tomato sauce. As the brave fell to the ground, a splash of soupy brains spilled out of the hole.

Buddy couldn't get a clear shot at the man carrying away Annabelle, so he ran after them and tried to wrestle her free. Meanwhile, Mabel was being dragged to the backdoor in a headlock, kicking and screaming the whole way. The scalped soldier summoned the courage to block their path. The brave swung his hand ax with his free hand and lopped off the soldier's ear. He still showed some grit and continued to fight. Finally, the soldier fell after a few more chops in the face, which looked a lot more painful than any scalping.

There was a loud crash that shook the whole building. The front door had split straight down the middle, and a pair of large hands wiggled into the crack. They grabbed each half and shoved them aside. Black Moon was standing in the cluttered doorway with a spear in his hand. He squeezed past the piano and the broken chairs that blocked the way. I raised my rifle and fired. The shot barely made him take a step back. The bullet was lodged in his chest with dozens of other lead plums that didn't seem to bother him. He continued marching straight toward Luther.

The wheat-haired giant was sapped of all strength, but still trying his damnedest to protect the plainest-looking whore from Arizona. He dragged down one last brave with his bare hands and snapped the man's neck. The effort left him too weak to move. He was completely defenseless to the unkillable Indian. Black Moon didn't bother wasting any time in trading blows. He just stuck his spear straight through Luther's heart. His long muscular body slid off a barstool onto the floor. Mollie let out a blood-curdling scream.

"Guess he's gonna meet his maker," Gut-Shot Granny said.

"Us too," I said.

Without Luther, we were licked, and everyone knew it. One soldier boy put a pistol in his mouth and pulled the trigger just to avoid getting scalped. The only one left with any pep was Buddy. After rescuing Annabelle, he went after the ax-swinging brave who had Mabel in a headlock. When Buddy got her clear, he cold-cocked the brave, then made a final charge at the rest of the warriors who had scrambled through the front door.

Buddy may have been leaner, but he still had his jolly, just like in the old days. He stood with a pistol in each hand, laughing his head off as he shot the invading braves. Black Moon pulled his spear from Luther's body and made ready to throw it at Buddy. Just as he cocked his arm back, a bullet knocked the buck's ear off. A scantily dressed woman up on the catwalk was holding the smoking gun. Mollie ejected the shell from her bolt-action rifle and took aim at the other ear.

The unkillable Indian was surprised to find he could be wounded. He reckoned it was wiser to retreat to the road where the numbers were to their favor, rather than face the cackling gunslinger and a sharp-shooting woman. On his way out the door, he turned and threw his spear at Buddy. He was tending to Mabel at the time and didn't see it coming. At the last second, Sergeant Silence, of all people, stepped in the way. The spear caught him in the chest. Even though Buddy had shot out the man's tongue for speaking poorly of Ms. Parker, he still sacrificed himself.

"I don't understand. Why would he do that?" Buddy asked.

"Musta known we'd have a better chance with you around than with him," Jake said.

"Dumbass soldier," a cowhand commented. "He prolly wanted to yell *duck*, but he didn't have the tongue to do. I bet he tried to use sign language to let you know there was a spear coming."

"Whatever the reason, his sacrifice is appreciated," I said. "Y'all done a good job fightin' off those Injuns, especially you, Buddy, and you too, Mollie."

"Yeah, but we're still surrounded," Kenny complained. Then he got back down on his knees to pray some more.

"It don't mean we gotta go down like a whiny Fre," Buddy told him.

"What the hell's a Fre?" he asked.

"I ain't exactly sure of the origin," Buddy told him. "It was before my time. Alls I can tell ya is, if a fella dies with tears on his cheeks instead of fire in his belly, then he's a Fre." Buddy uncorked the last remaining wine bottle that Mabel had stashed behind the bar. He took a big long gulp that spilled over his lips, staining his beard purple.

Just then a flaming arrow came through a shattered window. A soldier immediately stomped it out, but it was followed by two more. Then the flaming arrows struck high on the wall, which proved harder to reach. Kenny tore down some of Mabel's fancy tapestries to smother the flames.

"They're gonna smoke us out!" Jake said. "We can't put 'em out fast enough!"

"Looks like we're either gonna burn or be scalped," a soldier said.

"Never thought I'd say this," I admitted. "But right now, I wish I was Red, sitting comfy in the cellar of the Foggy Dew."

"Shit, he might be the only one of us to see tomorrow," Jake added.

Suddenly, the loudest noise I ever heard came from out in front of the saloon. It sounded like a thunderclap that kept repeating over and over again with just the teensiest pause in between.

"What the hell's that?" Blind Sal asked from the back of the room. He was pinned to the wall by a half dozen arrows. It looked like nothing vital had been hit, but he couldn't budge an inch. I went to the window to see where the racket was coming from, and I could hardly believe my eyes.

Chapter 41

Sal's Scheme

"Sal's sittin' on top of some kind of cannon!" I yelled over the clatter. "He's blasting away at them Injuns!"

"No, he ain't!" a newbie yelled back. "He's right over there, pinned to the wall by arrows."

"Not that Sal," I said. "The other Sal."

The racket outside stopped. It seemed to be on account of the cannon had jammed up. Sal had his foot up on the crossbeam that supported the barrels. It was bookended by two wagon wheels. He was using a knife as a lever to pry out a misfired shell casing, and there was no end to the cussing that came from his mouth.

"How the hell'd he shoot that cannon so quickly and go so long without reloading?" Old Moe wanted to know.

"It's a dang Gatling gun," a soldier told him. "Though I ain't got no idea where it came from."

"Guess it must've come out of the dust on an army wagon some time back," I said. Sal probably didn't even know what it was until he heard the soldiers describe one. Just behind Sal, Jarvis was sitting on top of a pony he had used to pull the gun into the road.

"He might've at least asked for help from someone who knows how to use that thing," the soldier said. "Those Indians are coming back and they're gonna take the Gatling gun from him if he don't start shooting soon."

Finally, Sal managed to unjam the gun, and just in time. The clatter started back up and an endless spray of bullets mowed down the advancing braves. The rest retreated out to the plains. Many of the Indians had been dead for decades, and they were just as mystified by the repeating canon as Old Moe.

"Let's get after 'em!" Sal hollered, and Jarvis spurred the pony to pull the gun out to the edge of town where the buildings wouldn't block his range.

Sal had the hang of it now. He swung from side to side, showering the flatlands like a water hose as the spent cartridges spit out the side. The gun had ten barrels that rotated around in a circle, so one of them was firing at every second. The Indians had nowhere to hide. Some dove for cover in their teepees, but the bullets tore right through the dried animal hides.

Not all of them ran away, though. Black Moon came charging straight for the gun. Maybe he remembered how he was killed the first time, and wanted to show that devil cannon he still wasn't afraid it. The first few rounds scuttled him back a step or two, like a hard shove, but he wasn't going down. He had big medicine, just as Little Bear had said.

A few other warriors were harkened by Black Moon's bravery, and they fell in behind him, marching straight into the line of fire. Sal had to pivot the barrels and shoot farther left and right to keep the flanks from overcoming him.

Black Moon walked calmly but with great determination straight up the center of the road. He was just twenty yards away from Sal now. The large caliber bullets ripped straight through his chest and came out the other side. Trails of blood streamed down his back, filling in his footprints. Still, he would not stop.

Sal had to concentrate his fire solely on the unkillable Indian. Round after round struck the big man's chest, enough to shatter his sternum and darken his heart with lead, but he would not retreat. Finally, both ankles gave out, and he dropped to his knees, pausing for a moment with arms outstretched. Black Moon seemed to be praying to his god for the strength to avenge his sister. Sal shot him one last time in the face, and he collapsed on the ground.

"You'd a thought he'd learnt his lesson last time about going against a Gatling gun," a soldier remarked.

"I reckon the lesson was ours to learn," I said.

The soldier looked at me cross. "How's that? What lesson you speaking of?"

"I can't rightly say. Seems like we ain't learnt it yet."

"Don't give me none of your circle-talking. You some kind of Injun lover?"

Jarvis brought over more ammunition, and Sal kept loading it into the gun. A cloud of smoke filled the plains, and you could hardly see twenty yards away. Just to be sure, Sal kept firing at the bodies of the hell-sent men until he was completely out of bullets.

When the gun clicked empty, he remarked, "That oughta do it." Then he doffed the silly hat, which he no longer needed since there was no sunlight.

Below the gun smoke, you could hardly see a speck of ground that wasn't covered by a corpse. The surviving Indians had retreated beyond the reach of the Gatling gun, all the way to the dust wall. A lot of them were just women and youngins. The fiercest fighters had charged right into harm's way with Black Moon. The ones with the biggest headdresses and brightest war paints lay just yards from the barrels.

The smoke began to clear. Not long after, Liam and the other miners surfaced from the tunnel. They timidly peered out from the shack that covered their hole. When they saw we were still standing, they seemed surprised.

"You ain't reached the other side yet?" I asked.

"Not sure," Liam answered. He wanted to count the footsteps from the shack where the tunnel started to the edge of the dust wall. He walked it off twice and still looked confounded.

"We shoulda reached it already!" he said.

"Then just dig upward and see where you're at," I said.

"We can't. There's nothing but solid rock above us."

"Go a little farther then," Jake suggested. "Whenever you get past the rock, dig upward. Maybe that's just the dust wall above you. No tellin' how thick it is."

"Ain't no rush to finish it now," I said. "Sal shot up all the Indians. You fellas can take a breather and start up again after you've rested."

A long solitary howl bellowed in the distance. This time it was followed by several more. Soon a dozen barks could be heard at once.

"Wolves!" Sal yelled.

"On second thought, maybe you should take that break later," I told Liam, and the miners hustled back to the tunnel.

Chapter 42

The Most Dangerous Ten Minutes in Damnation

At first, there were just the shadows of a few furry forms in the distance. Then they grew larger and doubled in number. Soon, there were thirty or forty wolves coming toward us, leaping over the piles of dead Indians. Their teeth were bared and they were drooling with hunger. They hadn't eaten in weeks, and they were all well-rested. A few soldiers posted at the side of the road and tried to make a stand. They got off some rifle shots, but the wolves closed the distance too quickly and overcame them.

"Seems like they took the mayor's plan," Sal said. "They were prolly waiting the whole time until we killed each other off."

"Now they're gonna finish us and have the whole damned town to themselves!" a cowboy cried.

This time, the wolves had no interest in getting us scared and hunting us down. They went straight in for the kill. Screams filled the road as the soldiers were mauled. Buddy provided cover so the rest of us could retreat back into the Rusty Nail. As we passed the dirt wall that the miners had built around the moss field, there was a long low groan from within. It was followed by a few angry snorts.

"Sitting Bull don't sound too happy," Kenny remarked.

Just then, the two-ton bull soared over the wall like he had wings carrying him. The dirt was piled about five feet high, and his hooves raked the top on the way.

It took a second to recognize what had maddened the beast enough to jump that high. It wasn't just that he had run out of moss to munch on. Rodeo

Bo managed to get a rope around his midsection while he was snoozing and climbed on top. Old Sitting Bull had probably been dreaming about some long-ago day when he was lazing by the riverside with his favorite squaw. Then the rope suddenly tightened around his ribs. It made him so furious that he couldn't be penned in any longer.

As soon as the flying bull touched down, he broke into a gallop. When he realized there was still something on top of him, he bucked recklessly, as if there were a pile of hot coals burning his back. With both hind legs in the air, he whipped his rear around sideways so fast that you couldn't tell which direction he might go next. Somehow, Bo managed to stay on top with one arm tied to the bull. Oddly, he didn't even bother holding on with the other hand, and just let it flail in the air for kicks.

Sitting Bull bucked so hard that the earth trembled every time his hooves crashed down. Then he started lifting his front legs off the ground before his hind legs came back down. He sailed three feet in the air while twisting all willy-nilly. It was a miracle that Bo wasn't thrown off in seconds. He didn't fight against the bull's motions. He took them with a broad smile, bending like a blade of grass in the wind. Bo must've found the beast's rhythm, because it looked kind of like they were dancing together. Maybe it was on account of the quarter Cherokee in Bo's blood. He sent a message through his spurs that the Lakota chief understood.

The wolves were crowding the road in front of the saloon, and Bo edged the bull straight into the middle of the pack. The sudden appearance of the huge angry beast must've confused them. If they'd had time to plan, three or four wolves could've taken him down. His movements were too hard to predict, though, and he kept knocking them down before they could attack as a group.

A shaggy brown mutt charged from behind, but Sitting Bull turned suddenly and rammed it head-on. Another nipped his heels, which made him even angrier. He was rising so high in the air that his hooves smashed into the wolves' heads. At every turn, two or three got trampled. They were hemmed in by the buildings, and the bodies scattered on the ground made it hard for them to bolt away. Before long, most of the pack got stomped to hell or had so many broken bones that they could no longer rise.

Argus, the pack leader, remained off to the side, waiting for his chance to strike. He had more heft than any of the others, and was only a few hands shorter than the giant bull, though still half as thick. He timed it so that the beast had his head in the dirt and his rear hooves kicking in the air. Argus lunged for the defenseless side of the neck.

Bo saw the big gray wolf coming, though. He smashed a spur into Sitting Bull's side, causing him to turn at the last second. Argus got gored by a horn. It pierced his throat, and he was left gasping for air. The fur fell away from his body, and his paws quickly shriveled up into man's hands. He changed back to human form and covered the hole in his neck with his fingers so that he could breathe.

After their leader was defeated, the rest of the wolves didn't see much reason in continuing to fight. They fled back to their side of town, licking their wounds. One of them dragged Argus with him, though it wasn't clear if he'd survive.

Bo kept riding the bull until he eventually tired out. It had only taken about ten minutes to lay out the entire wolf pack, but Sitting Bull had been bucking at full speed the entire time. It couldn't have been easy for something that large to move so fast for very long. Blind fury had kept him going. He finally collapsed in front of the door to the Foggy Dew. He was as gentle as a lamb. Bo softly petted his snout as Sitting Bull drifted off to sleep.

"Just how am I supposed to get into my saloon now?" Sal asked.

"I bet if we put a bullet in his eye at close range, that would do it," a cowboy suggested. "Then we can butcher him."

Bo wouldn't hear of it, though. "You're gonna have to go through me before you touch this animal," he declared.

"But I ain't ate nothin' in months! That sleepy stack of steaks could feed everyone for a week or two at least, and you wanna keep him as a pet?"

The rest of the men were also in favor of filling their bellies. I usually tried to avoid siding against popular opinion, but I'd already shot Whiny Pete. I wasn't going to heaven any time soon and didn't have much to lose.

"Now hold it there, boys," I said. "I understand you wanting to eat Sitting Bull, but there's still wolves out there. And there could be more of them coming out of the cloud any day now. Not to mention, there might be a whole tribe of new Indians at your doorstep tomorrow morning. Sitting Bull may look like a mess of rib eyes to you right now, but down the road he might be the only thing keeping us from getting scalped or eaten."

The cowpuncher saw my point, but more importantly he wasn't keen on going against Bo, who definitely wasn't backing down. Bo might not have been a gunslinger, but he had a knack for sending stuff to hell in a hurry, whether by twisting their necks or stomping on them with a bull.

"Guess we could just have wolf steaks," he suggested.

"Now, you're talking!" Sal said. "Get a fire going. Let's cook these dogs before they start to turn."

"I'll have mine with some of that sweet corn on the cob!" Jake called out.

Chapter 43

A Dozen Killable Pieces

After all the commotion died down, I strolled out into the plains to have a look around at all the bodies. It would have taken a hundred issues of *The Crapper* to account for the stories of all those hell-sent people. Most of them had no visible older wounds hinting at what had originally done them in. They could have been sent to Damnation by smallpox, measles, or just the plain old flu.

There'd never be any way of learning their stories, unless maybe Little Bear had survived and wanted to share what he knew with me. I kept my eyes peeled for his stubby corpse, expecting it would still bear a grin, as if going to hell hadn't bothered him much either.

Most of all, I was hoping I wouldn't find Rosalie among the trampled wolf carcasses. She didn't seem keen on attacking anyone, but maybe wolves didn't have any choice in the matter. Seemed like the pack did whatever Argus said. I had never seen her in wolf form, so I had no idea what she looked like, or if she had any features to distinguish her from the others.

Seeing so many Indian bodies with half-inch bullet holes, I couldn't help but feel we were the bad guys. Sure, we were just trying to survive, same as them, but if we were really the good guys, we might've put more effort into figuring out a way not to shoot anyone at all. Of course, that wasn't something I could share with the others.

There were too many loudmouths going on about what they were entitled to and what they were going to do if they didn't get it, from Red with the crazy-eyed squaw to the mayor and his meat. Even Nigel was angling for the end of times just so he might drink warm blood again. There wasn't a soul in Damnation trying to figure out how we might all just get along for whatever time we had left. They all wanted more of something—and there'd never be enough.

Some of the shot-up braves were still clinging to the afterlife. Moans of misery could be heard at every step. I wrapped up a few wounds for those who might not bleed out. I dragged bodies off of those who were being smothered. When I got to the edge of their camp, I noticed something odd. The ground beside the dust wall looked different from the rest. The dirt was a little darker, and I knew it hadn't always been that way. I called over Farmer Jake to have a look, since it was his area of expertise.

After a good long stare, he said in his slow way of talking, "This here newer dirt seems to form a ring around that there older dirt."

"No shit, I can see that," I told him. "What do you make of it?"

"I reckon the wall of dust has pulled back about a foot in all directions."

"Why would it do that?"

"Can't say. But I can tell you this. It means the town has grown some."

"Did you hear that?" I asked. "Sounds like crying over yonder."

It was louder than the moans of any of the wounded warriors. We hustled over, thinking it might be a child who had gotten caught in the crossfire. As we got closer, a squeaky voice called out from beneath a pile of bodies, "Somebody please help me!"

"That ain't no Indian," Jake said. "Unless he speaks American real good."

Sal and Jarvis weren't far away, and they came over to lend a hand. The four of us lifted the bodies one by one. Before long, we got to him. The feathers in his headdress were crushed and his face was bruised up pretty good, but we all knew those weren't new marks. My bullet had missed his heart by an inch and went clear through the other side.

"Guess you didn't kill Whiny Pete after all," Sal said.

"Guess not."

"So you're still in the running for heaven."

"It would seem so," I laughed. "If there is such a place."

Whiny Pete was so afraid that we might send him to hell that he took off running as soon as he got free. Nobody saw any use in chasing after the boy, and we didn't have any bullets left to shoot him anyway. We soon heard some muffled hollering beneath another nearby pile of bodies. This one was directly in the line of fire of the Gatling gun.

"It don't sound like that fella speaks American," Jake remarked.

"I ain't unburying him then," Sal informed us. "Seems like he still has some fight left in him. Let him stay under there till he bleeds out."

It turned out the man didn't need our help. A hand shot out from between the corpses and started wiggling around. Then his whole arm surfaced, all the way to the shoulder. Pretty soon, he wormed himself out all by himself. There were some new wounds on his shot-up chest, and now his cheeks had half-inch bullet holes too, but clearly Black Moon wasn't ready to leave Damnation.

"Guess he really can't be kilt," I said.

"It would appear so," Sal said.

The four of us were probably the least likely to wrestle a giant unkillable Indian. There weren't any reinforcements to count on. Luther had already been speared, Buddy was tending to his wounds, and Nigel still hadn't left the room where he was protecting baby Martin. Besides, if a Gatling gun couldn't kill him, what could we do to him? I reckoned there wasn't much use in running. We were clearly done for.

Black Moon picked up a spear from the ground and waved it in the air, letting out a furious holler. Then he jumped up and down in a fit. Clearly, he was still keen on avenging his sister with anybody that was left. After he was done with us, he'd surely go after Ms. Parker and the other women. If fifty rounds of a Gatling gun couldn't stop him, a tired British vampire probably couldn't either—if Nigel was even inclined to try. The only thing that I could think to do was get down on my knees and pray. My bad leg was acting up, though. Also, I didn't have much else to say to the Lord.

Just then, the ground began to tremble beneath our feet. I looked to the dust cloud and nothing was coming out of it. It shook even harder than when Sitting Bull was bucking. Black Moon wasn't bothered by it. He kept jumping up and down, hollering even louder. All of a sudden, the giant unkillable Indian vanished. He dropped straight down like the ground had swallowed him up.

"What happened?" Jake asked.

Naturally, Jarvis had his speculations. "Ya think he just got sucked straight into hell?"

We hustled over to the spot where he had been standing, and there was a hole about five feet across. As I looked over the edge, it took a moment for my eyes to adjust to the darkness. A dozen dirty miners stood below, and they were all holding blood-soaked shovels. Seemed like they had tunneled into the dust wall, and it somehow sent them coming back to the center of town from the other direction. That would've accounted for why it took so long.

The miners were just as surprised as Black Moon. They thought they were already outside of Damnation when a giant Indian fell in on top of them. Some reckoned it might be the devil, so they clobbered the big man before he could get to them first. Then they hacked away at his body, fearing he might still come after them. Black Moon was cut up into about a dozen pieces.

"Guess he ain't unkillable after all," Jarvis remarked.

"Guess not," I said. "Just needed to be chopped up instead of shot, I suppose."

"'Less you think maybe he's gonna come back together again somehow?" Jarvis asked. "We could spread his parts in different holes, just in case."

"Nah," I said. "That oughta do."

Liam was the only one who seemed disappointed by how things had turned out. It wasn't the chopping up of Black Moon that soured his spirits, though. It was the failure of his tunnel.

"You did all you could," I told him. "It just ain't possible to dig outta here."

"It ain't that exactly," he replied. "Now I can't rightly say that I'm the only miner who ain't had a mine collapse on him."

"Ah, you can't be faulted for that," I told him. "You did a darn good job with what little time and materials you had. There was a war going on above, and hardly a pencil's worth of wood left to support the walls. Then to top it off, a giant Indian jumped up and down right over your heads. I know it wasn't what you set out to do, but y'all killed an unkillable Indian. Now, that's somethin' you can hang your hat on, ain't it?"

Liam smiled as if he was proud, but he was just humoring me. He was a single-sighted bastard, and could only be pleased by the building of proper tunnels.

"Ah, that boy with the shot-up face is right," he added. "We can't really say for sure if that unkillable Indian is even kilt."

I reckoned Black Moon wasn't coming back again, but just in case, I found a loaded sidearm and strapped it to my leg.

Chapter 44

The Unmourned Piano Player

After Sal shot a couple hundred Indians, Bo trampled forty wolves on the back of a giant bull, and the miners killed an unkillable Indian, Nigel finally saw fit to leave the safety of the room on the second floor of the Rusty Nail. He carried baby Martin in his arms, and Ms. Parker was beside him. She immediately rushed over to Buddy, who had a few arrows in his back and a couple of bite marks on his behind, but was otherwise no worse for the wear.

"Now he shows up!" Sal said beneath his breath.

"Easy there," I warned him. "After all we've been through, don't go mouthing off and get yourself sent to hell by the only remaining vampire."

Nigel had a look around at all the bodies and said with some surprise, "I dare say you chaps have fared better than I'd have assumed."

"That's for damn sure!" a cowhand bragged. "And no thanks to you."

Nigel walked over with a polite smile. Then he grabbed the cowhand by the throat with one arm while holding Martin with the other. He let the man choke breathlessly for a moment before he crushed his outspoken windpipe with one quick squeeze.

"I see that my colleague Luther was not as fortunate... A shame," he said with no remorse. "From the window, I could see how the dark-skinned cowboy used the bull to trample the wolves. Very entertaining." He smirked. "It would appear you have gotten rid of everyone who might pose a threat to me."

Ms. Parker came back out into the road. She didn't like the mean look in Nigel's eyes, so she went to take Martin from him. He pulled away and gave her a shove, causing her to fall to the ground.

"I'll see to his care," he said, then, thinking better of it, he corrected himself. "You may nurse him until I find some warm blood, but the rest of you humans will stay clear of the unsacred child."

As he spoke, a beam of light broke through the cloud cover above. I reckoned it might be fixing to punish Nigel, but it shone down directly on me. It wasn't exactly like the light that had cooked the vampires. It was softer and warmer than the rays from the sun that wouldn't set. It felt kind of inviting, like it was pulling on me.

"Look!" Jarvis shouted. "Tom's getting lifted to heaven."

My whole body felt lighter, as if my beer gut had just vanished. Sure enough, my heels came off the ground all by themselves. I felt bad leaving everyone. Especially now that Nigel wasn't such a nice fella anymore. Also, they still needed someone to write *The Crapper* and keep folks informed. Another mayor could come along and start making things up again, like Hearst had. Maybe Jarvis would be up to the task someday, but he didn't seem ready yet. He had the curiosity and was steadfast about the truth. He just wasn't any good at talking to folks.

While everyone had their eyes on me in the center of the beam of light, they didn't take any notice of what was going on behind them. Whiny Pete had crept up beside Ms. Parker with a crazed look in his eyes. All those years of being scared had made Pete willing to follow whoever helped him feel brave. Even in hell, Black Moon still held his loyalty. He raised a tomahawk above Ms. Parker's head to avenge the squaw that Red had shot. Pete wasn't ever going to be a whiny cowpoke again.

I lifted the pistol in my holster and took aim over Ms. Parker's shoulder. She shrieked and covered her eyes. Then I shot that whiny bastard in the face. The light around me faded, and I eased back on my heels.

Nigel looked ready to tear my arms off, but then he saw his interests were served. Ms. Parker was still around to nurse the unsacred child.

"So it was true after all," Gut-Shot Granny noted.

"I told you so!" Regular Sal pronounced.

"Why didn't you just let it take you away to heaven?" Granny asked me. "You were so close after all these years."

"Guess I wasn't ready to leave y'all just yet," I answered. "'Sides, how could I laze around in the Lord's vineyard all day knowing I let Ms. Parker get sent to hell?"

The Crapper

Comings: *No animals or men have arrived, but there's plenty of corn and wolf meat to eat—if you have a taste for that sort of thing.*

Goings: *Most of the Indians got shot down by Sal's Gatling gun, a lot of the wolves were trampled by Bo and Sitting Bull, and Luther got stabbed through the heart while saving Mollie. I saw to it that Pete will never whine again. Our ranks have thinned considerably. The piano player was one of the casualties, so the saloon will be quieter for a spell. He only knew twenty or thirty songs, though, and we were all pretty tired of hearing them anyway.*

Chapter 45

The Little Gems Beneath Us

The remaining Indians huddled in a small camp on the far edge of the flatlands. Only five or six campfires could be seen burning in the distance. I never did find Little Bear's body. I reckoned he might be among the survivors, so I rode a horse out there to have a look. It was mostly squaws, and the little Iroquois was nowhere to be seen. I never found Rosalie either.

"What's the matter, Tom?" Farmer Jake said. "Ain't you gonna eat your supper?"

Annabelle had placed a plate in front of me on the bar. I pushed it forward. No matter how hungry I got, I couldn't stomach it. There was no way of knowing if one of those wolves they had butchered was Rosalie. I couldn't rightly eat a lady I'd held hands with.

"Suit yourself. More for me," he said and took the plate.

"So what do you make of the town growing bigger?" Jake asked.

"I got no idea," I confessed.

"Maybe the dust wall will keep moving back," Jarvis suggested excitedly. "Just think… someday, Damnation could grow to become the size of an entire planet!"

"The soil in the new territory is richer," Jake added. "It might grow trees."

"Maybe it'll turn out to be just like Earth," Kenny added. "It would be like we never died."

"Only one difference," I pointed out. "There's a bunch of shot-up folks wandering around here with memories of past lives."

"I don't remember a damn thing about my past life," Moe remarked. "Alls I know is y'all keep coming out of the dust yammering on about what coulda been."

The fellas laughed, but then fell silent as they gave it some serious thought. Finally, a lumberjack asked, "How long do you think it'll be before we all forget we're dead?"

"That ain't gonna happen," I told him. "Not with that hatchet in your back and the smell of decay coming from it."

"You gotta point there," Jarvis said. "But say Damnation does grow to become just like Earth. And maybe someday there's new people born here, just like Martin was. After we're all gone, do y'all think there'd be any way to tell this world apart from the one we left?"

"Maybe not," Jake speculated. "'Cept for what's written in Tom's paper."

Bo decided to stoke the fire a bit. "If any new folks came across *The Crapper* long after we're gone, they'd think it was just made-up stories instead of a record of what happened."

"Ah, hogwash!" Sal barked. "Ain't no damned new people gonna be born here!"

While they were bickering, I turned to Jarvis and said to him on the side, "You better brush up on your people skills, son."

"Why's that?"

"Writing's just a small part of the job. Talking to folks is the main part. Getting 'em to open up to ya and tell their stories."

"Why you telling me that?"

"I can't listen to these fools squabble for eternity. Next time a beam of light wants to lift me up to heaven, I'm goin'! And the town's gonna need a new reporter."

"Ah, you can't even say for sure if you were being lifted to heaven," Jarvis said. "You only had your heels up in the air. For all I know, you mighta just been standing on your tippy toes."

Just then, the door swung open with a thud. We looked up to see an old man in the doorway. He was hunched over on a cane with a long white beard. He was even older than Hearst had been. Looked like he might be pushing ninety years old. His clothes were worn out and moth-eaten.

He pointed a gnarled finger in my direction and snarled, "You ain't gettin' into heaven! Yer gonna burn in hell with the rest of us!" Right after he said it, the old-timer clutched his chest, then fell down and croaked right there in front of us.

"Guess folks are coming out of the dust again," Sal noted without any surprise.

"Hey, maybe there's whiskey out there!" a cowhand said, and everyone hustled outside in hopes of curing their thirst.

Some gunfire sounded within the dust cloud, followed by a mess of hooting and hollering. Moments later, a band of Indians appeared on the road. Their leader was a tall painted brave with a large stab wound in his belly. He sat atop of dead-eyed mare. His skin was pale blue, like he'd been dead a while.

"Holy shit!" the soldier beside me shuddered. "That's Crazy Horse!"

"How do you know?" I asked.

"'Cause I stabbed him myself, with a bayonet at Fort Robinson."

"Didn't he die 'bout twenty years ago?" I asked.

"More'n that," the soldier answered. "Where you suppose he's been all this time?"

"You could ask him," I suggested. "Though he prolly ain't much inclined to chat with the folks who kilt him."

More blue warriors followed behind Crazy Horse. They kept coming out of the dust, and none of them looked happy to see us. I looked over at the dry well, hoping to see Rosalie out there. Oddly, the lid on the well seemed to be moving all by itself. Soon after, a short squat figure climbed out from below. It was Little Bear. He had survived the battle by hiding out down there. I was happy to see that the smug little fella hadn't been sent to hell, even if he didn't care a lick what happened to me.

I thought I'd go over and have words with him, but then I saw something even more interesting. The Chinaman crept out from behind one of the abandoned buildings. He hadn't switched sides after all. He was hiding out the whole time. Trailing behind him on a leash was that big red boar Mei. Most interesting of all, her belly was swollen and her udder was full of milk. It looked like she was ready to birth a litter of baby boars any day now. The Chinaman led the hog into the shack where the miners had dug out the entrance of the tunnel to nowhere.

"What're you looking at, Tom?" Sal asked.

"Nothin'," I replied. Seeing as how Nigel wasn't such a nice fella anymore and Martin might grow up to wipe out the whole town, I reckoned I should keep it under my hat that the red gem might deliver a dozen piglets full of warm blood beneath the town.

Dawn in Damnation

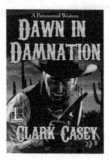

Having fun yet?
Here's a delightfully tempting little taste of the first book in the series.

WELCOME TO DAMNATION . . .
where every living soul is as dead as a doornail, except one.

Buddy Baker is a dead man. Literally. After gunning down more men than Billy the Kid—and being hung by a rope necktie for his crimes—the jolly, fast-drawing fugitive reckoned he'd earned himself a nonstop ticket to hell. Instead, he finds himself in Damnation: a gun-slinging ghost town located somewhere between heaven and hell.

There are no laws in Damnation. Only two simple rules: If you get shot, you go directly to hell. If you stay alive without shooting anyone for one year, you just might get into heaven.

Hardened outlaws pass the time in the saloon playing poker and wagering on who will get sent to hell next, while trying not to anger the town's reclusive vampire or the quarrelsome werewolves. Buddy winds up in everyone's crosshairs after swearing to protect a pretty gal who arrives in Damnation pregnant. Her child might end up a warm-blooded meal for the supernatural residents, or it could be a demon spawn on a mission to destroy them all.

"Total liberty for wolves is death to the lambs."
—Isaiah Berlin

Chapter 1

Fre...

"What happened?" asked the young man with a nickel-sized bullet hole in his temple.

"Well, what's the last thing you remember?" I asked him.

"Was playin' cards with some cowpuncher. Drew a flush, and he 'cused me a cheatin'. So I reached for my Colt. Reckon he did the same."

"My guess is he was faster."

The newbie had that stunned look they all got in their eyes when they first arrived. He was hardly old enough to grow a proper beard. Just another cowpoke born in a shitty little town who'd rustled some steer, made it with a few whores, then died over a two-dollar pot.

"So's this hell?" His voice quavered. Probably already browned his britches with fear shit.

"Not quite," I told him.

"Purgatory then?" He tried to put on a brave face.

"Kinda... the opposite, 'spose you could say."

"Huh?"

"Well, imagine if you was like a stone in a creek bed. After you die, a panhandler scoops you up with a bunch of other muck and runs you through his sifter. All the stuff that falls through goes straight to hell. The rest gotta be cleaned off to see if it's worth keeping. So you might say you're just here till the panhandler finds out whether or not you got any shine to ya."

"Is this hell's sifter?"

"Folks call it Damnation."

"Who's the panhandler?" he asked, "God?"

"Dunno," I shrugged.

He gave the room a squinty eye, trying to reckon if it wasn't all just a dream. The Foggy Dew had the same creaky chairs and sticky tables you'd find in any other saloon, though a little less flair perhaps. No trinkets on the mantel, just a simple dusty place to drink. Some cried when they found out where they were. Others were overjoyed they didn't end up someplace worse. The kid didn't look too impressed.

"What's there to do 'round here?" he asked.

"Drink, play cards... wait."

"For what?"

"Till you go to hell, of course."

"How's that happen?"

"Get yourself shot again, you'll likely find out. Otherwise, you could be here a spell."

"How long?"

"Fella in the corner was at Valley Forge with General Washington. Most don't last a year. Some don't make it an hour."

"Anybody ever come back from hell?"

"Not that I've seen."

"How ya even know they got there?"

"Hmm... Have to ask Sal that one, when he's got a moment."

As the suppertime crowd shuffled in, Sal was busy filling glasses. The bar was lined three deep with bullet-ridden outlaws. One thing you couldn't kill was a man's thirst.

"Say, you got any whores 'round here?" the kid asked.

"Whores go to heaven."

"Ain't what churchgoers say."

"Got some of them here." I pointed to the neatly dressed folks playing gin rummy in the corner. "Least the outspoken variety."

While we were chewing the fat, a short fella in a big fancy hat moseyed up beside the newbie. The brim of his Stetson cast a shadow over his face. All that showed was a whiskerless chin and a mouth that wasn't smiling. He paced back and forth impatiently. The newbie turned to see who was shadowing his backside. Must've figured he was the older of the two, 'cause he gave the little fella a mind-your-own-business smirk. The pacer lifted his face, and I recognized him. Jack looked like he was itching to put a lead plumb in somebody. It had been about a week, so that made sense. He was always taking flashy accessories off those he shot, shiny belt buckles and such. The hat must've been a recent acquisition. If it weren't so big, I'd have recognized him sooner and cleared out as fast as I could.

He pushed his duster over his hip real gently, showing a pearl-handled pistol in a greased black leather holster. I inched my stool away and shielded my face. Then, at the last second, the preacher burst through the door shaking his fists in the air all willy-nilly, hollering with the energy of a much younger man.

"I've had a premonition from the Lord!" he bellowed. "The end is nigh upon us!"

"The end done happened already, Preach," Fat Wally snapped back. "That's why you're here."

"A man of great girth will come from the dust, then fire will rain from above!" the preacher roared even louder. "The streets will muddy, and the seed of Satan will be born unto a woman beyond the grave. For that's how the devil canst reach where the Lord hath delivered us. The hounds will seek to destroy the demon spawn, but the portly pistoleer will protect it!"

"Good one, Preach," Wally laughed. "A dead gal wearing the bustle wrong—and with the devil's baby to boot! Now I've heard it all."

"I have seen it!" he hollered fearsomely. "The flying minions will multiply, and Damnation will grow in head and breadth! The light of the Lord will shine upon us all once more. Then weeds will sprout from the barren dust, but by then it will be *too late!* Once this domain is fattened like a calf, *the evil one will slaughter us all!*"

Jack, for one, had heard enough. He doffed his oversized hat and leveled his gun with his winking boyish face. The shot ripped through the side of the preacher's throat. The old coot gripped the wound and doubled over, then flopped back into a chair, sucking short, quick breaths from the hole as blood gurgled between his fingers. Jack reholstered his weapon, happy to have put a bullet in somebody, and he slowly wandered out of the barroom for a breath of dusty air. The newbie had no idea how close he'd come to getting a lead necktie.

"That preacher fella gonna go to hell?" he asked.

"When he bleeds out," I answered. "Reckon so."

"Ain't there some way of gettin' outta here, aside from goin' to hell?" the kid fretted. "Can I get to *heaven*, mister?"

"Some think so," I told him. "They reckon if you last a whole year in Damnation without shootin' no one, the Lord'll forgive whatever you done. After twelve months without sin, the gates of heaven open up."

"Anybody done it?"

"Record's six months. That fella wasn't right in the head though. Didn't leave his room for four of 'em. Came out to tell us all he was Christ. Then the preacher shot 'em in the gut just to prove he wasn't."

"You're tellin' me there might be a chance a gettin' to heaven if you don't shoot nobody for a year, and the only one to try it was some loon who thought he was Christ."

"Well, truth is I'm fixin' to give it a go myself," I told him. "I already got more'n two months under my belt."

"Is that all?" the kid sneered. Just then, a gust of wind pushed the swinging doors open, bringing in a cloud of dust. A figure in all black followed the dirty breeze into the barroom. The load of hay on his skull fell to his shoulders. It was combed back real neat like a girl's, with a gob of pomade. He wasn't real tall or thick, but looked powerful just the same, like a diamondback whose every muscle is made for striking. Otherwise, you might've took him for a tenderfoot with soft hands and fancy clothes.

The men at the bar all hot-footed out of his way. Sal placed a bottle of gin in front of him, then retreated to the far side of the bar. Most folks drank bathtub whiskey or flat beer, but he had himself an educated thirst for the juice of juniper berries. Some of the newer fellas let their eyes linger a little too long, so he hissed like an angry cat.

"What's that? Some kinda vampire?" the kid asked with a nervous giggle.

"Yup."

"You shittin' me? They're real! Thought they couldn't come out during the day—least that's what the storybooks say."

"Can come out at dusk, and it's always dusk in Damnation."

"*Always?*"

"Long as I been here, and that's nearly fifteen years."

"That vampire drink folks' blood?"

"Nah, everybody here's already dead. Blood's as cold as a crocodile's. That's why he's so ornery."

"Can he fly?"

"Leaps real far, almost like flying. Fast as a bugger, too."

"Any more like him around?"

"Nope, just the one. Musta done something halfway decent to end up here instead of hell. Don't think he appreciates it much though."

"Next you gonna tell me there's werewolves, too," he laughed.

"They drink down the road at their own saloon."

"Does everyone who don't go to heaven or hell wind up here?"

"Ain't seen my dead Uncle Joe," I said. "And he didn't seem ripe for neither place. Can't speak for the rest. It's a small town, though."

The kid eased back and took a gulp of the coffin varnish that passed for whiskey. Some folks were so relieved they ended up short of hell that they got a little cocky. Reckoned there wasn't much else to be afraid of. "Don't seem like such a bad place," he said.

"You just gotta watch what you say 'round here," I warned him. "Folks draw real fast. They get sick of being here. Puts 'em in bad spirits, and they'll draw if you so much as brush against a fella's sleeve."

"Like Dodge City."

"Worse than that. You risk getting sent to hell every time you leave the rooming house. But it gets more boring than church if you don't stretch your legs once in a while."

"Let me get this straight. If you get shot, you go to hell forever. But if you don't, you can hang out here long as you like, play cards, and maybe have a go at them old churchgoing ladies."

"That's about the size of it," I told him.

"Sounds like you need a sheriff," he said.

"Keep your voice down!" Sal hollered. "Somebody set this boy straight before Jack hears him and shoots up the whole bar!"

"What'd I say?" the newbie blathered.

"Pipe down!" Sal ordered. "No more of your lollygagging—that is if you're hoping to last the night." He stormed off, leaving the kid moping over an empty glass.

"Jack don't like to hear no talk of... ahem, law enforcement," I explained

"Who's Jack?"

"Member that short fella in the Stetson who kilt the preacher?"

* * * *

When he had first come to town some ten years earlier, Jack Finney was the measliest pipsqueak that'd ever darkened the doorstep of the Foggy Dew saloon. He needed a boost to get on a barstool. Hadn't made it all but two steps into the room before the betting began on how long he'd last—and nobody wagered a dime past suppertime.

Back then, the quickest gun in town was a sheriff from Lexington, Kentucky, named Jeremiah. He was a good old boy with a righteous streak. He might've taken a few bribes when he was alive, but he kept the peace and went to church every Sunday. He'd been the sort to give everyone a fair shake till they crossed the line, but the way he had met his end changed all that. He was scouting for rustlers, and a couple of two-bit thieves dressed as priests got the drop on him. They gut-shot him and stole his horse and guns, leaving him to die in the woods. It wasn't the bullet wound that did him in, though. They only shot him with a .22, but the pain kept him from walking. Couldn't even crawl to a creek for water. He went four days without anything to eat or drink. He was so parched his tongue blew up as big as a bullfrog's, and he began seeing things that weren't there. Reckoned it best to end his suffering while he could still think clearly. Didn't have no knife, so he widened his wound with his fingertips, trying to bleed out faster. Eventually his heart gave out. After he arrived in Damnation, the stretched-out bullet hole in his belly didn't mend properly, so bits of food and whiskey sometimes leaked out when he laughed. He claimed the spillage was the reason why he was always so damn hungry and thirsty.

Jeremiah wasn't officially appointed sheriff of Damnation. He just happened to be wearing a star when he died. Then he shot a mess of people right away, so folks quickly deferred to him. His suspicious nature wasn't helped any by having been gunned down by phony clergymen. He didn't like to go at anyone head-on who hadn't been tested. He preferred to see them show their stuff against someone else first.

Even someone as scrawny as Jack needed to be tested, and Jeremiah watched him closely as the boys bullied him. It gave them no small joy to hear the kid squeal. Just a few hours after he arrived, a Comanchero who had only been in town a couple of weeks stepped to Jack. He was a half-Mexican bandito who had made his living by stealing goods and livestock from gringos and trading them with Indians. His occupation had cost him an eye at some point, and he wore a black patch over the empty socket. The crosshatch scars on his cheeks and forearms attested to the many knife fights he'd managed to survive. He still had a sneaky way about him, always lurking in the shadows, ready to slit a throat. Now, he stared Jack down with the one good eye.

"My boots could use a shine, boy," he announced. Jack looked around the room, hoping someone'd laugh to let him know it was just a joke, but nobody said a word. "Well, don't just stand there," the Comanchero yelled. "Get down and give 'em a shine!" Jack slowly bent before the dirty boots. They were covered in blood and shit and dribbles of piss, then caked in so much dust you couldn't tell what color they were.

"Give 'em a spit shine!" the Comanchero ordered. Jack's eyes grew tearful. He puckered his mouth to offer a gob of spit, and sure enough the boot crashed into his face. The whole room erupted in laughter. Jack rolled over on the floor moaning, wishing he never did whatever he'd done to end up dead. A ribbon of blood leaked from his lip over his chin.

Jeremiah had been keeping a keen eye on the Comanchero ever since he'd arrived. Didn't trust a man who traded with Indians. The one-eyed bandito had already knifed a couple of fellas over card games. Nobody'd seen him shoot yet though, so there was no way of knowing how fast he was. He carried a greased Schofield revolver, which split in the middle so you could load all six chambers at once instead of one at a time, like the older Colts. It was a soldier's weapon, good for extended battle, but he seemed to prefer slashing throats by surprise. Jeremiah reckoned this would be a good chance to find out if his pistol work was as worrisome as his knife play.

"You don't gotta take no more ribbing today," Jeremiah told the boy as he tended to his lip. "Long as you outdraw somebody. And since Cyclops here is so keen on you, might as well be him. Winner gets free drinks and grub for the rest of the day."

The Comanchero glared at Jeremiah, but it was difficult for him to express himself properly with just the one eye. "In the land of the blind," he said solemnly, "the one-eyed man is king." Then he turned and headed outside.

"Well, shit... good thing we ain't all blind!" Jeremiah laughed and shoved Jack toward the door.

Mostly out of boredom, ten or fifteen men wandered out in front of the saloon. The sky was always an ashen yellow, no brighter than dusk. The clouds never lifted but streaks of orange and violet broke through in spots. It was pretty, only it never changed. I reckoned the living were so keen on sunsets because they didn't last. Even the prettiest lady in the world would get tiresome if you were stuck staring at her for eternity—especially if there was no chance of giving her a poke.

Most of the fellas didn't consider the gunfight worth vacating a stool, particularly if you had a good one near the fire. Most newbies didn't last their first week, and a skinny teenager like Jack didn't inspire any wagering. As a matter of duty, I went out to document his getting sent to hell. They stood in the center of the road as we lined the rotted-out boardwalk. Sal handed Jack an old Colt and a single bullet. The weight of the gun nearly caused him to drop it.

"Is that all I get?" Jack's voice cracked in disbelief. "Just one bullet!"

"Jeremiah don't want you gettin' no ideas. This way, if you take a shot at him, one of his men'll get you for sure."

"But what if I miss?" It was a fair question. The scared hand of the newbie could easily empty a six-shooter before hitting his target.

"Then I suppose the half-breed can take his sweet time returning fire," Sal answered.

They lined up back to back. Jack's head didn't reach the Comanchero's shoulder blade. On Jeremiah's mark, they each began marching in opposite directions. At the count of ten, they both turned. Jack's slight frame made him more nimble. His hips swiveled squarely in place, slightly ahead of the bandito's. He proved to have naturally quick hands, although they trembled with the weight of the giant Colt. His itty-bitty finger struggled to squeeze the rusty trigger. The bandito caught up with the steady arm of a practiced killer. The missing eye was a big disadvantage. He had to wait until he was fully turned around to take proper aim. Jack managed to get off a lucky shot, but it only winged the bandito's right arm. As he gripped the wound, tar-black blood spilled between his fingers, and the gun slipped from his hand.

They both looked at one another for a cold second. With no bullets left, Jack had two choices: stand there and wait to die or attack with everything he had. The little fella let out a blood-curdling shriek, then charged. The bandito debated for a split second whether he should pick up his gun with his left hand or pull the knife from his belt. Neither were necessary. He could have just knocked the kid down and stomped on him, but the moment of indecision cost him. Jack closed the distance between them and was on him like a saddle sore. Still hollering like a loon, he swung a wide haymaker with the rusty Colt clenched in his fist, braining the bandito above his ear. The edge of the cylinder ripped out a silver dollar-sized chunk of scalp. The Comanchero's eye stilled after the blow. Tears were running down Jack's cheeks. He was only 17 and had never murdered anyone before—let alone a dead man.

Those who hadn't bothered to come outside and watch the fight would hear the retelling of it for months afterward. The skinny teenager kept smashing the bandit's skull, fearing that if he let up for even a second, he'd be done for. First, the left ear shredded, then the flesh from neck to forehead scraped off. Hairy clumps of scalp clung to the gun barrel like leaves on a rake. Jack sobbed with one swing, then screamed with the next. Some of the noises didn't even sound human, more like a coyote's yelp. When he finally tired, there wasn't no more casing left to hold the brains together. A dark porridge spilled onto the ground like chuck-wagon stew. Jack collapsed on the body and lay there twitching and panting in exhaustion. When they pulled him off, he was as bloody as the bandito. He went back in the saloon and sat in the corner, still shaking as he nursed a beer. Sal gave him a couple of pork chops, and he wolfed them down hungrily. Everyone left him in peace for the rest of the day.

The next morning, Jack skulked into the saloon at breakfast time with dried blood still on his cheeks and hands. He looked like an Indian in war paint. Since he'd proven himself the day before, he wasn't expecting any trouble—at least not before he ate.

"You only earned a pass for one day, kid," Jeremiah announced. One of his men handed the boy the same rusty blood-stained Colt with a single bullet already in the chamber.

"Any volunteers to draw against this hayseed? Winner gets free drinks and grub for the day."

A cowboy with some experience stepped forward. He wasn't a trained gunfighter but had survived four or five draws since he'd arrived two months earlier. He didn't have much of a knack for cards, so he supported himself with his pistol work. Found it easier to spot a fella with a mess of chips in front of him, wait till he drank too much, then pick a fight. The winner typically claimed the loser's possessions.

Jack and the cowboy headed out to the road, and this time half the saloon followed. The rest still didn't consider the action good enough. The payout on the cowboy wasn't very good because nobody thought the newbie's luck could possibly last another day.

They stood back to back and walked off ten paces. This time, Jack was a little smoother and more deliberate in his draw. Meanwhile, the cowboy jammed his hand into his holster and plucked up his gun, letting off two screaming shots in rapid succession. Both struck the ground in front of Jack. He flinched but maintained his composure. He had learned it was better to squeeze the trigger instead of jerking it. The cowboy had just leveled his barrel to send the third bullet into Jack's chest when his own shirt reddened like a rose blossoming from his heart. He fell to the dust. Jack went back inside and ate some more pork chops.

Each day, Jeremiah called for a new volunteer, and each day Jack faced him. Wasn't any choice in the matter. With just a single bullet in the chamber, he couldn't raise the barrel at the man who handed him the gun. There were always two men beside Jeremiah that would've gunned him down. His best hope was to keep firing away at whoever they put in front of him. The first few men weren't very good, but it gave him a chance to learn. The best living gunfighters had upwards of thirty kills under their belt, but those were spaced out by months and sometimes years. Jack had the advantage of drawing every single day, which allowed him to fix his flaws while they were still fresh in his mind. And since he had just the one bullet, he put every bit of his concentration into aiming it.

At first Jeremiah was glad to be able to test folks out and separate the wheat from the chaff. He could see their weaknesses when they drew against the kid, and note if someone dipped their shoulder before they pulled. He figured he'd get the upper hand on whoever gunned the kid down. The thing was that nobody could, so all that information went to waste when they fell. Also, Jack learned something new every day. His hand got steadier and quicker. He didn't even bother asking for breakfast. Just marched straight up and stuck out his hand for the gun and the bullet, then he waited outside to see who'd follow. It didn't escape Jeremiah's attention that he was making a bona fide gunslinger out of the boy, who'd likely be even harder to control.

Everyone else found it a nice change of pace to start the day out with a gunfight. Gave folks something to look forward to, a reason to get out of bed. We all gathered beside the road each morning, even a few of the Indians who camped out in the dusty plains surrounding the town. People started to root for the little fella, and eventually the betting pool swung to favor him against the hardened outlaws who were just in it for free grub and drinks. After a few weeks, Jack gained a lifetime's worth of experience. Then the day came when there were no more volunteers to go up against him.

"All right, boy, you ain't gotta go against no one today," Jeremiah announced. "Drink and eat as much as you like. Nobody'll hassle you. But tomorrow, you go against me."

Everyone was itching to see the matchup. Jeremiah had been studying Jack for a month, but Jack had been practicing every day of that month. Wasn't even the teensiest bit nervous anymore. His aim was dead on and his hand as steady as a post. But Jeremiah didn't intend to get hoodwinked by another thief dressed as a priest. He had found one weakness that he could use to his advantage.

Jack was only given the one bullet each day, so he couldn't risk aiming at his opponent's head, where a couple of inches in either direction might miss it entirely. And he couldn't fire off a quick shot at a fella's legs, since a wounded man might still overpower him. He always shot at the center of the chest, where the target was the widest.

That afternoon, I overheard Jeremiah telling the blacksmith to mold him a sheet of tin. The next morning at breakfast time, Jeremiah was sitting at the bar with his back to the door. He was all by himself, carelessly gobbling down a plateful of beans. A glint of metal shined from under his collar.

He'd gotten up early so he could have the blacksmith fit it in place while everyone was still asleep. If it succeeded in stopping Jack's first bullet, he'd have all the time in the world to aim, and since he knew right where the bullet was going, he had extra metal layered in the center. Probably wouldn't stop a buffalo gun, but it'd do for a rusty old Colt. It was a pretty good plan… till Jack came through the door an hour earlier than usual.

The boy was through playing by another man's rules—that much was clear. He grabbed the sheriff's hair from behind and yanked his head back, exposing his neck to the ceiling.

"Ain't gonna be any sheriffs parsing out the bullets no more!" Jack said as he pulled out the Comanchero's knife. He must've pocketed it the first day he'd arrived, when he killed the half-breed and collapsed on top of him. We thought he was just twitching with fear but he was really fleecing that knife from the body. Ever since then, the boy had been biding his time, trying to stay alive till he got close enough and no one was by Jeremiah's side. Jack ran the blade across the sheriff's throat before he could say a damn thing.

By the time Jeremiah's men arrived, Jack had already helped himself to his pretty pearl-handled pistols. He smiled at them tauntingly. They wouldn't have pulled on him if he only had two bullets, let alone twelve. The next week, Jack shot one of the men for fun. The week after, he shot the other. He had learned from Jeremiah not to trust anyone, but also not to grow soft. He made a point of going up against someone at least once a week to keep sharp—and he wasn't too fickle about who. Unlike Jeremiah, he had no problem with shooting untested newbies. Felt it kept him on his toes. And the bullying he'd endured didn't make him sympathize with the misfortunes of others. He turned into the meanest son of a bitch in town, so nobody ever mentioned sheriffs around him again.

* * * *

"I still say you need someone to uphold the rules around here," argued the newbie with the nickel-sized bullet hole in his temple.

"Oh, and what rules would you suggest?" I asked.

"Well, no shootin' each other for one. You fellas are playing for keeps here. Ain't like before when we wasn't sure what happened after you died. This is *it!*"

"So, what if someone accuses you of cheatin', like the fella you said put that bullet in your head?"

"Could wrassle," he suggested.

"And if a fella ain't much for wrasslin'?"

"Well then, he shouldn't call nobody a cheater. And if somebody calls him a cheater, he could just go to the sheriff."

"Sounds like you got it all worked out," I said. "Lemme ask you another question— how's a fella get a bullet in the side of his head from an argument at a card table? Weren't you lookin' at the man when he called you a cheater? Or did he somehow sneak up beside ya?"

"No, I mean yes." He fidgeted nervously. "I guess I kinda turned away when he shot me."

"Is that so?"

"It happened real fast."

"Thought you said the last thing you remembered was that you drew and reckoned he done the same. You telling me you drew your pistol and looked away before you even pulled the trigger?"

"I dunno! What ya want from me, mister?"

"Why'd ya do it?" I pressed him.

"Do what? I tole ya, mister. He 'cused me a cheatin'. Then he shot me 'fore I could shoot him."

"Did he do it real close, or was he sitting across the table?"

"He was across the table," he blubbered. "We was sitting as far apart as them two fellas over there."

"Interesting," I nodded.

"How's that?"

"'Cause that bullet hole's got a ring around it like a hot barrel was pressed to your head. You know what I think? I think you pulled the trigger yourself and you're ashamed of it, so you cooked up a story about an argument over cards. And I'm damn sick of pissants like you coming in here and making stuff up. What I wanna know now is *why you done it*?"

Looked like his face was going to shatter from holding it all in. Finally, he broke down, "I had the sadness, sir. I always had it—long as I can remember. My pa had it before me and, from what I heard, his pa before him. Couldn't be helped. It made me do lots a bad things, and it weren't never gonna go away. So I done myself in."

"All right then." I scribbled down a note. "Sal, get this fella a drink on me."

"Thanks, mister. I appreciate it," he smiled. "And just 'cause I done myself in don't mean I'm wrong in what I'm sayin'. Matter of fact, killin' myself made me realize things."

"Oh?"

"Like how special stuff is. Even breathin' this dusty air and sittin' here in this dark saloon talkin' with you. It's all special! If y'all only knew what was good for ya, you'd stop shootin' each other this very day. Just think," his voice lifted, "if what you were sayin' earlier's true, then a year from today the whole darn town could march straight up to heaven together!"

Some sodbusters at a nearby table burst into laughter.

"Shit, boy, when's the last time you seen a fella do what's best for him?" I asked. "You think if you pluck a man from his life and stick him in a one-horse town with a hundred other rotten bastards he's gonna act *better*?"

"That's why you need somebody to keep 'em in line, *like a sheriff!*"

"Keep it down!" Sal scolded. "You say that word again, and I'll send ya to hell myself."

"Just out of curiosity," I asked the kid, "who you reckon might be capable of stopping these bored and hateful men from shootin' each another?"

It was a subject I'd given a fair amount of thought to. The last time I had preached pacifism, some old-timer tried to gut me, and I had to shoot him—much to everyone's amusement. That's when I took to practicing it instead of preaching it. Everyone could go on blasting one another over nothing. Hopefully, I'd slip between the cracks right into heaven. Sure, every so often a newbie'd come at me for asking the wrong questions, but I'd gotten a knack for avoiding them. Hadn't even heeled myself in a month.

The kid was still giving the question serious consideration. He peered down the bar to where the vampire was drinking by himself. "How 'bout that fella?" he suggested. "Looks like he could uphold rules well enough. He's gotta be quicker than Jack or any other man."

"I expect he is," I agreed. "And he probably could whip this town into shape real quick, if he was inclined to. And if anyone was compelled to ask him."

"Well, dang! That's exactly what I'm gonna do." The kid sprang to his feet and walked straight over before I could stop him. Wanted to show he was more than a cowardly suicide. Strutted up with the gumption of a mayor on Election Day. Didn't even seem to notice the yellow glow in the vampire's eyes growing brighter as he approached. He stuck out his hand real friendly-like and said, "Howdy, pardner. My name's Fre...!"

Didn't even get out his full name. The vampire snatched the outstretched hand like an apple from a tree and pressed the boy's wrist to his lips. Yellow fangs sprang from his gums and pierced the soft sunburnt flesh. He clamped down on the bone without swallowing the blood that was pouring out. With one yank of his neck, the hand tore clean off. The kid screamed like one of them lady opera singers, so high and loud I thought the chandelier'd shatter. The vampire tossed the hand to the ground with the fingers still twitching like a daddy longlegs. Then he spat out some blood in disgust. The kid gripped his stump in shock. Then for some reason, he started scooping up the veins and muck dangling out. Tried to put them back inside like he was stuffing a sausage. Suppose he thought it could be mended somehow. All the while he kept screaming.

"Aw, come on, Sal," Fat Wally complained from the poker table. "Hobble that measly cowpoke's lip. Some of us are trying to play cards here. Can't concentrate with all his yellin'. Shit, I think Red's finally got himself something better than a pair of bullshit," he said, and the others laughed.

Sal moseyed to the end of the bar in no particular hurry. Wasn't the type to break a sweat if he didn't have to. He wiped his hands off on his apron, then grabbed the scattergun from the umbrella stand. He came around the other side of the bar and pressed the barrel against the kid's chest to avoid any buckshot spray. He pulled the trigger, and the boy was thrown five paces backwards onto the floor with a wet thud.

"*Goddamnit!*" Red hollered. "You stood too close again, Sal. Done shot the guts clear out his back. Got it all over my dang cards. I call *re*-deal!" The other players grumbled and mucked their cards, arguing that Red probably didn't have shit anyways.

"He could've at least got sent to hell like a man, instead of a little girl that seen a bug," Fat Wally remarked. "When your time comes, boys, whatever you do, don't go out like a 'Fre...!'" Wally clutched his wrist imitating the boy's shock at seeing his hand torn off. The fellas laughed good and hard at that one, and from then on anyone who left Damnation in a cowardly manner was referred to as a "Fre...!"

The Chinaman who tended to the pigs came and dragged Fre's body to the pigpen. The preacher had bled out by then, so he took him, too. The pigs chewed the cold corpses to bits. There wouldn't have been any trace that they were ever in town if I didn't remember to write down a few words about them. On account of all the gunfights, the swine were always plump and juicy. Most folks agreed that the best thing about Damnation was you could eat all the bacon you'd ever wanted.

The vampire finished his drink, then left without a word. A little while later, Jack came back in and scanned the room to see if anyone else needed shooting. Those were the last of the simple days when everyone knew their place, and there was still peace between us and the wolves. Then, just like the preacher had preached, a new gunfighter came to town and stirred up a real shit storm.

Meet the Author

Clark Casey is the author of three novellas: *The Jesus Fish and Slaughter Bird, Pale Male and the Infertile Girl,* and *The Perfect Defective.* He was born in New York and currently resides in Northern California.

Printed in the United States
by Baker & Taylor Publisher Services